The Legionary Seduction

Roman Heirs, Book Two
Jenna Bigelow

To Frankie

CHAPTER 1

Outside Narbo (Narbonne)

MAX CROSSED HIS ARMS over his chest and took a deep inhale of the air, tinged with the scent of woodsmoke. Chainmail armor laid heavy on his shoulders, but after ten years in the army, he barely noticed its weight.

Tax day was everyone's least favorite day, from the provincial citizens who had to turn over their hard-earned profits, to the legionaries tasked with the tedious collection. Until a moment ago, the day had been painfully boring but peaceful. Max and five other legionaries had traveled from village to village around the southern reaches of Gallia Transalpina, watching the tax collector tally careful figures and weigh sacks of grain.

Now, a complainer had emerged. *Finally, something interesting.* A large man, sporting the mane of fair hair common to the provincial natives, approached the tax collector. He braced his weight against a tall walking stick and spoke Latin with a lilting Gallic accent. "I'll ask again for an explanation. Why have our taxes nearly doubled?"

The tax collector, seated at a table piled high with wax tablets, twirled his stylus between his fingers. "And I'll tell you again. The tax rate is set by acting governor Gaius Galerius Petronax."

The man raised a bushy eyebrow. "That's not an explanation. If we're to hand over nearly twice a share of our income, we deserve to know why."

Murmurs of agreement sounded from the crowd behind him. The tax collector fixed the man with a dispassionate stare. "It's not for you to ask questions. Only to pay the lawful taxes that are due of every man who has the honor of calling himself a citizen of Rome."

The man glanced behind him, as if gauging the support of the others. He turned back to face the tax collector. His hold on his walking stick changed from a casual grasp to the sort of grip that could wield the staff as a weapon if required. Max tensed, his hand going to the sword hanging at his hip. Out of the corner of his eye, he noticed the other legionaries making similar moves, chainmail rattling as they shifted.

"I reckon we could go to Narbo and ask Governor Petronax ourselves," the Gallic man said, the threat clear in his words. The men behind him shifted forward, fanning out at his back.

Metal rasped as the other legionaries drew their swords. Max kept his in its scabbard. He had only the haziest understanding of the intricacies of provincial tax code, but he did understand frustration. And he was no mathematician, but the arithmetic of this situation was clear even to him. There were at least thirty men of the village, against five legionaries. The legionaries had swords, armor, and training, but the villagers had numbers and righteous anger. If this turned to violence, it wouldn't go well for either side.

Max jumped in front of the tax collector's table, between the legionaries and the villagers, his hands raised. "Let's all take a moment before we do anything we might regret." He used the same tone of voice as when he was trying to calm a skittish horse, and glanced from the other legionaries to the villagers, making it clear that his message was for both groups. "We don't want any trouble."

The blond man walked forward to meet him, planting his walking stick in the ground at his side. "All you Romans are is trouble."

"Insolence," one of the other legionaries growled.

Max ignored the insult. It wouldn't help to appear as over-sensitive as some of his colleagues. "Listen, I won't pretend to know exactly how your tax money is going to be spent." Max hesitated, trying to summon the right words. He had no gift for rousing men with eloquent speeches—that was his politician father's skill, not his. But maybe this situation didn't call for an orator. Maybe nothing more than calm, reasonable words could defuse the tension humming between the legionaries and the villagers.

"I do know that the province's taxes have gone to building many roads here," Max said. "Travel is safer, and Narbo is connected to Hispania as well as Italy. I bet your wife enjoys all the goods she can buy at the market from around the world at decent prices. And she can visit her mother in the next village over without fearing that her wagon will lose a wheel to a muddy road. All because everyone pays their taxes."

The man surveyed him. Max wasn't sure if his words would be enough to avert violence, and his shoulders tensed. He forced himself to adopt a casual, relaxed posture, hands loosely clasped in front of him, as if they were chatting at a tavern. Usually, Max was getting chewed out for looking too casual—"slovenly," as his centurion was fond of putting it—but today, his natural ease might be useful.

The Gallic man glanced from Max to the other legionaries, their swords still drawn. He must have realized, as Max had, that even if the thirty villagers succeeded in overcoming the handful of legionaries, the might of the entire legion would crush them. It wasn't fair, but it was true.

The man hefted his sack of grain and dumped it on the tax collector's table. The legionaries sheathed their swords. Max caught the man's eye and gave him a small nod, hoping the man could sense his gratitude that he'd chosen peace. It wasn't right to make people give up their money without explanation, but today, it seemed more important to keep the peace than to question the entire system of government.

An hour later, Max helped load the last of the tax payments into a large cart to be taken back to Narbo. He mounted up on Elephant, his gray mare, and took up the rear of their little caravan.

Elephant was his favorite being, human or animal, in the entire world. His adoptive parents had gifted her to him as a filly when he was seventeen, just before he joined the army. She'd carried him all over the Republic, kept him safe in battle, and was always there to lend a listening ear.

As they left the village behind, riding single file on a narrow road, Max pulled Elephant to a stop and hopped down from her saddle. The legionary riding in front of him noticed and slowed his own horse. "Everything all right, Legionary Maximus?"

Max bent to lift one of Elephant's hooves, frowning as if concerned. "I think my horse has taken a stone in her hoof. You all keep going, I'll be right behind you."

The legionary shrugged. "Don't forget, we're expected back in Narbo for the arrival." He continued on.

Vesta's tits. Max had forgotten all about the event later today. The province's new governor was arriving this afternoon, and the legion was expected to assemble to welcome him. Max glanced at the sun's position in the sky and calculated that he had a bit of time. Worst case, if he was late, he'd just have to sneak into formation without attracting his centurion's notice.

Max pretended to diligently check all of Elephant's hooves until the other four legionaries had vanished around a bend in the road. Then he grinned in triumph, mounted back up, and steered Elephant off the road and down a small path between the trees. This was one of many paths he'd discovered that led straight to the beach. A gallop on the beach would be the highlight of his week, and he wasn't about to give up his chance, even if he was risking another punishment for tardiness.

Soon, Elephant's hooves pounded on flat-packed sand. A vast expanse of glimmering water shone to their right. Wind whipped at Max's hair. He let out a whoop of delight as Elephant effortlessly jumped a log of driftwood lying on the beach. Her hooves slammed down on the other side with only a minor jolt, her strong legs absorbing most of the impact. Waves crashed beside them, and flecks of sea spray cooled him.

He'd needed this, needed the freedom, the exhilaration. Army life, though it offered opportunity for adventure, was constricting. He should be grateful that Narbo was peaceful, far from the civil war currently seething in Greece, but sometimes he longed for a bit more excitement. Everything was rules and duty and saluting, and sometimes only the chance to gallop his horse on an empty beach made it worth it.

As the beach began to curve, he gently guided Elephant into a measured trot and lifted a hand to squint at the sky. The sun was much too close to the horizon. Oh yes, he was definitely going to be late. *Fuck.*

He wheeled Elephant away from the water and found the trail back to Narbo. Elephant snorted at the interruption, but allowed herself to be coaxed back into a canter once they hit the wider road.

"Sorry," he murmured to her. "Glabrio will skin me alive if I'm late again, and then who would spoil you?"

She flicked her ear back at him in a gesture that was the horse equivalent of an eye roll.

Max practiced excuses in his mind as they approached Narbo. Punctuality was not his strong suit, but he'd resolved to do better. He *needed* to do better if he was going to make decurion, after all. Then, he'd be responsible not just for himself, but for a squadron of thirty men. He should have been promoted already, given his ten years of service, but too many incidents of lateness or accidental impudence had held him back.

When they reached the stables, Max untacked Elephant, brushed her down, and released her into the pasture as quickly as he could. Then, he jogged outside the walls of the city to the field before the eastern gate that the legion used for drills and assemblies.

Shit, he was definitely late. The whole legion was assembled already, facing the road on which the new governor would arrive. Max held his breath and tried to make himself as unobtrusive as possible as he slipped through the ranks to find the spot that had been left for him in his cavalry unit. His height was usually an advantage, but today, he was fairly sure that all five thousand men of the legion were watching him fumble around.

He finally found his spot next to his friend and bunkmate, Drusus, and slipped into it.

"Where in Dis have you been?" Drusus breathed.

"Riding," Max replied.

"Idiot."

Max nodded in agreement. His one consolation was that Glabrio, his centurion, was at the front, facing forward, so might not have noticed Max's tardy arrival. Then again, the man seemed to have eyes in the back of his head, so Max doubted he'd get off easy. Besides, someone else would probably rat him out to curry favor.

Between the heads of the men in front of him, Max could just glimpse the legion's commander, Petronax, pacing before the ranks. He wore a bright white cape, and sunlight glanced off the gold filigree in his ceremonial breastplate. Petronax had been acting governor of the province in the months since the previous governor finished his three-year term. Petronax probably wasn't looking forward to giving up the power and prestige that came with governing a profitable and peaceful province like Gallia Transalpina.

They waited for several minutes. Then, a scout on a fast horse came riding down the road, hooves thumping, and relayed a message to Petronax, likely announcing the imminent arrival of the traveling party. At the front of the legion, trumpeters lifted their instruments and launched into a loud, jaunty tune.

Moments later, a small procession rounded the curve of the road and came into view. A few men rode horses in front, followed by a small, enclosed carriage. Several carts packed high with crates and boxes brought up the rear.

The frontmost rider surveyed the assembled legion with an air of command as he drew his horse to a halt. He must be the province's new governor. His close-cropped hair was graying at the edges, but he sprang down from his horse with energetic ease. He patted the horse on the nose before handing the reins to an eager legionary. A good sign—Max liked men who were kind to their animals.

Petronax stepped forward, ready to greet the new governor, but the other man turned toward the carriage, which had pulled up behind them. He waved away another attendant and opened the door himself, extending a hand up to assist the woman inside the carriage.

A jolt of shock pulsed through Max. He sucked a ragged breath through his teeth at the sight of the woman who emerged from the carriage.

Over the past ten years, he'd often had moments like this, where he'd thought he'd seen her. But it was always just another woman with the same shade of dark-honey hair, or a build similar to hers, petite and slender.

Though other women might share the same hair color or figure, no one had ever matched her bearing: prim but not haughty, dignified but not cold. She'd carried herself like that even when they were adolescents, and the woman who stepped down from the carriage moved with the warm grace he remembered.

It was Volusia, his childhood friend and source of deep infatuation. He hadn't seen her in ten years, not since one disastrous kiss had ruined everything between them. He knew she married shortly after they had parted. He didn't know her husband would become the new governor of Gallia Transalpina, or that she would accompany him all the way from Rome.

He swallowed hard. Petronax and the governor were exchanging a formal greeting, but Max couldn't tear his gaze from Volusia. She stood patiently behind her husband, glancing over the ranks with a small smile. A fair-haired attendant stood at her side, and Volusia leaned over to whisper something to her.

His chest felt tight. He had never expected to see her again, had resigned himself to it, despite comparing every woman he flirted with or the few he bedded to her. Now, she was to live here, in the same town.

But they would probably never see each other. He didn't often cross paths with the governor's household, and Volusia would have no reason to venture outside of the comfortable house she'd soon be installed in. She was married now—to a governor, no less—and he was just a soldier who couldn't even land one promotion.

Regret pulled at him. Once, they were the best of friends. But fate had torn them apart, and they'd never be able to recapture what they once had. He'd keep his distance, and she'd never even know he was here.

CHAPTER 2

VOLUSIA SURVEYED THE flurry of unpacking happening in her new quarters. They had just arrived in Narbo after a month of travel, and so far, the city seemed to consist only of surly, grim-faced soldiers.

Iris, her maid, attempted to shake the wrinkles out of the linen and silk dresses that had been crushed into trunks for the duration of their journey. Some other women made the bed with fresh linens.

Volusia rifled through her trunks to locate a small wooden box containing her jewelry. She opened it and glanced over the contents, making sure nothing had gone missing on the journey. She wasn't given to dousing herself in jewels as some women were, but the jewelry represented security. She was in a strange city, hundreds of miles from everyone she knew, except Iris and Avitus. The jewelry was a promise that she could take care of herself, if the need arose.

She sifted a pearl and ruby necklace through her fingers. It brought forth a pang of longing. Avitus had given her this necklace upon the birth of their son, Lucius, nine years ago. Lucius remained behind in Rome with his grandparents. He was a bookish lad with a delicate constitution, and she worried about the effect of the journey on his health. Also, his education was paramount if he was going to follow in his father's footsteps as a successful statesman, and she didn't want to interrupt it. But she'd missed him from the moment the carriage rolled away from their house in Rome.

"All well, mistress?" Iris asked quietly.

Volusia hastily put the necklace down. Iris had been given to her as a wedding present, and over the past ten years, Iris had become a trusted confidant, always attuned to Volusia's moods. "I'm just tired from the journey."

Iris nodded. She clapped her hands. "Out!"

The other women immediately dropped what they were doing and left the room. Volusia smiled. Iris had run the household in Rome with a firm hand, and it seemed she was poised to do the same here. "These army men could learn a lesson from you, Iris."

Iris finished making the bed, tucking the linens beneath the mattress and plumping the pillow. "Indeed, mistress."

"Your family lives hereabouts, don't they? Does the country seem familiar?" Iris's family in Gaul had sold her into slavery to pay a debt, which was how she'd ended up in Volusia's service.

"I remember passing through Narbo on my way to Rome," Iris said. "It was the biggest city I'd ever seen, until Rome, of course. My family is several days' ride north of here."

"Perhaps you could visit them. Or invite them to come here to see you." Volusia had always sympathized with Iris's plight, being torn from her family and sent to a far-off land. Volusia had known upheaval in her life, as her father died when she was a child. But her mother remarried soon after, and Volusia grew to love her stepfather, Rufus. It was nothing compared to what Iris had suffered.

"That would be very kind, mistress."

"We'll speak about it more once things are settled here." In truth, Volusia had been thinking of freeing Iris. Iris deserved it, after ten years of loyal service, and now that they were in Gaul, near Iris's family, it seemed right. But she didn't want to send Iris back to a life of poverty and struggle, so she needed to convince Avitus to gift Iris a sum of money upon her emancipation.

"Would you like to rest, mistress?" Iris suggested. "I'm going to have a talk with the kitchen to make sure they know what you like to eat."

"Thank you, Iris."

Iris nodded and left. Volusia sat on the bed, but she wasn't precisely tired. Everything here was so strange, and she felt out of her depth. The air tasted different and this house, though a relatively new construction, was much smaller than she was used to. Before, she had only ever gone between Rome and her family's summer estate in Baiae. Now, she was separated from everything she knew by a stretch of hundreds of miles and a towering mountain range. Rome was crowded, smelly, and loud, but it was home.

She sighed and lay back against the pillows as a sudden surge of loneliness overwhelmed her. She'd accompanied Avitus here not because she wanted to, but because it was a wife's duty to go where her husband went. But now, it hardly seemed to matter. They'd barely seen each other on the journey. Avitus rode with Silvanus, his favorite secretary, and she'd been sequestered in the carriage most of the time, though on pleasant days she did insist on riding her gelding. Now, Avitus had barely stepped foot in their new home before going straight to the government offices to speak with Petronax, the stern commander who'd been in charge of the province until today.

Whatever her regrets, it was too late to turn back now. She had no option but to make Narbo her home.

Drusus nudged Max in the ribs. The legion had begun to disperse once Volusia, her husband, and the rest of their household disappeared through the city gates. "You sick or something? You've gone pale."

"I know her," Max replied under his breath, not wanting anyone else to overhear. "I was just surprised to see her."

"The wife?"

Max nodded. "Volusia. We used to be friends. Before she married, and before I joined the army. My father and her stepfather, er, worked together." Max's adoptive father and Volusia's stepfather had been consuls in the same year, occupying the two highest positions in the Republic. Max had decided to conceal his father's political history from his legionary comrades, not wanting them to think him some sort of spoiled prick. Max and Volusia had spent many hours sitting through interminable dinners while their fathers talked politics. They'd quickly built a friendship rooted in mutual boredom and the urge to see how much mischief they could get away with.

Drusus opened his mouth to reply, but his face settled into a blank mask as his attention fixed on something behind Max's shoulder. His fist snapped to his chest in a salute.

Max whirled around to see Glabrio, their centurion, wearing his customary scowl. Max stood at attention and saluted.

Glabrio lifted his chin. "Report to my office immediately, Legionary Maximus."

"Yes, sir," Max said. Fuck, he was in for it now.

The centurion turned on his heel and strode off. Max exchanged a grim glance with Drusus, then set off in Glabrio's wake.

He trudged behind Glabrio to the low stone building that housed administrative offices for the legion, next to several rows of barracks. The military buildings were separated from the town by a wall and a guard, but the barrier was perfunctory. There was little restriction on who might enter the camp, and soldiers were free to move around the town when off duty.

Max found the close-clustered buildings oppressive and cramped; he preferred living in a tent on campaign, but the legion was too well-established in Narbo for such primitive measures.

When he entered the centurion's cell-like office, he saluted once more, clasping his fist to his chest in a practiced gesture. Glabrio was a stickler for protocol and convention; he regularly disciplined legionaries if he deemed their salutes too slow or not crisp enough. For this reason, he and Max generally did not get along.

Max privately thought that Glabrio had a stick so far up his backside he should be chewing woodchips. He did, however, respect Glabrio's experience, so managed to maintain a façade of compliance...most of the time.

Glabrio settled behind his desk and surveyed Max with a dissatisfied frown. "I look forward to hearing the explanation for your behavior today."

Max swallowed and clasped his arms behind his back. "The explanation, sir, is that I was hoping you wouldn't notice."

Glabrio's glower intensified. "You showed a clear lack of regard and discipline in front of our new governor."

"With respect, sir, I was there by the time the governor arrived. He wouldn't have noticed anything."

Glabrio's eyes narrowed. "Don't talk back to me, legionary."

"Of course not, sir." This was not going well. Max wondered what he was in for. He braced himself for weeks of latrine duty or hard labor.

"Tell me what you were doing that was so much more interesting than greeting our new governor." The centurion's voice was as clipped and cold as cracking ice. "I suppose you were hungover, or warming some harlot's bed."

"I was exercising my horse, sir." Max enjoyed a good drink and a bit of flirtation as much as the next man, but if given the choice, he'd always rather spend time with Elephant.

Glabrio leaned back in his chair. "I see." He considered for a long moment.

Max stood stock still, gaze fixed straight ahead, as he waited for his sentence to be delivered.

"It's clear you need freedom from distractions," Glabrio finally said. "Governor Avitus's residence requires a security detail. You will serve there for two weeks."

Max bit his lip, his stomach sinking. Guard duty at the governor's house would not only be mind-numbingly boring, it would almost certainly ruin his plan to keep his distance from Volusia.

"In addition," Glabrio continued, steepling his fingers atop his desk, "you are hereby banned from the stables for the duration of those two weeks."

Disbelief made Max splutter. "But, sir—Elephant needs to be exercised and brushed and—"

Glabrio held up a hand. "Your horse will be well looked after. Just not by you." He opened a wax tablet on his desk and began to read. "Dismissed."

Max managed another salute, and trudged from the office. Shock still numbed him. Two weeks without being able to see or ride Elephant? Glabrio's punishment bordered on cruelty. He would gladly have volunteered for latrine duty at this point, but Glabrio knew him too well. The bastard knew that two weeks of boring security detail, combined with the inability to see Elephant, would be near torture.

And then there was Volusia to consider. He would have to see her. Would she recognize him after ten years? Would she deign to speak to him, or would she ignore him? He wouldn't blame her if she did. Once, they could pretend to be equals, both the children of elected consuls. But now, he was a mere legionary, and she was the governor's wife. There would always be a gulf between them, and Max could never forget it.

CHAPTER 3

MAX WAS IN A foul mood for the rest of that day. He carried out his afternoon duties, which included helping to repair a sagging roof along with polishing and sharpening a dozen swords. In the evening, he returned to his section of the barracks, a narrow room that housed four sets of bunk beds, sleeping eight men. He muttered a greeting to Drusus, who was sitting on one of the top bunks, legs hanging down, as he attempted to patch a hole in his tunic.

Drusus set down the needle and thread. "So? What's the sentence? Ulpius was betting you were in for at least a month of latrine duty."

Max grimaced, dropping onto a bench that rested against the wall. "Two weeks of guard duty at the governor's residence. *And* I'm banned from the stables."

Drusus shrugged. "Guard duty isn't so bad. You'll be inside, just standing around."

"Just standing around" sounded like a nightmare. "Would you check on Elephant a few times for me? She'll miss me. And she's gotten accustomed to a certain routine."

"By routine, you mean stuffing her with as many apples and carrots as you can pilfer from the provisioner." Drusus grinned good-naturedly. "Don't worry, I'll look after her. You spoil her more than a husband spoils his wife."

"Well, a wife couldn't carry me on her back all the way from Rome, could she?" Max allowed himself a brief laugh, but the mention of wives brought Volusia to mind. The last time he'd seen her, she was on the verge of a betrothal. Now, she was ten years into a marriage. He chewed his lip, wondering if marriage had changed her.

Drusus eyed him. "You're thinking about her again. The governor's wife. What was her name? Valeria?"

"Volusia," Max murmured.

"You said you knew her. Is there a story there?" His eyes lit up. Drusus loved gossip, though he would never betray a confidence.

"I told you the bulk of it. We became friends as adolescents. Of course I was besotted with her. What boy wouldn't have been?" He hesitated, remembering those heady days of infatuation. "I had reason to believe she returned the interest. But..." He shook his head. "It was just a childish fancy."

"Do you think she'll remember you?"

Max considered. They hadn't exactly parted on good terms. His last memories of her consisted of shouted threats reverberating around her family's atrium, her distraught face pale in the twilight. "I'm beginning to hope she doesn't."

The next day, Max reported for duty at the governor's residence. It was a newly constructed house near the center of Narbo, built like all Roman houses with rooms arranged around a central atrium. The house bustled with activity as slaves carried boxes and bundles to and fro. Unpacking efforts must still be underway.

Max stood in the antechamber near the front door, making sure no one got in who wasn't supposed to. It was, as he feared, extremely boring. Without the sun overhead, he had no way to estimate the time. He busied himself trying to count the tiny floor tiles, seeing how many he could get to before losing track. How would he survive two weeks of this?

The governor, Avitus, left early in the day, likely to conduct business in the offices nearby. A slender young man with an armful of scrolls and wax tablets followed him, probably a secretary of some sort. Max kept his ears pricked for sign of Volusia throughout the rest of the day. Occasionally, he heard a trill of female laughter emanating from elsewhere in the house, but he couldn't tell if it was her or not.

He realized it was midday when Avitus returned for lunch, secretary on his heels. Max saluted as he held the door open for the governor, who acknowledged him with a nod.

Quick, light footsteps approached from behind him. "Avitus, is that you? I've just had lunch set out in the—" The flurry of words stopped short.

Max turned away from the door to see Volusia, standing a few feet away and staring at him with an open mouth.

He'd been bracing himself for this meeting all day, but he couldn't suppress the bolt of *something* that ran up his spine at the sight of her. There were subtle differences in her appearance from the seventeen-year old Max remembered: her hair was done in a more complex style, and she carried herself with a mantle of cool maturity befitting a lady of her station. But the warmth filling her eyes was just as he remembered.

Avitus raised an eyebrow at his dumbstruck wife. "My dear?"

Volusia blinked and recovered herself. Her mouth closed and her lips curved in a smile. "Lunch is in the dining room, of course. You must be hungry after a morning of hard work."

"Indeed." Avitus walked toward the dining room, the secretary following. Volusia cast a lingering look at Max, hesitated as if to say something, then turned and went after her husband.

Max let out a long breath and leaned against the wall. He watched her figure recede among the columns that lined the atrium. She had clearly recognized him—and clearly didn't want her husband to know of their connection. He wasn't sure what to make of that. On its face, there was nothing so scandalous in mentioning a past acquaintance, especially as they were the same age and had moved in the same social circle in Rome.

An hour or so passed. Avitus, Volusia, and the secretary reappeared once more when the men left, their lunch concluded. Max tried to look anywhere but at Volusia as he closed and locked the front door. He waited for her to leave, but she lingered.

"Is it really you, Max?" she asked.

Finally, he looked at her. She had stepped only an arm's length from him. He could smell the flowery perfumed oil she wore. His mouth was dry, but he cleared his throat. "It's me."

A broad smile spread over her face. He remembered what it was like to bask in one of her bright, warm smiles—like stepping into a shaft of sunlight.

"Oh, how wonderful! Forgive me for acting so strange earlier—only I was just so surprised and didn't know what to say. I was half-sure I was seeing things."

An answering smile tugged at his lips. "I couldn't believe it either when you stepped out of that carriage yesterday."

"It's been a long time, hasn't it? You look well. Of course you always looked well—not that I meant"—she stumbled over her words, a pretty flush rising to her cheeks—"I just meant the army seems to suit you."

"It does, most of the time." *Just not when my centurion is being a massive prick.* "Marriage seems to suit you likewise." He was taking a risk with such a personal comment, but he couldn't resist trying to recapture the ease that used to exist between them.

She tucked a curl of hair behind her ear. "As you say. It does, most of the time."

Something lurked beneath that comment, but he'd be pushing his luck to pry. "I thought I recalled you had a son. He's not here with you?"

Her gaze turned wistful. "We decided to let Lucius remain in Rome with his grandparents. His constitution is delicate, and we didn't want to interrupt his studies."

"Studies? He can't be more than nine."

"Ten in a few months. Unlike you, he takes education very seriously. He wants to be a consul like his grandfather."

Max's mouth twisted at the mention of Volusia's stepfather. "Good luck to him."

Volusia gave him a stern look. "He could do much worse."

A heaviness settled between them. Volusia's stepfather, Rufus, was one of the reasons she and Max hadn't spoken in ten years.

According to Rufus, Max was not fit to breathe the same air as his precious stepdaughter, due to Max's unconventional upbringing. Max had been born into poverty and fled an unhappy home, preferring to take his chances on the street as a child of seven. Then, he'd been adopted by Aelius and Crispina, unable to have children of their own. Rufus knew of Max's ignoble origins and had never seen him as anything more than a delinquent.

It didn't help that Max, as a child, had once attempted to attack Rufus. During a contentious election between Rufus and Aelius, Rufus had stooped to threatening Crispina. Max had witnessed Rufus lay hands on Crispina, and the best he could do was kick Rufus as hard as possible in the shin in an effort to defend her. No doubt Rufus remembered the incident keenly, which contributed to his hatred of Max.

"I must return to see how the rest of the unpacking is going," Volusia said, her voice turning brisk. "It was very nice to see you, Max." She nodded to him, then turned and walked further into the house.

Max watched her go, a tugging feeling in his chest urging him to follow her. He ignored it, and resumed his post by the door.

CHAPTER 4

Ten years ago

P RAISE ALL THE GODS, it was almost over. Max's adoptive father's year as consul was nearing its end. In a matter of weeks, Max would be free from his suffocating position in one of Rome's two most scrutinized families.

Volusia, sitting across from him at dinner, knew just how he felt. He could tell it from her smile as they listened to their fathers discuss the upcoming election, speculating who might win the next term.

The past year had been dismal, full of dinner parties and banquets and state occasions where he had to stand up straight and pretend to pay attention. He'd been kept on a tight leash, forbidden from carousing and gambling with his friends. He'd only endured it because his parents had struck a bargain with him: one year of exemplary behavior, and he would be sent off to join the army's cavalry division with a horse of his choosing.

He'd already chosen the horse, a graceful young mare whose gait was the smoothest he'd ever felt, and he endured every boring dinner party by imagining the adventures they would have together. He pitied Volusia; all she had to look forward to was marriage to some magistrate her parents had selected.

Volusia caught his eye across the table. Her delicate eyebrows twitched twice in quick succession. He smothered his grin into his napkin. That signal meant "escape at the first opportunity." They had developed their own language of twitches and nudges over the past few months, after an unfortunate incident resulted in them being forbidden from sitting next to each other. The incident in question had been almost worth it: Max had endeavored to make Volusia laugh by spelling out inappropriate words with his food. He'd been halfway through "farthole" when she'd burst out in an unbecoming peal of giggles, drawing the attention of every guest.

After that, he'd received a stern talking-to from Aelius and Crispina, his adoptive parents, and there had been no more sitting next to Volusia. They'd gotten more creative in finding ways to slip away unnoticed and escape into the atrium of whatever house they were at.

Tonight's gathering was a small one, just their parents at Volusia's house. Their fathers were avidly talking politics, and their mothers were discussing Crispina's endeavor to fund a school for children whose parents couldn't afford school fees or private tutors. Volusia, moving with the gentle grace that never failed to catch his attention, rose from the table and slipped from the dining room.

Max counted to fifty in his head, then languidly lifted himself off the dining couch and walked as casually as he could to the door.

His pace increased once he left the dining room behind, and he hurried down the hallway. He'd probably find Volusia in the atrium, enjoying the quiet twilight.

He was right; she sat on a bench between two flowering bushes in stone planters, looking like some sort of forest nymph among the greenery.

"You found me," she said with a smile.

"Were you hiding?" He lowered himself onto the bench next to her.

"Not from you." Their shoulders brushed on the narrow bench, and a flare of heat traveled through him. He'd been smitten with her since they'd first met, but he'd been told in no uncertain terms that she was not for him. Volusia's stepfather scorned Max's low birth, but neither Rufus's contempt nor the fact that Volusia was on the verge of an engagement could dull the sparks Max felt whenever he was near her.

"Only a few more weeks of this." Max stretched his legs in front of him. "Then we're free."

"Hardly free," Volusia said with a rueful smile. "I'll be married before winter, no doubt, and you'll be in service to the army."

To Max, joining the army was freedom—the chance to escape the oppressive city, to see new lands and test himself in battle. One day, he might be a great general. He imagined leading a triumphal procession through the streets, basking in the respect and adoration of the whole Republic.

But then it settled over him like a heavy, uncomfortable toga: the end of his father's term meant he wouldn't have an excuse to see Volusia anymore. Once she was married, she would be even further out of his reach.

He tried to ignore the unpleasant thought. "I found my horse the other day. She's a gray mare. Guess what I'm going to name her."

Volusia propped her chin in her hand as if thinking hard. "I don't know, but I'm sure it's something *very* respectable." Her voice dripped with sarcasm.

"Her name is going to be Elephant," Max said, his chest puffing out with pride. "On account of her coloring, and because I want to ride an elephant into battle like Hannibal."

Volusia covered her mouth against a shriek of giggling. "You're naming a *horse* Elephant? That's the stupidest thing I've ever heard."

"It's very clever," he protested.

She rolled her eyes. "If you say so."

He huffed and changed the subject. "What about you? Anything new with the engagement?"

"Mother and Father are negotiating the dowry. I expect the betrothal will be official once that is finalized, and then it will just be a matter of finding an auspicious date."

"Have you even met this man you're supposed to marry?"

"Several times. He's very kind, and his prospects are excellent. He even gave me this." She flashed a blue-stoned bracelet on her slender wrist.

Max, who had admired the deep blue stones against her fair skin earlier in the evening, now thought it was the ugliest piece of jewelry he had ever seen.

"I could have a child by this time next year," Volusia said, her eyes lighting up. "Wouldn't that be wonderful?"

The thought of Volusia having children with some unknown man sent a sickening pang through him. "Juno's cunt," he muttered.

"Max!" Her eyes widened in scandalized horror, as they always did when he swore. "You really shouldn't talk like that. The gods don't like being mocked."

"I think they have more important things to worry about." He seized on her shock, needing something to distract himself from their talk about marriage and children and parting, and leaped to his feet. He held up his arms as if addressing the gods directly. "Juno's cunt," he intoned. "Mars's balls. Jupiter's hairy—"

Volusia leaped up and clapped a hand over his mouth. "Stop it!" She was half-scandalized, and half-laughing.

The touch of her hand on his face made him fall silent. He stared down at her, swimming in her luminous hazel eyes. Her hand gently slid from his mouth, her touch becoming a caress down his jaw, his neck.

His arms slid around her of their own accord, pulling her close. Her slim body felt so good, so *right* in his arms—just like when he'd ridden Elephant for the first time.

He only wanted to hold her, but then she tilted her face up and rose on her tiptoes to brush his mouth with hers.

A shiver ran down his spine. Everything faded away—the columns in the atrium, the smell of food from the kitchens, even his excitement and anxiety about their futures. There was only Volusia, her gleaming eyes and pink cheeks and soft mouth.

Their lips met again in a hard, searching kiss. She pressed against him, and he allowed her slight weight to push him backward.

They almost fell over, but he managed to right them and guide them to a column for support. Her hands slid down his chest, finding places Max didn't even know could be pleasurable. Emboldened by her touch, he drew one hand up her waist, still kissing her with mindless desperation. His fingers splayed on her ribs, resting just beneath the curve of her breast. He waited for her to tense, to draw back, but when she didn't, he allowed his hand to shift further upward. She let out a little gasp against his cheek as his fingers brushed against her breast, warmth filling his hand.

He braced himself against the column, Volusia nestled into him. She was still grabbing at him, pulling him ever closer.

A shout split the air. Volusia jerked, shoving Max away from her. He stumbled back and whipped his head around to see Volusia's stepfather bearing down on them, his sallow face purpling with rage.

"What villainy is this? How dare you come into my house and assault my daughter?" Rufus skidded to a halt an arm's length from Max. His wife, Sabina, latched on to his elbow, which seemed to be the only thing stopping him from hurling himself at Max.

"Father!" Volusia gasped.

Rufus kept bellowing about disrespect and virtue and honor. His voice had an unfortunate habit of growing higher the more incensed he became, until he sounded like an enraged mouse. He finally freed his arm from Sabina's grasp and stepped right up to Max, shaking his fist in Max's face.

Max spoke evenly. "Get your hand out of my face, or I will break your fucking fingers."

"You insolent animal," Rufus hissed, but he did lower his hand. "I will have you sued for assault. Your name will be dragged through the *mud*—"

Two more figures entered the atrium, and the calm voice of Max's father interrupted Rufus's threats. "I'm sure you don't mean to be speaking in such a manner to my son, Rufus."

"What my husband means," Crispina said, her voice icy, "is that if you don't moderate your tone, I will dunk you in the atrium pool."

Rufus turned to her. "Your brat deserves much more than some harsh words. I saw him with his *filthy* hands all over my daughter!"

"Father!" Volusia interjected again. Angry tears glimmered in her eyes. One spilled down her cheek, and Max's heart clenched at the sight of it. Sabina went to her, wrapping an arm around her shoulders and trying to lead her away, but Volusia evaded her mother's gentle grasp. "Listen to me! It's not what you think."

"Don't try to defend him, Volusia. I know what I saw," Rufus snarled.

"Perhaps you should let the young lady speak," Aelius said. He had a knack for speaking quietly yet commanding the attention of a room, even in chaos like this.

Rufus glared at him, but fell silent. Volusia took a breath and cast Max a glance. "No offense was given," she said in a small voice. "It was—"

Max knew that she was about to take the blame for their kiss, to insist that it was all her fault and he'd done no wrong. Maybe it was true—she had initiated the kiss—but in an instant, Max knew he couldn't let her take responsibility for this. She'd face her parents' displeasure and anger. Word of this might even get out, if the household slaves gossiped, and jeopardize her engagement.

"All my fault," he finished her sentence. Five pairs of eyes snapped to him. "It was a silly joke. I meant no harm."

"No harm? No harm?" Rufus exclaimed.

Volusia bit her lip. Max could tell she was on the verge of confessing, but he held her gaze and gave a slight shake of his head.

Aelius cleared his throat. "If Volusia is not offended, then no more needs to be said. I think it's time for us to be going." He beckoned to Max.

Max stepped toward him, but Rufus blocked his path, his face still blotchy and red. "You will never set foot in my house again, is that understood? Much less speak a single word more to my daughter."

"Father—" Volusia protested, but Rufus held up a hand and she fell silent.

"You are not worthy of breathing the same air as her," Rufus said, his voice hoarse from shouting. "You will never be anything more than a dirt-grubbing stray—"

"That's quite enough." Crispina took firm hold of Max's elbow and steered him from the room. He craned his head back for one last glimpse of Volusia, who was standing with slumped shoulders and tearstained cheeks, before they left.

Outside, Max climbed into the waiting litter with heavy limbs. Aelius and Crispina followed.

"Really, Max, what were you thinking?" Crispina demanded as the litter lurched into motion. "You can't go around kissing girls at dinner parties."

"I don't kiss girls at dinner parties," Max muttered. "I kissed one girl. And, if you must know, she kissed *me*. I lied."

Crispina's eyes widened. "You lied to Rufus?"

He nodded, staring glumly at his knees. "I figured if he hates me that much, he'd be even angrier at Volusia if he thought she'd kissed me. Things would be easier for her if I just said it was my fault."

"Oh, Max," Crispina whispered. She pulled him into a tight sideways hug, awkward in the confines of the litter. "That was so gallant of you."

Aelius laid an approving hand on his shoulder. "Very well done."

Usually, his parents were chiding him for being late or not trying hard enough at his studies or spending too much of his allowance at dice, so the fact that he'd actually done something right should have filled him with bliss. But even their praise couldn't lessen the heavy feeling in his gut, couldn't erase the sight of Volusia's distraught face.

"I'm very sorry," Crispina murmured, almost as if reading his mind.

"Why?"

She gazed at him, her eyes dark and serious. "Because to act as you did—to bring displeasure and wrath upon yourself to spare Volusia from discord with her parents—well, I fear that means you love her."

CHAPTER 5

A FTER SEEING MAX FOR the first time in ten years, Volusia was scattered for the rest of the day. She endured a quiet dinner with Avitus and Silvanus, then went to bed early on her own. Lying in bed, she replayed her conversation with Max over and over again. It had been mundane, but every word they exchanged was like a spark to tinder, rekindling feelings she'd thought long extinguished.

The past ten years had been good to him. He'd always had a carefree handsomeness about him, but ten years' service in the army had filled out his boyish lankiness. Now, he was all broad shoulders and muscled limbs, though his untidy bronze hair and lively brown eyes were just as she remembered.

It was improper for her to think of him this way, but she let the prick of guilt pass. Her husband, after all, was sharing a bed with Silvanus at this very moment. Avitus had made her aware of his preferences very early in their marriage. *"I have every intention of conceiving a son with you, Volusia,"* he'd said, *"but once that is achieved, you need not worry that I'll bother you further."*

Bother. There were moments she longed to be *bothered*, but she'd had ten years of practice in resigning herself to a decidedly unbothered existence. Avitus was kind, respectful, and unflinchingly honest with her. He didn't try to hide his affairs, and Volusia repaid his candor by tolerating them. Nevertheless, it had been a shock when he'd suggested that Silvanus, his most talented secretary and latest lover, move in with them once they arrived in Narbo. But, like everything else, she had accepted it.

Max's reappearance seemed an answer to a prayer she hadn't known she was making. She'd been homesick, lonely, regretting her decision to leave Rome and travel to Narbo. Max was a friend from a simpler time. In the dark, a smile curled her lips as she remembered the mischief they used to get up to—surreptitiously tossing nuts into someone's wine goblet at dinner, spelling dirty words with the food on their plates, and the like. It was all childish nonsense, but it warmed her to remember how things used to be.

She fell asleep thinking of Max, and woke with the realization that he could be helpful to her in making Narbo feel like home. She knew him, and he knew the city. At dinner last night, Avitus had encouraged her to see the town once she was settled at home, and Max would make the perfect escort.

After Avitus and Silvanus left for the day, Volusia found Max in his post by the door. He was leaning against the wall, arms crossed over his chest and a bored look on his face—hardly the picture of military discipline. As soon as he saw her, he snapped into a straighter position.

"Good morning," she said.

"Morning," he replied with an uncertain half-smile.

"I was hoping you could help me with something. I wanted to see a little of the town, and I need an escort. Would you accompany me?"

His face brightened. "Of course. I'll just need to find a replacement for my duties."

She waved a hand. "Hermes can keep an eye on the door for an hour or so. I'll get a cloak and find him."

She went briefly to her room to fetch a small purse and don a light linen cloak to protect her dress from any dirt they might encounter outside, then asked Iris to have Hermes, one of the household slaves, man the front door.

Then, she returned to Max. He opened the front door, and escorted her out of the house. She blinked in the bright sunlight. It was the first time she'd been outside since arriving here.

"What do you want to see?" he asked.

She hesitated, glancing around the quiet street. "I don't know. What is there to see?"

"Not as much as you're used to, probably. There's no amphitheater, no circus, or anything like that. We could go to the market square, if you like?"

She nodded, and he gestured her to follow him. The streets were narrow, and became more crowded with people and animals as they headed toward the center of the town. The buildings, though nowhere near as grand as those in Rome, looked new, or newly refurbished, with clean concrete walls and neat brickwork. The legionaries must have been hard at work improving the town.

Volusia walked at Max's side, their arms occasionally brushing. How strange it was to walk through the streets beside him. Even in Rome, she had almost always been carried in a litter whenever she wanted to go somewhere. The streets were dangerous, and mugging was always a risk. But today, with Max at her side, she felt completely safe.

In the road ahead, a large ox pulling a cart full of boxes made its lumbering way toward them, a man tugging at the rope connected to its halter. The street was barely big enough for the huge animal, causing everyone to squeeze themselves out of the way on both sides. Volusia followed Max's lead and carefully stood to the side, waiting for the ox and cart to pass.

As the ox reached them, its path swerved toward them. Max's arm shot out and swept Volusia backward, until her back pressed hard against the building behind her. The ox's hooves missed her toes by barely a handspan.

"Watch your beast, cocksucker!" Max bellowed at the ox's driver.

The other man made an impolite hand gesture. "Bugger off, Roman swine."

Max replied with a hand gesture so rude Volusia blushed. The ox finally trudged past them, the cart so close it brushed her skirt. A little unsettled by the aggressive exchange, she glanced at Max's face, only to see that he was grinning.

"You haven't lost your taste for profanity, I see," Volusia said.

"If anything, the army has only increased my vocabulary." Max put a hand on her shoulder. "You're all right? You look a little shaken."

The warm, heavy feel of his hand on her shoulder, even through her linen cloak, was making her feel even more unsettled than the incident with the ox. "I–I'm fine. I was worried you'd come to blows." She knew plenty of men—stepfather and husband included—who wouldn't have let such insults pass. But to Max, it seemed to be all in good fun.

He removed his hand and shrugged. "If I got into a fistfight with every man who swore at me, I'd be too busy to get anything else done. Now, if that beast had injured you in any way, it would be a different story."

Her stomach gave a pleasing yet disconcerting lurch at the thought of him taking action to defend her.

They continued walking in silence. Soon, they arrived at a small square that was lined with shops. Temporary stalls filled the open space in the middle. A display of colorful pottery caught her eye. "Let's go look over here." She wanted to make a good first impression on the residents of Narbo by supporting their industry and craftsmanship.

Max followed her around the market as she browsed everyone's wares. He was a steady, mostly silent presence at her back, occasionally murmuring in her ear if a certain shopkeeper was known to be dishonest or their items of poor quality. She made several purchases, including a set of blue-glazed water jugs, a bolt of flowing turquoise fabric, and a delicately carved ivory comb for her hair. She arranged for the items to be delivered to her home later.

Shopping never failed to whet her appetite, and her stomach growled as the scent of something savory wafted over her. "That smells delicious."

Max pointed to a stall across the square. "Carmo's chickpea fritters. They're good. He drizzles them in rosemary-flower honey. It's a specialty of the province. Have you tried it yet?"

"Oh, everyone loves rosemary-flower honey in Rome. It comes from here?"

Max nodded. "Want me to get you some fritters?"

It would have been more proper to return home for lunch, but Volusia was much too tempted by the prospect of some warm, crispy chickpea fritters doused in sticky honey. "Yes, please." She handed Max the remains of her purse. "Will you get some for both of us?"

Max took her money and obtained a pile of fritters wrapped in a clean white cloth. He guided her away from the market to a quiet side street, where they sat on an empty stoop and dug into the fritters. Volusia bit into one in delight. The fritter was warm, slightly greasy, crispy on the outside beneath the thin coating of honey but light and delicate on the inside.

Max shoved one into his mouth whole and chewed loudly, which made her smile. His table manners had always left something to be desired. A vestige of his childhood spent on the streets, along with his penchant for foul language. As a mother, Volusia's heart broke to think of him being abandoned by his birth family and forced to fend for himself, but the fact that he had survived proved his strength and resilience.

Comfortable silence stretched between them for a few minutes as they ate. Volusia had never imagined she would find such enjoyment sitting on the street, eating greasy food with her hands, but this was the most fun she'd had in ages.

Max leaned back with a contented sigh after polishing off his half of the fritters. He licked his fingers and wiped his mouth with the back of his hand. "Is there any news from Rome? I haven't been home in two years."

Volusia cleaned her fingers on the edge of the napkin. "All anyone talks about is the civil war. It's somehow tedious and trying at the same time. Avitus says that Octavius will likely invade Sicily soon. It makes me nervous to think of fighting so close to Rome. Are you disappointed to be missing the excitement?"

Max shrugged. "Sometimes, but I think I'd rather be bored here in Gaul than have to fight other Romans."

Volusia grinned. "Finally, a sensible man." She turned to more interesting topics. "I don't see much of your family, but I understand all is well. I heard from my stepfather that Aelius is considering another run for the consulship next year. Assuming we still have a republic after this war, that is. And if your father runs, you know mine will have to as well, to prove he can beat Aelius."

Max groaned. "Again? At least this time I can hide out here in Gaul. Maybe I should ask for a transfer to Syria." He chewed his lip pensively, as if he were actually considering it.

Volusia laughed. "Nothing is certain. Don't you miss Aelius and Crispina?"

He nodded. "Of course. But I don't miss Rome. You can hardly take a step without someone asking you for money or trying to distract you so their friend can pick your pocket. If it weren't for my family, I'd be happy if I never saw the city again. I'd much rather be out here in the provinces. We may not have a theater or circus, but at least there's fresh air to breathe and room to gallop a horse."

"The countryside does seem beautiful," Volusia agreed. "I admired it on our journey, and I'd love to see more of it."

"I could take you," he offered immediately. "There are some perfect trails just outside the city. That is—I don't suppose you know how to ride." His face fell.

She hurried to correct him. "I do ride, a little. I brought a horse and sidesaddle on the journey, and rode whenever the weather was pleasant enough. The carriage gave me a terrible headache." She was not an experienced rider, and riding sidesaddle meant that someone else had to lead her horse, but it was worth it for the fresh air.

His expression warmed. "Perfect. I can escort you on a tour of the countryside anytime. Just say the word."

She smiled, but a flicker of unease rose in her chest. Spending an hour or two shopping with Max was one thing, but riding out into the hills and forests alone with him?

The proper thing would be to thank him for his offer but demur. Instead, she nodded. "I need a few more days to make sure everything is settled in the house. But after that, I will look forward to it."

That evening, Volusia joined Avitus and Silvanus for dinner. It should have been odd to dine with her husband's lover, but she was used to it by now. Even before her husband had struck up a relationship with Silvanus, he'd been a fixture at their table in Rome. There were always decisions to be made, letters to be dictated, and Silvanus was a dedicated, hardworking secretary. He didn't flaunt his status as Avitus's favorite, for which Volusia was grateful. She suspected that Silvanus liked Avitus's power and position more than anything else, but his presence helped dispel the silence that often fell on the rare occasions Volusia and Avitus were left alone together.

Tonight, the men were deep into a discussion of the province's finances, which didn't hold Volusia's interest. Instead, she reminisced about the day she'd had with Max: the way he'd shielded her from the ox, the ease with which he traded insults, and the comfort she felt in his presence.

She was in the midst of recalling the taste of the chickpea fritters when she realized silence had fallen in the dining room. She glanced up to see Avitus watching her expectantly.

"Volusia?" he asked, as if repeating himself.

She straightened up. "Forgive me, I was lost in thought. Did you say something?"

"I said I'd noticed some packages were delivered earlier. Did you make some purchases?"

Even in the mundane question, she recognized that he was trying to be kind, to include her in the conversation. "Yes, I went shopping and purchased some things at the market. Just little trinkets, really."

His brow furrowed. "You didn't go alone, did you?"

"Of course not." Even in Rome, the city where she'd lived her entire life, she never went anywhere unaccompanied. "I asked one of the legionaries to escort me."

"Next time, take someone from the household. Even Iris would do. These soldiers answer to Petronax, not me. I'm not sure I trust them yet. Especially not with my wife."

The mention of Iris made her remember what she needed to ask Avitus. "I've been meaning to talk to you about Iris. I want to free her."

Avitus glanced at her in surprise. "Whyever would you do that?"

"Because she's served me well for ten years. And her family lives here in Gaul. It seems right to allow her to go back to them."

Avitus exchanged a glance with Silvanus. "It may be difficult to find a well-trained replacement out here."

Volusia shrugged. "I'll manage. But I don't want Iris to leave empty-handed. I know her family is poor, and I'd like to give her some money. I believe she cost around a thousand denarii to purchase, so I'd like to give her that much." She hated that she had to ask permission, but there was no way around it. Iris belonged to her alone, but Avitus controlled the rest of their wealth and property.

"A thousand denarii!" Avitus chuckled as if she'd suggested gifting Iris a minotaur. "Freeing a slave is already a waste of money. This would be a waste twice over."

Her lips tightened, but she forced herself to remain placid. Arguing would not help her cause. "It's not as if we can't spare it."

Avitus looked over at Silvanus. "What do you think, Silvanus? Should I give my wife's slave a thousand denarii?"

Volusia flushed. She didn't mind Silvanus attending their dinners to advise Avitus on affairs relating to their work, but this was a matter that should remain between husband and wife.

"I'm sure it's not my place to have an opinion on a matter such as this," Silvanus said with his usual diffidence. "But if you insist, I must agree that it does not seem like a worthwhile expenditure."

Avitus gave a careless shrug, as if the matter was completely settled, but Volusia was not willing to give up so easily. "It's my birthday in three months," she said. "You can either gift me the money directly, or whatever gift you select, I'll sell it and give the money to Iris." Despite his flaws, Avitus had never been stingy with presents.

Avitus sighed. "As you wish, wife."

"Thank you." She turned back to her meal, until something else occurred to her from earlier in the conversation. "What did you mean when you said you didn't trust the soldiers because they report to Petronax, not you? Doesn't Petronax report to you?"

"I only meant that we are still strangers here." He exchanged a glance with Silvanus that seemed to bear some unspoken meaning.

A tendril of anxiety unfurled in Volusia's stomach. "Do you mean there could be some danger here?"

Avitus waved a dismissive hand. "A transition of power always brings some tension."

"You worry too much," Silvanus murmured into his wine goblet.

"Worrying is at least two-thirds of a governor's job," Avitus said with a smile, and the conversation turned to other things.

CHAPTER 6

A WEEK AND A half after Volusia's shopping excursion with Max, a suitable day for their riding tour finally arrived. Volusia had taken a few days to make sure the household was arranged as she liked it. Then, there had been a stretch of rainy weather, but this morning finally dawned clear and bright. Max told her to come fetch him whenever she was ready to leave.

First, she had to tell Avitus where she was going. He was conducting business in his study at home this morning. As she approached the closed door, raised voices echoed from within. She paused, not wanting to interrupt at a bad moment.

Her husband was speaking loudly and forcefully. "…don't care if that's the way you've been managing things, we must go about things properly."

She recognized the stern, clipped voice of Gaius Galerius Petronax, the legion's commander. "I'm sure if you spend some more time with the financial records, you'll see how my prior procedures can benefit you."

Volusia didn't want to interrupt, but she also didn't want to eavesdrop. She had no idea what the men could be discussing, but it seemed to be of a sensitive nature, involving money. She tapped gently on the door. "Avitus?"

"Come in, Volusia."

She pushed open the door. Petronax was on his feet, as if he'd been pacing, and Avitus sat at his desk with his fist clenched atop a stack of tablets. Petronax gave her a stiff nod, but did not smile or offer her a greeting.

"Forgive me, I did not mean to interrupt," she said.

Avitus unclenched his hand. "You're not. Petronax was just leaving."

The commander's shoulders tensed, but he turned on his heel and pushed past Volusia through the door.

Volusia watched him go. Was it wise to dismiss the province's second in command like a chastised lackey?

She shook the thought from her mind. Avitus had matters well in hand, no doubt.

"Did you need something?" her husband asked.

"I just wanted to tell you I'm about to go riding. I've asked one of the, er, household to escort me around the countryside." She carefully avoided mentioning that her escort was a legionary, given Avitus's earlier warning. Max was, she reasoned, technically a part of their household for the duration of his guard detail. "I'll be home well in time for dinner." *Though I doubt you'll notice if I'm not there.*

He nodded. "Very well. Enjoy the day." He bent his head to focus on the tablets in front of him, and she left the room.

She went to her room, where Iris was folding some clothes. "Could you find my traveling cloak?"

Iris went to a trunk and rifled through it, then pulled out a cloak. "Going somewhere?"

"Riding," Volusia said. "With Max—the legionary. You know, the one who's always at the front door."

Iris's blue eyes locked onto Volusia's face. "That big one who took you shopping?"

Volusia nodded.

"You like him, don't you? You should be careful, mistress. These soldiers, they might have pretty faces, but they're all just big dumb killers. And somehow that one seems dumber than most."

"Max isn't like that. I knew him before I got married. We were...friends." She blushed. They had been more than friends by the end.

"Hmph," Iris said. "I still think you should watch out. I know it's fashionable for married ladies to have their fun, but I think you can do better than a *soldier*." Her voice dripped with disdain.

"I don't want to have *fun* with him," Volusia insisted. "I just enjoy his company, and he's offered to take me riding. My cloak, if you please." She took the cloak from Iris. "I'll be back before dinner."

"Very well, mistress."

Volusia left her bedroom and went to the kitchens to pack a small bag full of bread, cheese, and a wineskin. She wasn't sure how long they'd be riding, and she didn't want either of them to go hungry.

She met Max at the front door, and held up the bag of provisions with a smile. "I brought sustenance."

He gave her an answering grin. "Excellent."

They set off. Hermes had once again been asked to watch the door in Max's absence. Really, Volusia wasn't entirely sure why a legionary had been assigned to do a job that one of the household slaves could easily manage, but perhaps there had been a desire for extra security.

"Am I finally to meet the famous Elephant?" Volusia asked as they reached the military stables on the outskirts of Narbo.

"You remember her name?" Max said, looking pleased.

"Of course. It's the stupidest name for a horse I ever heard."

He chuckled, then paused before entering the stables. "In case anyone asks, this outing was entirely your request."

She raised an eyebrow. "What's that supposed to mean?"

A trace of guilt flitted across his face. "I'm technically banned from the stables for another week. But if I'm acting on the orders of the lady Volusia, then I think I can get away with it."

"So you're just using me to get access to your precious horse?" She couldn't help smiling. Max was always in some sort of trouble.

"I guess you could look at it that way." He hauled open the heavy stable door, and beckoned her inside.

The earthy scent of horse droppings and hay greeted her as she stepped into the stables. A few grooms glanced at them, their gazes lingering on Volusia with curiosity. Max went straight for a stall toward the end of the aisle. A large gray head poked out through the slats in the stall door, and Max quickened his pace into a half-jog until he reached the horse.

Volusia hung back, watching as Max ran a gentle hand down the horse's cheek and pressed his forehead to hers. He tapped at the underside of her head, and she lifted her head until her nose was level with his face. He planted a kiss on her nose, after which the horse gave an appreciative snuffle of his hair.

"This is Elephant," Max said. "Come introduce yourself."

Volusia was not in the habit of introducing herself to horses, but she approached and obligingly patted Elephant's silky nose. "You are quite pretty, aren't you?" The name Elephant was apt; the horse was large for a mare, and her coat was a dappled gray like raindrops on stone.

Elephant found the gold bracelet on Volusia's wrist and snuffled at it. Volusia yanked her wrist back, tsking at the horse.

"She does have a taste for finery, like any lady," Max said. "Now, where's your horse?"

Volusia helped Max locate the docile gelding she'd brought from Rome, along with the sidesaddle, which had been stored in the stable's tack room. He saddled both horses with practiced efficiency, then led them out into the stable yard.

With gentle strength, he boosted Volusia onto her horse. His hands moved over her legs, checking that her knees were properly positioned. His touch was businesslike, not lingering, but she still suppressed a shiver.

Once satisfied, he mounted Elephant in a fluid, effortless movement, and took hold of the lead attached to her horse's bridle. Sitting sidesaddle unfortunately did not allow her to control her own horse, but it was a small price to pay for the exhilaration of riding.

Max signaled Elephant to walk. Volusia's horse dutifully followed as they left the stable yard.

With Volusia riding sidesaddle, the fastest they could go was a gentle trot as they took the flat road away from Narbo. Ordinarily, Max would have been simmering with irritation at the slowness, but he would have been happy to move at a snail's pace if it meant spending time with Volusia.

He stole a glance at her. She appeared to be comfortably seated on her horse and was tipping her face up, as if enjoying the sun and fresh breeze on her face. It had rained yesterday, and today the air smelled pure and clean. He tried not to look at the way the horse's motion made her hips sway.

They passed several small farms on the outskirts of Narbo. He raised his hand in greeting to the farm workers who stopped their labor to watch him and Volusia pass.

Soon, the dwellings became less frequent, and the road turned to a rutted dirt path. The further they got from civilization, the more Max's shoulders relaxed. He loved being out here in the countryside, with only Elephant and the birds for company. And today, Volusia.

"It becomes wooded just over that rise." Max gestured to the rolling hill before them. "Do you like redcurrants? There's a spot I know with bushes of them."

"How lovely," Volusia said. "Perhaps I can bring some back for the kitchens. Avitus is fond of them as well."

The casual mention of her husband threatened to dampen his good mood, but he strove to keep the conversation light. "How does the governor find his province so far?"

He expected her to have a cheerful, meaningless response about how busy Avitus was or how well he'd settled in, but instead her mouth drew into a small frown. "To be honest, I don't know. I walked in on him arguing with Petronax before I left. I'm sure it was nothing, but…" She shook her head. "Do you know Petronax well?"

The question caught Max off guard. "Not really." It was probably for the best that he didn't have much direct interaction with the legion's highest commander, given how much his own centurion already disliked him.

"Is the legion loyal to him?"

"Of course." It went without question that every member of the legion would be blindly loyal to their commander.

"Do you think he's a good leader?" she pressed.

Max had never stopped to consider that question. "I-I don't know."

"What about the people of the province? Do they like him?"

Another question Max had never thought about, but there was the whole business of the mysterious increase in taxes that no one would explain. "Lately there's been a bit of agitation around taxes. Petronax raised the tax rate this year, and of course everyone is displeased. It's to be expected, I suppose. No one likes paying taxes."

"Especially not citizens of a conquered province," she murmured.

Max gave her a surprised glance. A comment like that bordered on radicalism, especially coming from a governor's wife.

Volusia lapsed into silence, and Max left her alone with her thoughts. They crested the hill and passed into forested territory. Slowing to a walk, the horses picked their way along a narrow path, avoiding fallen logs and rocks underfoot. Elephant was familiar with this trail, and moved confidently, while Volusia's mount proceeded with more caution.

Birdsong echoed through the trees, and shafts of sunlight dappled the ground. Max took a deep inhale, filling his lungs with the fresh woodsy air. The rush of moving water grew louder, and Max guided them toward the spot he'd mentioned, where several large bushes festooned with red berries grew next to a narrow, fast-flowing stream.

He drew the horses to a halt and hopped off Elephant, then went to help Volusia down from her horse. His hands encircled her waist, and she grabbed his shoulders for steadiness as he lowered her gently to the ground. The pressure of her hands on his body, even through the fabric of his tunic, sent his mind straight back to that heady, foolish kiss ten years ago.

But she released him as soon as her feet touched the ground, and he didn't allow his hands to linger on her waist. He busied himself securing the horses' reins to the branch of a nearby tree. Elephant could be trusted not to wander off, but they had to set a good example for Volusia's horse.

"Beautiful," Volusia said, glancing around at the quiet scene. Her gaze lingered on Max. "You look so at home out here. One would never guess you're a city boy through and through."

"I'm no such thing," he said with mock offense. "Just because I grew up on the streets and didn't know anything existed outside the city walls doesn't mean I have any love for the city."

Her mouth opened, her cheeks flushing. "I didn't mean—I know your childhood wasn't—"

Dis, she thought he was actually affronted. "I'm joking, Volusia."

"Oh," she said. "Well, let me apologize anyway. You never really spoke of your childhood, and I shouldn't have brought it up."

It was true; their friendship had never extended to discussion of Max's upbringing, but he knew she knew the broad strokes. "I'm sure your stepfather filled you in. What did he tell you?"

She approached one of the redcurrant bushes and plucked a berry, then rolled it between her fingertips, inspecting it. "He said you were a street thief who conned Aelius and Crispina into adopting you. I'm sure that's an exaggeration."

Max let out a short laugh. Trust Rufus to cast Max in the worst light possible. "I was seven years old when Crispina found me on the streets. Barely smart enough to keep myself alive, let alone pull off a con."

Volusia bit her lip. "I didn't know you were that young. How did you—forgive me, I shouldn't ask."

Max usually didn't like to remember that he had a life before Aelius and Crispina plucked him off the streets. As an adolescent, he'd gotten into many fights with posh boys who tried to shame him for his humble birth. Max never hesitated to use his fists to defend himself against their taunts, which led to many angry fathers marching to his house and demanding that Aelius punish Max for his insolence. Aelius always shrugged and promised to punish Max when their brat received an equal punishment for thinking they were better than anyone else.

But Volusia wasn't taunting him. She had never held herself above him, even though she outclassed him in every way. She, for some reason, wanted to know about him, his past, and the thought made him feel warm. "You were going to ask how I ended up on the streets."

She nodded as she plucked another berry.

"There's not much to it," he said. "I was unhappy, so I ran away." His childhood memories were hazy and shifting, like trying to look at his reflection in flowing water. He could only ever seem to remember his father's booming voice and hard fist, and his mother's cold, dismissive face.

"You never tried to go back and find your family—your birth family, I mean?" she asked.

"No." He shrugged. "I don't need them. Aelius and Crispina have given me everything I needed, and more."

She let out a soft sigh. "It breaks my heart to think that any child could end up without a home. I felt guilty leaving Lucius in Rome with his grandparents, even though I know he's much happier there than he would be here. We would have had to take a whole extra carriage for his books." She smiled wistfully.

It was still strange to think of Volusia as a mother, even though he'd always known she would be. "Your son is lucky to have you as a mother."

"I do my best."

They picked handfuls of berries and sat on the grassy bank to eat them, along with the bread and cheese that Volusia had thoughtfully brought. Volusia saved some of the berries and tucked them into a handkerchief.

"For your husband?" Max asked.

She nodded. "He'll be pleased."

"You told him where you were going today?" He assumed she would have had to come up with some subterfuge to be allowed to go on an excursion like this.

"We keep no secrets from each other. For better or for worse," she added in a lower tone.

Max laid back on the ground, lacing his fingers together behind his head. "What's that supposed to mean?" He stared up at the treetops cutting through the blue sky, expecting her to demur and avoid his prying question.

Volusia let out a small sigh. "Avitus is a great man. I always wanted to marry a great man."

"There are plenty of great men I wouldn't want to be married to," Max said, giving his words a joking lilt. But that was yet another reason they were ill-suited; he was as far from a great man as Elephant was from a hydra. He couldn't even secure one minor promotion, after all.

She rewarded him with a small chuckle. As an adolescent, making her laugh used to be his greatest aim, and he felt the same warm flare of satisfaction at the sound now.

She lapsed into silence a moment later, and Max thought the conversation was finished. Until she spoke once more. "Avitus and I...our marriage is...different from what I expected," she finally said. "I appreciate his honesty, but sometimes it's difficult to know you're married to someone who will never truly desire you."

Max sat up straight. It was inconceivable that a man could be married to Volusia and not be consumed with desire for her.

"He prefers to spend his nights with his secretary," Volusia said, in response to the question that must have shown on Max's face.

"Ah." He recalled the handsome secretary he often saw dogging Avitus's heels. "So you don't...you never...but you have a child together!"

She nodded. "He was very clear that he would endure what he had to until we produced a son. Luckily that did not take long at all."

Endure. Several emotions warred in his chest: anger at Avitus for not appreciating her, regret that Volusia had suffered so much loneliness, and admiration for the dignified way she spoke of it, absent of any resentment toward her husband.

"Vesta's tits," he muttered.

"Max!" A trill of laughter entered her voice. "I'm sorry, I shouldn't have told you all that."

"I won't repeat it, if that's what concerns you." Impulsively, he reached out and closed his fingers around her hand. "You can trust me, Volusia. Always."

She gazed into his eyes. "I know."

Max wanted to ask if she would ever take a lover herself, and if so, could he please be considered for the role. But even he knew that would be inappropriate, and not what Volusia needed right now, so he merely squeezed her hand and let it be.

As the sun began to stretch toward the horizon, they prepared to return to Narbo. Volusia fought regret as she gathered up her harvest of redcurrants and tucked them into Max's saddle bag.

Max untied the horses. "Are you up for an adventure?"

"Hasn't this already been one?" Volusia smiled. "What did you have in mind?"

Max checked to make sure Elephant's saddle was still securely fastened. "We could circle around to the beach and have a gallop. You'd have to ride with me on Elephant."

"I've never galloped on a horse before." The prospect of being wedged tight on horseback against Max, flying down a stretch of beach, made her stomach quiver. "Will that be quite safe?"

"Do you really think I'd take any risks with you? I'd be ejected from the army in disgrace if I let any harm come to you."

"With that assurance, I suppose it could be fun."

He grinned at her. "It will be more than fun, I promise."

He helped her onto the gelding, mounted Elephant, and they set off on a circuitous route toward the coastline. Soon, the trees cleared, and the dirt beneath their horses' hooves turned to sand. The sea appeared, endless and gently rolling. Volusia was accustomed to spending summers at Baiae, the coastal retreat of Rome's wealthy, so the sight of a vast expanse of shifting turquoise water was familiar, but it still took her breath away. The afternoon sunlight sparkled on the water. In the distance, a little fishing boat skimmed the waves.

Her gelding snuffled with distaste as his hooves sank into the sand. She and Max dismounted, and Max secured her horse's lead under a boulder near the edge of the beach, so he wouldn't wander off while they galloped.

Max lifted her into Elephant's saddle. Riding astride, her dress bunched up around her knees, exposing her calves. Elephant sidestepped beneath her, causing Volusia to grab at the saddle for support.

"Are you comfortable?" Max asked.

"I-I think so."

Max vaulted up in front of her, squeezing them both into the saddle. Volusia tucked her feet around Max's ankles for security. They were pressed together from hip to ankle, and she could feel every movement of his body as he adjusted his position in the saddle.

"Hold on tight," he said, and then nudged Elephant into a trot.

Volusia wrapped her arms around his middle, having no choice but to nestle her chin atop his shoulder. Oh, yes, he had filled out deliciously since seventeen. All she could feel was warm, hard muscle beneath his linen tunic.

Elephant trotted down the beach toward the water, where the sand became hard-packed. Max turned her to face down the beach, and she smoothly shifted into a canter. Volusia felt Max's knees tighten around Elephant, and the horse reached a breakneck gallop.

Wind rushed in Volusia's ears, blocking out all sound but the rhythmic thump of Elephant's hooves. To her right, waves crashed onto the beach. Ahead of them was nothing but an empty, gently curving shoreline. They could gallop all the way to Rome at this rate.

Her heart raced, the only thing that could exceed Elephant's speed. She clutched at Max, afraid she'd go tumbling off Elephant's back otherwise. Her hair streamed behind her, wisps loosening themselves from her braids. Iris would have quite a time putting her back to rights later.

Max tilted his head back toward her. "You all right?" he asked, raising his voice over the roar of the wind and waves.

She squeezed him even tighter. "Better than all right!"

He laughed. "Dare you to close your eyes."

An answering laugh bubbled up from deep in her chest. "Only if you don't." She closed her eyes. Exhilaration spread through her. Her stomach lurched in a way that was somehow thrilling. Nothing existed but the feeling of flight and the body clutched in her arms, the only thing solid in a world of rushing wind and pounding hooves.

Elephant slowed eventually, and Volusia opened her eyes, squinting in the sunlight. Max turned Elephant around, and they trotted down the beach to rejoin Volusia's patient gelding. Her breathing calmed, but the thrill didn't leave her.

"Thank you," she murmured as Max lifted her back onto her own horse. She thanked him not just for the mounting assistance, but for everything—this day, the gallop, the way he listened to her.

"Of course," he said, and swung up onto Elephant. He took hold of her horse's lead, and guided them back in the direction of Narbo.

CHAPTER 7

VOLUSIA AND MAX RETURNED to town in late afternoon. Volusia regretfully parted from Max at the front door with a smile and a murmured goodbye. She had revealed too much to him, but it had felt good to talk to someone. Iris knew the state of her marriage, of course, and Volusia did confide in her, but Iris received all of Volusia's confidences relating to Avitus with a calm, almost expressionless demeanor. Volusia understood—it would be inappropriate for a slave to express any frustration or rancor toward the master of the house, even if she was only sympathizing with Volusia.

But Max had seemed near outraged at the revelation of her passionless marriage. *Vesta's tits,* he'd said. His language should scandalize her, but it brought a smile to her face, just like when they were adolescents. She sent a silent plea of forgiveness to the goddess of the hearth, and vowed to make a few extra sacrifices on Max's behalf next time she was near a temple.

Volusia paused at the door of Avitus's study. She heard no voices from within, so surmised that he was alone. She tapped on the door. "Avitus?"

"Come in."

She entered, and crossed the room to lay the bundle of redcurrants on his desk. "I harvested some redcurrants for you."

His face brightened, and he picked a berry from the top of the pile. "Your excursion was satisfactory?"

"The countryside is beautiful." It was, but what she most remembered from the afternoon wasn't the swell of hills or sparkle of sunlight on water, but Max's face, the press of his hand on hers, his promise that she could trust him, always.

She shoved the memory aside. "I was chatting with the legionary who escorted me. He mentioned some interesting anecdotes about Petronax that I thought you should know."

Avitus raised an eyebrow as he ate another berry. "Yes?"

Volusia seated herself in the chair across from his desk, wondering if she was overstepping by mentioning this. Ordinarily, she didn't interfere in her husband's affairs. But here, so far from home, she felt vulnerable, despite their high position. "There's been some dissatisfaction since Petronax raised the taxes here."

He waved a hand. "There is always dissatisfaction about taxes."

"But isn't he overstepping by hiking up the tax rate? He's meant to be in charge of the legion, not the province."

"He was acting governor before I arrived, Volusia. He was entitled to do as he wished. With respect, you understand little of these matters."

She flinched at the dismissiveness of his tone. "I'm only trying to help. I heard you with Petronax earlier. I don't think you should antagonize him. What were you arguing about?" she pressed.

His gaze became stony. "It's none of your concern."

"Is it Silvanus's concern?" she shot back. "I bet you're going to tell *him* everything. Maybe you already have. You tell him too much. He is your subordinate, after all."

Never before had she questioned his relationship with Silvanus, but Max's outrage at the state of her marriage had changed something inside her. Maybe she'd been wrong to be so accommodating, so amenable. Maybe she deserved more than a disinterested husband.

"You are my subordinate too, wife." Ice coated his words. "I will speak of my business as I please, and your opinion is not required." He rose from behind the desk and strode past her to the door, pausing in the doorway. "Tell the kitchen that I will take dinner in my room."

With Silvanus, no doubt.

She gave a stiff nod, and he left. The pile of redcurrants remained forlorn on his desk.

Volusia bit her lip until it hurt. They had never argued like this before, perhaps because Volusia had never broken her role of the dutiful, agreeable wife. But now, the boundaries of their marriage, once safe and comfortable, felt oppressive, constricting, like a hairstyle braided too tight.

She rose from the chair and left the study. In the hallway, her feet itched to turn right, toward the atrium and front door where Max no doubt stood, silent and dependable. But she forced herself to turn left, and retreated to her bedroom.

As the sun dipped low in the sky, Max left the governor's residence and returned to the buildings that comprised the legion's camp at the edge of the town. Almost as soon as he set foot within the walls, one of Glabrio's lackeys informed him that the centurion would like to see him.

Jupiter's balls. Max stifled a groan. One of the grooms in the stables must have reported his presence to Glabrio.

Max set his jaw and turned in the direction of the centurion's office, practicing excuses in his head. He entered the office and saluted in a way he hoped looked especially deferential. "Sir, you asked to see me?"

Glabrio, seated at his desk, steepled his fingers and fixed Max with an intensified version of his usual disapproving glare. "I was told you violated the terms of your punishment."

Max endeavored to look as innocent as a newborn kitten. "Sir?"

"You were seen at the stables today. Were you not expressly forbidden from visiting the stables?"

"Yes, sir, but the lady Volusia requested to go riding. I thought it would be inappropriate to refuse her."

Glabrio's brows drew together. "What reason does a lady have for riding?"

"I believe she wished to see some of the countryside, sir, but I did not think it respectful to question her motives."

"So you abandoned your post to go gallivanting around the countryside with the governor's wife," Glabrio said.

"On the contrary sir, I assumed I was carrying out my duty by ensuring the lady's safety. And…" Max risked a small elaboration of the truth. He had a feeling he was on the verge of another punishment, so he needed to think fast to convince Glabrio that he'd acted correctly. "Governor Avitus himself encouraged it. He wished his wife to see more of the province but did not have time to escort her himself." At least it was true enough that Avitus knew of their outing—even if he hadn't explicitly encouraged it.

Glabrio's lips tightened at this new information. "Be that as it may, I would urge you to be cautious of how you conduct yourself, legionary. I would never dare to impugn the lady's honor, but it's well known that Roman ladies who have been married for a time often seek distraction. And any legionary who dares to take such liberties will be dishonorably dismissed without delay."

Max flushed. Could Glabrio tell how much he wanted to take liberties with Volusia? "On my honor, sir, nothing untoward happened while we were riding."

"Nor will it in the future," Glabrio said. "If the lady asks to ride again, you will decline. Is that clear?"

Max strove for a chastened expression, despite his relief that he seemed to have avoided a second punishment. "Yes, sir."

"Dismissed."

Max saluted once more, and hurried from the office before Glabrio could change his mind.

The day after his riding excursion with Volusia, Max's mind was full of Volusia's confession about her marriage as he stood guard by her front door. It wasn't fair. She deserved a husband who worshiped the very air she breathed. Avitus never should have married Volusia if he couldn't be the loving husband she deserved.

Would you be happier to see her blissfully satisfied in her marriage? an unpleasant voice in his head questioned.

Perhaps there was a small, selfish, uncharitable part of him that was glad he didn't have to witness her marital bliss. But still, his heart ached at the thought of what the past ten years must have been like for her.

A throat cleared. Max straightened up quickly, hoping to see Volusia.

It wasn't Volusia, but Iris, her fair-haired maid. Max leaned back against the wall and crossed his arms over his chest, trying to suppress his disappointment. He hadn't seen much of Iris, but the few times their paths had crossed, she'd looked at him as if he were a pile of horse droppings in her way.

Nevertheless, he addressed her with respect. "Hello, Iris. Does Volusia need something?" Even if she did, she had a whole household full of servants to attend to her every need. She wouldn't need anything from him.

Iris shook her head and moved closer to the front door. She regarded Max with what he now recognized as her customary suspicious, disdainful stare, lips pursed and nostrils flared. "I wanted a word."

He shrugged. "All right. I've got nothing but time."

She glanced over her shoulder, into the atrium, and lowered her voice. "I wanted to warn you. Because it seems you're too thick to understand the situation for yourself."

He raised an eyebrow. "What situation?"

She rolled her eyes. "Volusia, of course. Dis, soldiers really are stupid."

"You don't have to insult me, Iris."

She ignored him. "I tried to tell Volusia as much. Soldiers are just big dumb killers, every one of them. All you know how to do is say 'yes sir, no sir, how many innocents should I slaughter today, sir?'" She clutched her fist to her chest in a mocking salute.

This was the most Iris had ever spoken to Max, and he noticed a Gallic lilt to her words. That, coupled with her curly, fair hair and sprinkling of freckles, made him realize she must be a native of Gaul. Thus, she'd have plenty of reasons to hate the Roman army.

Few of his legionary fellows would let such insolence—especially from a slave—pass without retaliation, but Max allowed the insults to roll off his back like water from a duck's feathers. "Why are you discussing me with Volusia?"

"I merely advised her that she should be careful. But of course there are limits to the advice I can give to my mistress. Which brings me to you." She folded her arms. "If Avitus catches wind of what's going on between you, he will divorce her. She'll be separated from her son. And no doubt I'll be sold off somewhere terrible. You have no reason to care about me, but for the sake of Volusia and her son, you need to watch it. Keep your cock in your braccae, or you'll have me to answer to."

Max stared at her. "Nothing's happened between us."

Iris arched an eyebrow, clearly unconvinced. "You mean to tell me that you went off to the countryside for an entire afternoon, alone, and nothing happened?"

"Nothing happened," he insisted. *As much as I wanted something to.* "Besides, her husband spends his nights with Silvanus. Why should he care what Volusia does?"

"Because men are hypocrites. Not that you know what that word means, I expect."

"I know what a h-hypocrite is," Max said. At least, he was pretty sure he did. "I'm telling you again, there's nothing inappropriate between us."

"Then it should be easy for you to stop staring at her like a lovesick donkey," Iris said.

"Well, I only have three more days on guard duty here," Max snapped. He hadn't realized his feelings for Volusia were so plain, if Iris had picked up on them. "You'll be rid of me in short order."

On one hand, he was looking forward to resuming normal duties. But on the other hand, that would mean giving up the moments of delight when Volusia found an excuse to come see him. She took an uncanny interest in checking whether the front antechamber was perfectly swept, or ensuring that the lamps were properly filled. They were usually able to steal a few minutes of conversation each day.

"That's the best news I've heard all week," Iris said with a wide, sarcastic smile. "Good day, legionary. May our paths never cross again." She turned on her heel and left.

"The feeling is mutual," Max muttered in the empty antechamber.

Later that day, Volusia found him, a mournful look on her face as she pretended to check the corners of the antechamber for dust. "Iris told me you'll be leaving soon."

Max nodded. "This was only meant to be a temporary stint. So I'll be returning to normal duties soon."

"Oh. I see. Normal duties."

His heart twisted at her obvious disappointment. For a moment, he debated asking Glabrio to station him here permanently. He could see Volusia every day.

But despite the pleasure that seeing her brought him, guard duty was as monotonous as he'd feared. Even the endless drills that the legion undertook were better than this. He needed excitement, activity. And besides, he was still angling for a promotion to decurion. He needed to prove himself worthy to command his own men, and standing guard in a governor's house was not the way to do that.

"I'm sorry," he said.

"There's no need to apologize," she replied. "You have your duties. I have mine. Seeing you here was a pleasant surprise, and I've appreciated your friendship, but I think it best if we go back to the way things were."

She meant the ten years of never seeing each other. Maybe Iris had succeeded in warning her away from him. He knew there was no other possible response she could have, but her words still made his chest feel tight with regret. "Yes."

She turned to go.

"Wait," he said. He crossed to her and took her hand—a shocking liberty in her own house, but she didn't pull away. "Volusia, if you ever have need of me..." As the words came out, he realized how stupid they sounded. What need could she have of him? She had a husband and an entire staff to see to anything she might require. "I'll be at your service," he finished lamely.

But she looked up at him with a serious gaze. "Thank you, Max."

He dropped her hand, and she left the antechamber. As she disappeared, he closed his fist, trying to preserve the warmth of her hand in his. He would likely never feel her touch again, and these memories would soon be all he had left of her.

CHAPTER 8

MAX SERVED OUT THE last day of his guard detail, and returned to normal duties. A month passed in which he saw nothing of Volusia. His days consisted of a rotation of cavalry drills, building maintenance, sharpening weapons, and patrolling the countryside. He tried to forget Volusia, to be grateful he could now visit Elephant whenever he pleased.

But thoughts of Volusia surfaced at the most inopportune times. He remembered the feel of her plastered to his back whenever he galloped Elephant, and the sight of a redcurrant bush made him think of the blissful afternoon they'd spent among the trees.

One morning, he sat in his bottom bunk attempting to shave with the aid of a blurry silver mirror. A hubbub of voices rose in the hallway outside, but Max didn't pay enough attention to parse out the words, focusing instead on making sure he didn't cut himself with the razor. No doubt his fellow legionaries were just gossiping about something inconsequential.

Hurried footsteps sounded, and Drusus threw open the door, poking his head into the room. "Have you heard? We're to form up immediately."

Max ran a hand over his chin. He was only half-done shaving. "What's the matter? Are we under attack?"

Drusus shook his head. "People are saying…" He hesitated and came fully into the room, letting the door close behind him. "People are saying Governor Avitus is dead."

Max dropped the razor, which clattered to the floor. "Juno's cunt." His mind immediately went to Volusia. *What happened? Is she all right?*

"I imagine Petronax wants to address everyone, to get the news out there and stop gossip from spreading. So get dressed quick." Drusus left the room.

Max rushed to dry his half-shaven face and throw on a tunic. His mind raced. Could this be true? Governor Avitus had seemed in the best of health from the little Max had seen of him.

He tried to imagine Volusia swathed in the dark clothing of mourning, her hair left loose. Would she be distraught with grief, despite what she had shared with him about their marriage? Avitus was still the father of her child, after all.

Max hurried out of the barracks and followed the horde of soldiers assembling in measured ranks on the field before the city. He found his spot next to Drusus. At least this time he wasn't late.

Once everyone had assembled, Petronax appeared before the crowd. As one, the legion saluted.

Petronax wore a charcoal black toga, more somber than his usual chainmail armor and scarlet cape, though gold bracelets and rings still glimmered on his arms and fingers. "I come before you with tragic news," he said, his voice carrying across the crowd. Those at the back would have a hard time hearing, but the message would filter through the ranks. "Our esteemed governor Avitus was taken ill a few days ago, and succumbed to his illness last night."

A murmur swept through the assembled legion.

Petronax kept talking. "No doubt he is in Elysium now, and we will honor his memory as he deserves. To turn to more mortal concerns, the Senate will be alerted of this tragic development, and they will appoint a replacement in due course. In the meantime, I will resume my role as acting governor." A note of smugness broke the solemnity of his voice. He paused.

The legionaries stamped their feet in dutiful approval. Petronax nodded in acknowledgement, then made a gesture of dismissal. The legion saluted once more, then began to filter off the field.

"He didn't mention Volusia," Max muttered to Drusus.

"Why would he?" Drusus said. "The widow doesn't concern us."

"I was just wondering what might happen to her."

"Well, she'll return to Rome, I expect," Drusus said. "Or wherever she came from. She has no reason to stay here now, does she?"

A pang of shock shot through Max, leaving devastation in its wake. Of course, it was that simple. He just hadn't wanted to acknowledge it. Volusia was going to leave Narbo, and he would never see her again.

Volusia sat at her dressing table, an open box of jewelry before her. She ran her fingers over the pieces. Each held a memory that stabbed deep into her chest. There was the carnelian ring Avitus had given her upon their wedding. The sapphire bracelet, a betrothal present. The pearl and ruby necklace for Lucius's birth.

He'd even given her a golden hairpiece when he'd been made governor of Narbo, as consolation for having to leave Rome.

The remains of her life with Avitus glimmered back at her from the silk-lined box.

She was still in shock at the suddenness with which it had happened. Not even a week ago they'd been eating dinner, herself and Avitus and Silvanus as usual, when Avitus had complained of a stomachache. Nothing odd in that, though Avitus usually boasted a robust digestion.

From there, it had only worsened. The stomachache had become a piercing pain that wouldn't relent. He'd grown feverish and listless, and couldn't seem to draw a full breath.

For once, she'd been grateful for Silvanus's presence. He'd sat with Avitus during the nights, while Volusia kept vigil during the days. When Avitus finally died, Silvanus had been at his side. She began to think that maybe Silvanus had truly cared for her husband.

Her gaze went to the one piece of jewelry that wasn't in the box—her wedding ring. It shone too brightly on her finger, polished by ten years of daily wear. She took a deep breath and twisted it off her finger. It yielded easily, and in a moment, her finger was bare. A swell of emotion rose within her, too thick to name.

Footsteps sounded behind her. Volusia dropped the ring into the jewelry box and turned to see Iris enter the room.

"Petronax is here to see you, mistress. I can turn him away if you like."

Volusia shook her head and rose. "I'll receive him in the atrium."

Iris clasped her hands together. "Are you sure, mistress? You've hardly slept. You should be resting."

"I'll rest later." Between funeral arrangements and preparing for her inevitable departure from Narbo, there was too much to be done. Something else occurred to her as she thought of their departure—a conversation she needed to have with Iris. "Petronax can wait for a moment. There's something I need to speak with you about." She beckoned Iris closer.

Iris closed the door and came to stand before her. "Yes, mistress?"

Volusia gazed at the face of her faithful companion. "Iris, I want you to know that I was planning on freeing you here in Gaul, close to your family. I only waited because I didn't want to send you off with nothing, and Avitus had promised to gift me some money to give to you on my birthday."

Iris's face remained blank, but Volusia knew her well enough to catch the flicker of emotion in her pale blue eyes. "That would have been most generous, mistress."

"No more than you deserve. But now that he's gone, I have nothing to give you. Not now, at least. Avitus's will transferred his entire estate to my control, to keep in trust until Lucius comes of age. Once I return to Rome, I can give you what you deserve. So I wanted to give you the choice. I'll free you now, if you desire it. Or, if you stay with me until Rome, I can send you off with enough money to set up a life for yourself wherever you choose."

Iris met Volusia's gaze for a moment, as if trying to ascertain whether she was serious. Then, Iris dropped to her knees and pressed her forehead to Volusia's feet in a quick, formal gesture of gratitude. "Thank you, mistress. I will go with you to Rome."

Relief filtered through her at Iris's choice. At least, after having lost Avitus, she wouldn't have to lose Iris just yet. She bent and raised Iris to her feet, clasping her hands. "Thank you. I wasn't looking forward to making that journey alone, besides the escort. Now, I should go speak with Petronax. Likely he wishes to discuss the arrangements for my departure."

Iris nodded and stood aside. Volusia exited her bedroom, and Iris fell into step behind her.

The legion's commander waited in the atrium, garbed in a black toga. Volusia herself didn't have any black clothing, so wore her most drab gray dress with a matching palla pinned to her head to cover her hair, which she'd left unbound as befitted a widow in mourning.

Petronax gave a small nod when she approached. "My condolences on your loss, lady."

"Thank you."

"I came to tell you that an escort is being prepared as we speak for your departure from Narbo. You may leave at your earliest convenience."

"The funeral rites have not even taken place." Petronax seemed quite eager to rush her away, as if to remove every trace of the province's former governor.

"Of course you may stay to see the formalities observed. Will you wish for your husband's ashes to be interred here, or will you take them back to Rome?"

"They belong with our family in Rome." She thought the loss would be easier for her son to comprehend if she could present some physical proof of his father's death, even if just an urn of ashes. "If that's all, commander, I have much to attend to."

He gave a stiff nod, then turned on his heel and left the house.

Volusia watched him go. His visit brought to mind the dark thoughts that had plagued her as Avitus had inexplicably sickened. It seemed impossible that his death could be nothing more than tragic happenstance. As she had watched her vigorous husband waste away before her, foul play seemed the only thing that made sense.

But no sooner could such a thought enter her mind than she recalled all the reasons it didn't add up. Firstly, how could anyone want Avitus dead? True, she'd overheard him and Petronax arguing, but a mere argument was hardly a reason for the legion's highest commander to murder a Senate-appointed governor.

Furthermore, even if Petronax had wanted Avitus dead, she couldn't think of how it might have been accomplished. Avitus had been taken ill after dinner, so poison seemed likely, but she and Silvanus had eaten from the same dishes and drank the same wine, and neither of them had suffered any illness.

It just didn't add up, but something in her refused to believe a healthy, vital man like Avitus could be struck down so easily.

She heaved a sigh. There was one person who might be able to sympathize with the frazzled workings of her mind right now, so she dismissed Iris and went to find Silvanus. She had to ask him about his plans to leave Narbo anyway.

The door to Silvanus's bedroom was closed, and she hesitated before knocking gently. This was the room Avitus had spent his nights in, the room he'd died in.

"Yes?" came the call from within.

"It's Volusia."

She heard footsteps, and then the door swung open. Silvanus looked gaunt and exhausted, as if the last few days had aged him ten years. Despite herself, a twinge of sympathy pained her.

"What is it?" he said, his voice almost a snap.

"I just wanted to ask what you plan to do now. I'll be returning to Rome after the funeral. You are welcome to join me."

Silvanus shook his head. "Petronax has offered me a position here, with the provincial administration."

"You're staying in Narbo?"

He shrugged. "Where else would I go?"

Volusia recalled that Silvanus hailed from a rustic town in northern Italy and did not have much in the way of family. There was likely nothing for him there, or in Rome, so perhaps it made sense he'd stay here. "Very well. Speaking of Petronax...may I come in?"

He frowned at her for a moment, then stood back from the door and allowed her to enter the bedroom.

Volusia closed the door behind her and tried not to look at the bed where Avitus had died. "Did Avitus mention anything to you about Petronax? Any quarrel they might have had?"

Silvanus crossed the room and sat heavily in a chair by the wall. "What are you getting at?"

She bit her lip. To think such things was one matter, but to actually speak them aloud... "Do you not think it strange how he died?"

His gaze flicked up to her, as quick as an arrow, then slid away. "People get sick all the time. Some of them die."

"I just...did the thought of foul play really never cross your mind?"

"I think you should be careful about throwing around accusations about the most powerful man in the province," Silvanus said, lowering his voice.

"I'm not throwing around accusations. Just asking questions in the privacy of my own home."

Silvanus let out a tight sigh through his teeth. "Of course the idea of foul play crossed my mind. But I can't see how anyone could have accomplished it. The three of us ate the same food that night."

"Did Avitus share anything with you that might point to a reason for someone to want to..." She couldn't say the words: *to kill him.*

Silvanus shook his head slowly. "Not that I recall." A flash of pain crossed his face, as if he were recalling every conversation he'd ever had with Avitus.

Impulsively, Volusia went to him and laid a hand on his shoulder. "I know how much you cared for him. And I'm grateful for everything you did for him, especially at the end."

Silvanus pushed her hand away with surprising force. "It's over, Volusia. We don't have to pretend to be the best of friends anymore."

"I-I wasn't pretending—"

Silvanus rose to his feet, shoved past her, and left the room without a backward glance.

Volusia stared after him in shock for a moment, then gathered herself. Silvanus was entitled to his frustration, and he was clearly still reeling from Avitus's death.

With a sigh, she left the bedroom and made her way to Avitus's study. She wanted to make a start on clearing things out to determine what should remain here and what should be taken back to Rome. It felt strange to rifle through her husband's things, and perhaps Silvanus was better suited for the task as his secretary, but she didn't want to bother him right now.

She found a pile of wax tablets and sorted through them to separate blank ones from ones containing writing. Silvanus would have to advise on which of the filled ones needed to be kept. As she glanced over one blank tablet, something caught her eye. A slight indentation in the wax, revealing words not completely removed.

Curiosity took hold, and she tilted the tablet to find the best angle to read the letters. It appeared as if the tablet had once been full of writing, but only the barest trace of a few words remained. She squinted, moving a lamp nearer to better see.

…ax revenue…counting irregular…ruption….

These words made no sense. Ax revenue? She looked closer, trying to see the ghosts of missing letters.

It wasn't *ax revenue*, but *tax revenue. Accounting irregularities. Corruption.*

At the very bottom of the tablet, there was a hazy stroke and curve which might have formed a P.

Petronax.

Volusia set the tablet down with shaking hands. Avitus had a habit of writing out his thoughts when he was struggling with a problem or question. Was this tablet evidence of him figuring out that Petronax was up to something unlawful?

If this was true, and if Petronax had gotten wind of Avitus's suspicions, it was easy to see how Avitus might have ended up dead.

Silvanus's words came back to her. *"I think you should be careful about throwing around accusations about the most powerful man in the province."* She shivered. If Petronax really had done something to Avitus, Volusia had to tread carefully. This province was full of people who were loyal to Petronax, people who would believe him over her without a second thought.

She ran a finger over the wax surface of the tablet. She could just take a stylus and rub away the traces of writing. She could return to Rome, start a quiet life as a widow with her son, and forget all of this.

That choice tempted her. It would be so easy to turn a blind eye, to pick the safe, comfortable option.

But Avitus, though he wasn't perfect, deserved better. If he really had been killed, he deserved justice. And if Petronax was misappropriating tax revenue, then the people of this province deserved better.

Volusia closed the tablet and tucked it under her arm. She needed to keep it with her, as it was the only shred of evidence she possessed. Evidence that Avitus, at least, had suspected something.

She went to her bedroom. Iris was there, starting to pack a trunk. Volusia wrapped the tablet in a shawl and placed it into the trunk. "Make sure this isn't disturbed," she said to Iris.

Iris glanced at the bundle and nodded. "Yes, mistress."

Volusia longed to tell Iris everything she suspected, but held back. She trusted Iris, but these suspicions were dangerous, and for the time being, it was safer for Iris not to know. Silvanus's warning about throwing around accusations stuck in her mind. The fewer people who knew her suspicions, the better. But there was one thing Iris could help with.

"Iris, do you remember that legionary who was on guard duty here when we first arrived?"

Iris looked up from her packing. "The one who couldn't stop staring at you like a puppy?"

Trust Iris to make her smile barely a day after her husband's death. "Yes, that one. I need to see him. Do you think you could ask around and find out where he might be tonight?" Max might be the only person she could trust with her suspicions, and even he was a risk given that Petronax was the legion's commander.

Iris raised an eyebrow. "Really, mistress? Are you sure that's wise? I know you're no longer married, but—"

Volusia blushed. "It's not that. I just need to speak to him, and I can't trust a messenger." Summoning Max here would be too suspicious—why would the governor's widow need to speak with a lowly legionary? So she'd have to go to him, as discreetly as she could.

Iris nodded. "All right. I'll find out what I can."

CHAPTER 9

In the evening, Max sat with Drusus and a few of their comrades around a low fire outside an open-air tavern. The soldiers had been subdued for most of the day after the announcement of Governor Avitus's death, but now, with the help of some wine and the company of certain ladies, the mood was lifting. Laughter and jokes echoed back and forth. Drusus had a dark-haired lady nestled firmly in his lap, and they were in the midst of negotiating a price for her company that night.

One of her colleagues paused in front of Max, giving him a questioning look. He shook his head, and she moved on to flirt with another soldier. Since being stationed in Narbo, Max had occasionally sought nighttime company, but not since Volusia arrived. For some reason, it felt wrong to consort with another woman while Volusia was in the same city.

But now, Volusia was leaving, returning to Rome, and he'd never see her again. He heaved a mournful sigh. Apollo's balls, when did he become so pathetic, moping around after a woman he could never have?

Across the fire, a female figure caught his eye, and his gaze snapped to her. *Volusia.*

No, you idiot. It was just another woman who bore a passing resemblance. At this rate, he was going to spend the rest of his life jumping every time he saw anything with breasts.

The figure lifted a pale hand to the scarf she wore over her head and shoulders, pulling it away from her face. Max caught a glimpse of golden hair. Firelight flickered on hazel eyes, and the woman's gaze locked with Max's.

Max nearly dropped his cup of wine. *Fuck, it's actually her.* Behind Volusia, Iris lurked, glancing over the group of carousing soldiers with a sour expression on her face.

Volusia held his gaze for a moment, then moved away, into the shadowy alley between two buildings. Iris followed.

Max hastily put his cup of wine on the ground next to his stool and hurried after them, weaving through the maze of stools and benches that were clustered around the fire. What in Dis was Volusia doing here?

He entered the alley, squinting in the gloom as his eyes adjusted after the bright firelight. He didn't see the two women, and took several steps further into the alley, his feet slipping on uneven cobblestones.

A hand grasped his arm from behind. Instinct and years of training kicked in, and he didn't think before his other hand flew to the knife at his belt. He whipped out the blade and whirled around, breaking the person's grip on his arm. He thrust the blade forward.

A feminine shriek made him stop short. Awareness slowly returned. He wasn't being attacked by an enemy soldier or brigand. It was just Volusia, and now he'd pinned her against a wall with a knife to her throat.

She raised both hands, eyes wide. "Max," she gasped. "It's me!"

Iris marched forward and batted at his arm. "Get that thing out of her face."

Max hurriedly lowered the dagger and sheathed it at his hip. "Sorry, but you shouldn't sneak up on someone like that at night. Especially not a soldier."

Iris snorted. "Only a soldier is stupid enough to mistake a tiny woman for an attacker."

Max resisted the urge to roll his eyes. "Speaking of attackers, don't you know it's dangerous to be out at night?"

"Of course we know that," Iris said, her voice dripping with condescension. "My esteemed mistress has decided that this excursion to find you is worth being raped and murdered."

Volusia crossed her arms. "I told you several times, we're not going to be raped and murdered, Iris. If anyone bothers us, all I have to do is show my face"—she pulled down the scarf that covered her hair—"and they'll leave us alone. No one would dare lay a hand on the governor's wife—widow," she corrected with a flinch.

She was probably right; military discipline was strict enough that no one would dare bother her. But that only went for the soldiers. There were plenty of others in Narbo who weren't bound by military honor.

But Max sensed that she had not come here to be lectured about taking risks with her safety, so he set the matter aside. "I am sorry about Avitus. This must have been a great shock."

Her face clouded. She glanced at Iris. "Would you keep watch over there, Iris? Make sure no one disturbs us."

Iris gave a reluctant nod and headed to stand at the mouth of the alley, looking out over the street.

Volusia stepped nearer to him, and lowered her voice. "The reason I came here has to do with Avitus, actually."

Max had to lean close to hear her. The scent of lavender from her clothes washed over him.

"I fear...I'm afraid..." Her words faltered, but Max waited patiently. "I think Avitus might have been murdered. By Petronax, or someone working for him."

Murdered? A bolt of shock rippled down his spine, somehow managing to surpass even the surprise of Volusia being here. "Fuck," he breathed.

Volusia went on to explain her reasoning, describing the tablet she'd found hidden in Avitus's study and the words she had pieced together from it. Max's stomach sank as he realized he believed her. Petronax had used his power as acting governor to hike up the tax rates for his own gain. And if Avitus had found out and objected, it made a horrible sort of sense that he'd end up dead.

"So what are you going to do?" he asked when she'd finished speaking.

She blinked at him. "You mean to say you believe me?"

Max shrugged. "Petronax may be my commander, but I know you better. And like you a lot more."

She gave him a long look he couldn't decipher. "Even if you believe me, I don't think anyone else here will dare to side with me against him. So I'll wait until I return to Rome and then bring my evidence to the consuls. My father has influence, as a former consul. He can help make sure I get listened to."

It sounded like a good plan, so Max nodded. "All right. Is there anything I can do to help?"

"There is something I would ask of you." Her hand stretched out in the shadows to find his. A spark of heat ran up his arm as her fingers brushed his palm. "I need someone I can trust on the journey to Rome. I know it's asking a lot, but if you could arrange to be part of my escort—"

He tightened his fingers around hers. "I'll speak to my centurion in the morning," Max said without hesitation. It was a sacrifice; spending months journeying to and from Rome was not the kind of assignment that would be impressive enough to help in his quest for promotion. Furthermore, he hated Rome, even though his family lived there, and he had little desire to return.

But if Volusia asked it of him, he couldn't say no.

"Oh, Max," she whispered. "Thank you." Suddenly, her arms were around his shoulders, pulling him into an embrace.

Her warmth surrounded him, blocking out all rational thought. His arms slid around her. Her head rested on his shoulder. For a long, blissful moment, nothing else existed but Volusia in his arms. Not Petronax, not the shade of Volusia's dead husband, not even the increasingly raucous yells emanating from the group of soldiers on the street.

Volusia shifted, and he thought she was moving to break their embrace, but instead she tilted her face up and pressed her lips to his.

For ten years, he had wondered if his memory of their first kiss was colored by childhood exaggeration. Now, he discovered that kissing her was as heady as he remembered, if not more.

Her lips were tentative at first, but grew bolder after that first gentle brush. Instinct took over in Max. He anchored one arm around her waist. His other hand went to her chin, fingers brushing her throat. He gently angled her face to his, tilting her head back so his tongue could delve into her mouth.

She let out a soft sigh against his lips. Her hands tangled in his hair, giving a slight pull. He choked back a groan.

Iris coughed loudly from her position at the top of the alley. Volusia drew back, removing her hands from Max's body. She gazed up at him, her eyes luminous in the darkness. "I-I'm sorry," she whispered.

He had no idea what she was apologizing for, but he nodded as if he understood perfectly.

"I should go." Volusia replaced her head covering, pulling it around her face and draping the ends over her shoulders.

"I'll escort you back."

She looked as if she wanted to refuse, but let out a sigh of acceptance. "Thank you."

When they reached the start of the alley, Iris gave Max a scorching glare—as if he was the one who'd kissed Volusia. Nevertheless, Iris did suffer Max to walk ahead of them on the street that led back to the governor's residence, keeping a wary eye out for trouble.

Max glowered at anyone who dared glance at the two women behind him, and they reached the house without incident. Volusia gave Max one last nod before she disappeared within the house.

Max ambled back to his comrades, still reeling from the events of the last quarter hour. Volusia thought Petronax had murdered her husband. He passed a hand over his lips. Even more shocking than her suspicions about Petronax, Volusia had kissed him.

And he'd promised to journey to Rome with her. Despite himself, joy surged in his chest at the prospect of at least one more month with her. Of course, he wouldn't be free to speak to her on their journey, as he'd have to maintain the appropriate decorum in front of others, but at least he could look at her. Maybe they could steal a few moments alone...

He quickened his pace, trying to rein in his thoughts. There was no use in pining after her. Even though she was no longer married, she was still not for the likes of him. Her duty was now to her son, and no doubt she would soon find another powerful statesman to become her son's stepfather. Max's duty was to the army, and he had no business chasing a woman he could never have.

CHAPTER 10

T HE NEXT MORNING, MAX managed to convince himself that Volusia's appearance—and their kiss—last night hadn't been a dream. If he had been dreaming, a murder accusation probably wouldn't have been part of it.

To keep his promise to Volusia, he went in search of Glabrio to ask if he could be assigned to the escort that would take Volusia back to Rome.

The centurion wasn't in his office, and one of his lackeys said he'd gone in the direction of the stables, so Max headed that way. As he walked the short distance from the camp to the stables, he caught sight of Glabrio walking up ahead next to another man. Though both had their backs to Max, the other man's tall, proud bearing was unmistakable: Petronax.

Max hung back, seeing the commander in a new light after hearing Volusia's suspicions. Was he capable of treason and cold-blooded murder?

As an experienced soldier, killing would be familiar to Petronax. Max, too, had killed men in battle. But there was a difference between the unavoidable violence of war and stooping to poison a governor to keep him quiet.

Petronax and Glabrio finished their conversation, and Petronax turned to head back in the direction Max had come. Max stepped out of his way and saluted as he passed. Petronax didn't even look at Max.

Max hurried up the path to draw level with Glabrio. "Sir." He saluted once more. "I was wondering if I could ask a favor."

Glabrio kept walking toward the stables, shooting Max a scowl. "Are you in a position to be asking favors, legionary?"

"Well, probably not, sir, but I was wondering if there might be a spot for me on the escort that is taking the governor's widow back to Rome. Do you know whom I might speak to about that?"

Glabrio stopped and turned to look at him. "As a matter of fact, Petronax has just asked me to lead that escort."

"Oh." It was somewhat surprising for a centurion to be put in charge of something so banal as escort duty, but perhaps Volusia's station as a governor's widow warranted it. The prospect of a solid month on the road with Glabrio was supremely unappealing, but he thought of Volusia. He was doing this for her, so she would feel safe until she got to Rome.

Glabrio raised an eyebrow at Max's evident reluctance. "Are you rescinding your request?"

"No, sir. I would still like to go. It's been quite a while since I've seen my family in Rome."

Glabrio surveyed him dispassionately. Max knew this assignment was not one that would be coveted; few soldiers would want to undertake a tedious journey, and escorting a woman would not be seen as a particularly distinguished endeavor.

"All right," Glabrio finally said. "The funeral is to be the day after tomorrow, and we leave the day after that. Go speak to the provisioners about setting aside enough supplies for the trip. If we go hungry, it will be your fault."

Max saluted. "Yes, sir. Right away, sir." He hurried off.

Avitus's funeral took place with due solemnity. With Iris's help, Volusia had managed to find some black clothing, and garbed herself appropriately for the occasion. She walked at the head of the funeral procession from their home to the place outside the city gates where a pyre waited. The people of Narbo gathered to watch. Everyone stared at her, and her skin prickled with awareness of their curious gazes. Volusia kept her eyes trained straight ahead on the bier that bore Avitus's body, dressed in the purple-edged toga which honored his status. Iris walked at her elbow, a steady, reassuring presence.

Outside the city gates, the legion had assembled. She allowed herself a quick scan of the crowd, but didn't see Max. Still, it comforted her to know that he was out there somewhere.

Volusia stood nearest to the pyre, Silvanus and other members of Avitus's staff behind her, as a priest chanted. Petronax stood a short distance away at the head of the legion. His head was bowed in a somber posture. Volusia stared hard at him, but his face revealed nothing.

Someone handed her a flaming torch, and she stepped forward to lay it at the base of the pyre. She took one last glimpse of Avitus's face, pale and still, then set down the torch and stood back to watch the flames consume his body.

No doubt everyone expected her to sob and rend her clothing in grief, but she felt no urge toward such extravagant displays of emotion. She would miss the stability that Avitus had given her, but there was no love to render her heartbroken at his loss. He hadn't deserved to die, and she would seek justice, but it was for the sake of her son, not for Avitus.

Lucius should be here to witness his father's journey into the afterlife, to know that he was now the head of their little family. She hadn't yet found the words to tell him of his father's death, but she had several weeks to ponder on the journey. Lucius would be devastated, and though she felt no pain for Avitus, her heart already ached in sympathy for her son's loss.

Thinking of Lucius made her think about the future. Regardless of whether she was successful in bringing Petronax to justice, a long future stretched before her in which she had to act in her son's best interest. Avitus had always meant for Lucius to follow in his footsteps and make a success of himself, whether as a consul or senator or other magistrate, and Volusia needed to ensure that Lucius didn't miss any opportunities just because he'd lost his father. She would need to consider remarriage; a stepfather of the right caliber could open many doors for her son.

Besides, she didn't want to be alone for the rest of her days. After ten years of a lonely marriage, she wanted a companion—or at least someone who would show her more affection than Avitus had. She wanted to feel important to someone, to be cherished and esteemed, though she feared that may be too much to ask from a marriage designed to benefit her son.

Smoke rose into the sky from the pyre, and Volusia's eyes watered. She glanced back over at the legion, even knowing she wouldn't see Max's face. Kissing him—again—had been a mistake, though at least this time it hadn't ended with her stepfather shouting threats and insults at him. Max made her heart flutter as he always had, but for all his virtues, he was not the sort of man who could help her son climb the ladder of Roman politics.

Besides, he'd always spoken of wanting a career in the army, and soldiers weren't permitted to marry. In any case, Volusia didn't want to be with a man who was gone for months and years at a time, always worrying if he'd get himself killed or injured. She resolved to tuck her feelings for Max away like an out-of-style dress, difficult as their impending journey might make that. She couldn't let a silly childhood affection jeopardize something as important as her son's future.

The morning after the funeral, Max assembled with the other five men of the escort, including Glabrio, outside Volusia's house. Ulpius and Calvus loaded provisions into the back of a large cart, and Pullus and Sextus checked the harness of the horses that would pull Volusia's carriage. Glabrio oversaw it all with a frown.

Volusia's belongings had already been loaded into the back of another cart. Volusia exited the house, followed by Iris. Volusia was garbed for traveling in a simple dress covered in a long linen cloak, but gold jewelry shone at her throat and wrists, and her bearing was regal as a queen.

Max had strategically positioned himself closest to the covered carriage, and thus was the one to extend his hand and help Volusia in. She barely spared him a glance, but her fingers gave his an extra squeeze as he handed her into the carriage. Iris followed, giving Max an assessing look laced with suspicion.

Once the carriage door was closed, the six soldiers mounted up, and they set off through the streets of Narbo. Outside the city, another wagon of provisions joined their train, and their journey began in earnest.

Max's chest expanded as they left the city behind. Riding Elephant on the open road always made him feel invincible, even when confined to the slow pace required by the carriage and carts.

A month of this wouldn't be so bad, Max reflected as they made camp at the end of the first day. It was high summer, but they were taking a coastal road so enjoyed a fresh sea breeze. The only improvement he could imagine would be if Volusia were riding next to him, instead of sequestered in a carriage. And maybe if Glabrio had stayed in Narbo.

As the sun set, Max took his time rubbing Elephant down in the area where the other horses were tethered. It had been a while since she'd been ridden for a whole day, and he wanted to make sure he dried her thoroughly so she wouldn't catch a chill from any sweat. He ran his fingers through her mane, gently working through the tangles that had arisen throughout the day, and offered her an apple he'd filched from the supplies.

A figure approached in the gathering dusk. Max glanced up from Elephant to see Volusia.

"Good evening," she said. "I needed to stretch my legs after a day in that carriage."

"Good evening," he replied. They were alone out here, but he could still hear the noise of the others at the camp and see the flickering firelight just a little ways in the distance. He wasn't quite sure how to treat her—as a legionary escorting a Roman lady, or the childhood friend he couldn't seem to stop kissing.

He settled for somewhere in between, and gave her a friendly smile as she patted Elephant's nose.

"I wanted to thank you, again, for arranging to be here," Volusia said. "It comforts me to know you're here."

Warmth bloomed in his chest at the thought that his presence could bring her comfort. "It was no trouble." He drew closer to her, resting an arm atop Elephant's back.

"If there's anything I can ever do for you in return, never hesitate to ask." Elephant was snuffling at her hair, but Volusia didn't look away from Max's face. Invitation glimmered in her eyes, and it spurred Max to boldness.

"I will never ask anything of you," Max murmured, "except perhaps another kiss."

The words hung in the air for a moment, and Max opened his mouth to backtrack, but Volusia smiled. "Rather a bold request, but one I'm happy to grant."

He slid an arm around her waist and pulled her to him, then dipped his head down and brushed her lips with his. It struck him that this was the first time he was the one to kiss her; both of their previous encounters had been initiated by her.

His chainmail armor rattled as she grabbed his shoulders and lifted herself onto her tiptoes to take more of his mouth. Desire raced through him. Max's back pressed against Elephant, who gave a disapproving snort and sidestepped away. Max stumbled, pulling Volusia with him. She giggled as they found their footing.

"Elephant is more sensible than either of us," she said, looping her arms around his neck. "She knows we should not be doing this."

Volusia—and Elephant—were right, but he couldn't resist the temptation of holding her, touching her, kissing her. Their time together was running out, and they both knew it.

He slid a hand under her chin and moved to kiss her once more—but the rustle of footsteps through grass made him jump away from her. He hastily picked up the cloth he'd been using to wipe down Elephant, and began rubbing at her flank once more, even though she was perfectly dry.

Glabrio approached and surveyed them with distaste. The twilight shadows clung to his craggy face, intensifying his scowl. He acknowledged Volusia with a nod. "Lady."

She nodded back, offering no excuse or explanation for straying from the camp. Good: she wasn't one of his legionaries, and didn't need to account for herself to him.

Glabrio turned to Max. "If you can tear yourself away from your horse, legionary, there are tents that need to be put up."

Max tucked the rag into his belt. "Right away, sir." He gave Volusia a parting nod.

As he left, he glimpsed Glabrio clumsily offering his arm to Volusia. She smoothly ignored him, and followed Max back to camp, leaving Glabrio to hasten after them.

CHAPTER 11

I N THE DAYS THAT followed, the travelers alternated between making camp and sleeping in roadside inns. Though she was grateful for a bed, Volusia almost preferred sleeping rough. It afforded more excuses to steal time alone with Max, whether feigning a desire to check on the horses or asking him to lead her to a nearby stream so she could wash her face in fresh water.

They stole kisses, as well. At night, Volusia retired to bed warm with the memory of the taste of him, the way his arms felt wrapped around her. This was dangerous—both in the short term, if Max's grim centurion discovered what they were up to, as well as in the long term, as she knew they could have no future together.

But the exhilaration she felt at his touch was irresistible. Too long, she'd been trapped in a passionless marriage. She hadn't even known what she was missing. Now, at least for a short time, she had a measure of freedom, and she refused to feel guilty about finding some pleasure with Max.

Almost better than his kisses was simply the way he looked at her—hungry, covetous, and worshipful all in one dark-eyed glance. She could always feel his gaze on her whether they were alone with the horses or sharing dinner around the campfire. She had become so used to Avitus's apathy, though it was never meant unkindly. But with Max, she never doubted that she was his focus, his anchor, whenever they were in sight of each other. Feeling so important to someone was deliciously seductive, and no doubt it would be difficult to give up when their paths inevitably diverged.

Four days into their journey, Volusia woke in a cramped inn room to the sound of vomiting. She sat up in the creaky bed she'd shared with Iris, fumbling to light a lamp. The sun was just beginning to rise outside, and the room was still cloaked in shadows. "Iris? Are you all right?"

The lamp flared to life, illuminating the pale form of Iris, crouched over a chamber pot with a hand pressed over her eyes.

"Oh, dear." Volusia swung her legs out of bed. "Is it the headache again?" Iris was prone to terrible headaches that incapacitated her for a day or more, often so painful they made her vomit.

Iris nodded miserably. "I'm sorry, mistress."

"Nonsense. You must come straight back to bed." Volusia blew out the lamp, knowing that light made the ailment worse. She wrapped an arm around Iris's shoulders and helped her into bed, then set the chamber pot on the floor next to the bed in case Iris threw up again.

"I'll ask the kitchen to prepare some clear broth, and I'll see if they have any lavender for a cold compress. That helped last time, didn't it?" After ten years with Iris, Volusia was familiar with the best ways to manage her maid's attacks. Above all, Iris needed rest, darkness, and quiet. "And of course we cannot travel today. I'll inform the soldiers."

"Thank you, mistress," Iris said weakly.

Volusia dressed and braided her hair in two simple lengths, twisting and pinning them into a simple bun with a long bone hairpin. She donned the few pieces of simple jewelry she'd chosen to wear on the journey, and covered her hair with a long green palla before venturing downstairs.

The six soldiers, Max among them, were readying the horses in the inn yard as the sun rose. They must have slept outside or in the stables, as the inn couldn't house them all. Max winked when he saw her, and Volusia stifled a smile. A wink meant "hello" in the language of little gestures they'd developed as children.

She winked back, and then cleared her throat until Glabrio, the sour-faced centurion, turned to see her. "Iris is sick," she announced. "We'll have to remain here for at least a day until she recovers. Perhaps two."

Glabrio looked befuddled. "Who is Iris?"

Volusia raised an eyebrow. "My maid."

"Ah, the slave." He crossed his muscular arms over his chest. "There's no point in delaying for such a trivial reason. It's not as if she has to sit a horse. Just put her in the carriage. She can sleep the whole day."

Volusia matched his posture by drawing herself up and crossing her own arms. "She absolutely cannot travel. Any movement pains her and makes her vomit."

His lips thinned in distaste. "Then leave her here. You can buy a new slave in the next town we come to."

Outrage sparked at the callous way he spoke about Iris. She knew she'd disliked Glabrio for a reason. "I will do no such thing! Iris has been with me for ten years. I will not just cast her off like—"

"What is she sick with, anyway?" Glabrio demanded. "If it's catching, we have to leave her. I won't risk the lot of us taking ill."

"It's not contagious," Volusia said. "She's prone to attacks of terrible headaches. It will resolve in a day or two."

Glabrio took a step closer, so she had to tilt up her chin to look him in the eye. "That's a day or two of additional food and lodging for six men and eight horses. I'm not undertaking that expense for the comfort of a *slave*. You have two choices: either leave the slave, or get her into a carriage by the time the sun has risen."

Volusia bristled. The centurion was trying to intimidate her, and he was used to being obeyed. But she wasn't one of his legionaries, bound by duty and oath to obey him. "You do not give me ultimatums, *sir*."

His thick brows drew together, anger flashing in his eyes. "You might think you're in charge here, *lady*, but these men"—he gestured to the five legionaries, all avidly watching the exchange—"these men all obey my orders. Not yours. And if I tell them to get you and your slave into that carriage, they will."

"How dare—"

Max sidled up next to her. "Forgive me, sir, but it might do the horses good to rest for a day. One of the locals mentioned they expect rain this afternoon. Wouldn't be the worst thing to be in shelter. Perhaps we can see how Iris feels tomorrow and reevaluate."

His tone was relaxed and his bearing deferential, but Volusia knew him well enough to see the tension humming in the lines of his body.

A muscle in Glabrio's jaw pulsed, but Volusia knew they had him. Arguing with a woman was not an honorable pursuit for a centurion, and Max had given him an out without making it seem like he'd lost the argument.

"Very well," Glabrio ground out. "One day." He turned on his heel and stalked away.

"Thank you," Volusia murmured to Max.

"He can be an ass about the stupidest things," Max said. "I was enjoying watching you argue with him, though. Do you think you could pick another fight with him sometime? It's top-quality entertainment."

She grinned. "I'll do my best." In truth, standing up to the centurion had set her heart pounding, and her palms were still sweaty, but knowing that Max's steady gaze was on her gave her courage. She'd been right to ask him to come on this journey. He'd stood up for her, even in a small way, against his centurion.

"Does Iris need a physician?" Max asked. "I don't know if this town will have much in the way of medical expertise, but if you want me to try to find someone to attend to her, I can."

Volusia shook her head, though the offer was touching. "She'll be fine. I just need to ask the kitchens for some clear broth and see if they have any lavender for a compress. I should go do that now." She smiled at him again, and, before she could waste the whole day trading smiles with him outside the inn, turned away to find the kitchen.

CHAPTER 12

To Max's delight, Glabrio was even more irritable and short-tempered than usual for the rest of that day. Volusia's insubordination—as Glabrio would no doubt see it—had really gotten under his skin. Though the legionaries were the ones who suffered the effects of Glabrio's displeasure, it gave Max no end of satisfaction to see someone needle him, especially Volusia.

It did rain, as the locals had promised, and they were all grateful to be under shelter amid the downpour. While looking after the horses in the inn's stables, Max and the four other soldiers discussed the incident between Glabrio and Volusia in hushed tones of wonder.

Max was careful not to reveal the depth of his relationship with Volusia. It was clear that they knew each other, as he was the only soldier she ever directly addressed, but Max passed it off as an effect of the two weeks he'd spent on guard duty in her house. If the other soldiers knew he was the childhood friend of a lady like Volusia, they'd start treating Max as if he were some sort of snobby patrician, and he'd never live it down.

The morning after the argument with Glabrio, Iris evidently was recovered enough to travel, as she and Volusia boarded the carriage without complaint. They passed another night at an inn. As they journeyed toward the huge mountain range that split Gaul from Italy, the terrain became rougher, and the towns sparser.

Because they were sticking to the coastal road rather than venturing inland, they didn't have to cross the Alps proper, but the landscape still became rocky and densely forested. They would have to spend several nights in a row sleeping rough, as they wouldn't encounter another town until they crossed into Italy.

After a long day of riding, Max gave Elephant her customary extended brush and rub down. He gazed at the distant peaks outlined against the twilight sky. What would it be like to explore such unforgiving terrain, to conquer one of those mighty peaks, to see the world spread beneath him? He thought of Elephant's namesake, the animals that Hannibal had crossed the Alps with to attack Rome almost two hundred years ago, and imagined the huge beasts navigating such a harsh landscape.

Raised voices echoed from the camp, pulling him out of his fantasies. Elephant's ears pricked, and she swished her tail. One of the voices was female. Max hastily finished brushing Elephant, and started back toward the camp. Volusia might be arguing with Glabrio again, and he didn't want to miss that.

The female voice turned into a scream. Without thinking, Max broke into a run, closing the short distance to the camp. His hand reached for the short sword strapped to his belt. What was happening? Were they under attack? Why—

He skidded to a halt as he took in the scene at the camp. His mind struggled to make sense of it, as if everyone had suddenly started speaking a different language.

Juno's cunt.

Ulpius had grabbed Volusia, restraining her arms behind her back. Sextus had Iris in a similar grip. Glabrio stood between them. He drew his sword and pointed it straight at Volusia's throat.

Pullus and Calvus stood off to the side, shock and confusion clear on their faces. Even Ulpius and Sextus looked unsure as they restrained the two women. Only Glabrio seemed to know what was going on.

Max strode forward and planted himself in front of Volusia, shielding her from Glabrio's menacing blade. "What the fuck is going on?" Max demanded.

Glabrio's eyes flashed. "Stand down, legionary. And address your superior officer with more respect."

Max folded his arms across his chest. "Not until I know why you are threatening two women."

Behind Glabrio, Iris struggled against Sextus, trying to break free. "Hold her, legionary," Glabrio snapped at Sextus.

Sextus hesitated, then twisted her arm behind her back, immobilizing her. She cried out in pain. Sextus bit his lip and glanced desperately at Glabrio, as if hoping for an order to release Iris.

Volusia let out a growl of rage behind Max. "Take your hands off her! Whatever problem you think you have with me, she's no part of it."

Glabrio smirked. "I suppose you should have listened to me and left her behind in Nemausus if you didn't want her to be harmed."

Max could hear Volusia gasping, struggling against her captor, but Ulpius held her firm. "You will pay for this indignity many times over," she shouted. "When we reach Rome—"

"Quiet, woman!" Glabrio barked.

Ulpius spoke from behind Max. "Sir, there must be some mistake. Surely this can't be right."

Glabrio fixed the legionary with a scorching glare. "There is no mistake. My orders were clear. Legionary Maximus"—he fixed Max with a cold, steady gaze—"once more, I order you to stand aside."

The meaning behind Glabrio's words sank in. Glabrio had been ordered to make sure Volusia never arrived in Rome. He had been ordered to kill her.

And he would do it, if Max didn't stop him.

Max put his hand on the leather-wrapped hilt of his sword.

Glabrio's face purpled. "Do not dare to draw arms against your commanding officer, legionary. You have already earned yourself an appearance before the tribunal for insubordination. You know the penalty for mutiny. Is this woman really worth dying for?"

Max wrapped his fingers around the hilt. He turned around to look at Volusia, as if assessing the answer to Glabrio's question. Volusia stared at him, her hair askew, her eyes wild.

Max raised his eyebrows twice in quick succession. Understanding lit her gaze. That was one of the signals they'd developed as children, meaning "escape at the first opportunity," though it usually applied to escaping a boring dinner party.

Max turned back to Glabrio. "Yes," he said.

In one quick motion, he drew his sword and smashed the pommel into the side of Glabrio's head. The centurion fell backward and lay motionless on the ground.

Volusia broke free of Ulpius and ran for the trees surrounding the camp. "Run, Iris!" she shouted.

Iris elbowed Sextus hard, and he released her without much protest. Pullus and Calvus froze for a moment, then ran at Max with swords drawn. Max parried Calvus's strike and kneed him in the stomach, forcing him to drop to the ground gasping for breath. Pullus advanced, but there was hesitation in his movements. Max paused, breathing hard. He wasn't going to attack his comrades without cause, but he would defend himself.

Pullus cast a glance at Glabrio's prone body. His jaw set, and he lunged at Max with a shout. Max evaded the blow and rammed the pommel of his sword into Pullus's head. The soldier dropped like a stone.

Max rounded on Sextus and Ulpius, brandishing his sword. Both legionaries dropped their weapons and raised their hands in surrender. On the ground, Glabrio stirred.

Ulpius jerked his head to the left. "They went that way."

"Thanks." Max sheathed his sword and ran after Volusia and Iris.

He caught up with the two women easily. Volusia let out a small shriek when he came up behind them.

"It's me," Max gasped. "I knocked Glabrio out, but he'll wake any moment, and he's not going to let us get away easily. We have to run." He cast a frantic gaze around the darkened forest, searching for something that could serve as a hiding place.

Volusia grasped his hand in cold, shaking fingers. "Max, you have to go back. Your life is the army, I can't let you—"

"I attacked my commanding officer, Volusia. Whatever life I had in the army is done." A pang went through him at the realization, but he couldn't stop to reflect on what he had just sacrificed. "Now, we have to go."

He grabbed Volusia and Iris by a hand each and tugged them further into the forest. Iris's pace flagged, so Max threw her over his shoulder unceremoniously and kept running, Volusia's hand clutched tight in his.

CHAPTER 13

A S THEY RAN, SOMETHING sparkling up ahead caught Max's eye. Moonlight on water. He angled toward it, and they came to a halt on the banks of a wide, fast-flowing river, still swollen from the heavy rain two days ago. Rivers in this area were often icy cold and rapid, carrying snowmelt from the nearby mountains.

Volusia bent over, bracing her hands on her knees and gulping in air. "Can we...cross it?" she gasped.

He heaved Iris off his shoulder and set her on her feet as gently as possible. "Can either of you swim?"

They both shook their heads.

"Then we can't risk it. It will be freezing cold, and if you lose your footing once, or if the river grows too deep in the center, you'll be swept away." He racked his brain, trying to come up with a plan that had an acceptable chance of survival for all three of them.

Noise echoed from the direction they'd come—rustles and shouts, growing closer every moment. Glabrio must have recovered from the blow to his head and ordered everyone to follow them.

Max bit his lip. Time was running out. He stared hard at the river. A hazy, idiotic plan emerged, but it was the best he had.

Glabrio wanted them dead, so why not give him what he wanted? "They'll expect us to try to cross the river, so we'll make it look like we did, or tried to."

He unbuckled his sword from around his waist and dropped it by the bank, as if he'd taken it off to shed weight before crossing the river. He didn't like being without a weapon, but he still had a knife strapped to his waist. He also shed his red legionary cape and chainmail armor, and dumped the items atop the sword.

He beckoned the women to follow him, and they raced upstream, following the bends and curves of the river. Voices echoed from behind him, but they were talking, not shouting. The party of soldiers must have stopped at the riverbank upon finding Max's discarded items.

Max drew to a halt and beckoned Iris and Volusia to hide behind nearby trees. He closed his eyes and listened hard to the voices downstream. The next part of his plan hinged on the camp being empty.

Once he was satisfied that he heard all five voices, he opened his eyes. Volusia met his gaze, her face pale and panicked. "What now?" she hissed. "We can't outrun them, and we can't run all night."

"We're not going to," Max said. "The one place they won't check is the camp itself. We'll go back there—it's empty now—and hide ourselves in one of the supply carts. We'll escape in the middle of the night once they've given up searching."

"That's insane!" Volusia whispered. Iris nodded vehemently.

"Do you have a better plan?" Max demanded. "They outnumber us. They can fan out and search faster than we can find hiding places. The only place we can hide is somewhere they won't search." He reached out and took Volusia's hand. "Once, you said you trusted me. Do you still?"

Her fingers tightened around his. "Yes," she murmured.

"Then let's go." He led them back into the forest, following his vague mental map to lead them back in the direction of the camp. They walked as quickly and as quietly as possible, traveling in a wide arc to avoid running into the other soldiers.

The flickering campfire appeared through the trees ahead. Max drew them to a halt, pausing to make sure the camp was truly empty. Once he was certain, he pointed to a supply cart on the edge of the camp. It was laden with boxes and crates of Volusia's possessions as well as food and supplies for the journey, and a canvas tarp lay over everything. "We can hide in there."

Iris gave him a look that said she clearly thought he was crazy, but Volusia nodded resolutely. On his signal, they sprinted across the short open distance between the trees and the cart. Max lifted the tarp and helped the two women in, then climbed in behind them, pulling the fabric back down over them. There was just enough space between the trunks and crates for the three of them to fit.

Volusia and Iris squeezed into the back of the cart. Volusia wrapped an arm around Iris's shoulders, and they huddled together. Max stayed near the front, his hand on the hilt of his knife. If anyone did try to investigate the cart, they'd meet him first, and he could give the women time to get away.

Max quickly gave up trying to find a comfortable position for his long legs, and sat crammed between two crates, his knees pressed tight against his chest. He let out a long breath, his body still humming with shock, fear, and anger. The image of Glabrio's sword levelled at Volusia's throat was imprinted on his mind. And resounding in his skull was the question that had changed everything: *is this woman really worth dying for?*

His gaze sought Volusia out in the near pitch-darkness of the covered cart. Iris's head rested on her shoulder, and Volusia held her close, whispering something comforting in her ear. Somehow, Volusia had gone from a childhood infatuation to a woman he would sacrifice everything for. His chest squeezed at the thought of losing her. He made a vow to himself in the darkness: no matter what the future held or didn't hold for them, he would see her safely out of this mess, whatever the cost.

Volusia couldn't stop shaking. She wrapped an arm tight around Iris to try to quell her tremors. Her heart was still pounding as fast as it had when they'd been running.

She rested her gaze on Max's shadowy form at the other end of the cart. The sight of him calmed her, but guilt twisted in her stomach. He had given up so much in a moment's decision to defend her. If it weren't for his bravery, she and Iris would both be dead, their bodies dumped in the river by now.

Her mind struggled to process the events of the last hour. Clearly, Petronax had known that she suspected his involvement in Avitus's death. But how? She'd given nothing away.

Maybe the corrupt commander just wanted to tie up any potential loose ends, hence his order to Glabrio. This attempt on her life was all the proof she needed of Petronax's guilt. Now, it wasn't only about justice for Avitus, but for herself as well. If she could make it back to Rome, and with Max as a witness, she could bring Petronax to justice.

But right now, making it back to Rome seemed as impossible as traveling to Mount Olympus. They were still in the camp of the men who had just tried to murder them, and they needed to sneak out without being discovered. She shivered. Max had gotten them this far. She had to trust that his plan would work.

Volusia estimated they'd been hiding in the cart for about an hour when voices filtered back to the camp: the other soldiers returning, having given up their search. Volusia tensed, and felt Iris stiffen next to her. But no footsteps crossed near the cart.

"Idiots," someone spat, his voice sounding from the direction of the campfire. The voice had Glabrio's gravelly burr. "The river must have swept them away. No doubt we'll find their bodies downstream in a day or two."

"With respect, sir," another soldier said, "if the order was to kill the lady, doesn't that mean our mission was accomplished? Do we return to Narbo now, or continue on to Rome?"

"We continue on," Glabrio said. "Once the Senate nominates a new governor, we will return with him to Narbo. As far as any of you are concerned, there was a tragic accident while fording a river, in which the lady, a legionary, and a slave perished. If I hear any rumors otherwise, each and every one of you will face severe consequences. Is that clear?"

There was a subdued muttering of "Yes, sir" from the men.

"Good," Glabrio growled. "Now, Ulpius takes first watch. The rest of you, dismissed."

Noises sprang up around the camp as the legionaries readied themselves for bed. Gradually, the camp quieted. Another hour passed. Volusia's legs were sore and stiff, and her bottom had gone numb from sitting on the unforgiving wood.

When she thought she couldn't take it anymore, Max finally shifted, his movements slow and careful. He lifted the edge of the tarp and peered out.

He lowered it and turned toward her and Iris. "Ulpius is sitting by the fire with his back to us," Max breathed. "We should be able to escape into the trees from here…as long as he doesn't turn around."

Volusia's stomach tightened. As torturous as sitting in this cramped cart was, staying here suddenly seemed preferable to a risky escape.

"Are you ready?" Max asked. "You both should run for the trees as soon as you're out of the cart. I'll follow."

Volusia and Iris nodded. Max gave a swift, businesslike nod in return, as if they were his legionary comrades rather than two frightened women, then raised the tarp up once more. He created a small opening and eased his tall body out. He extended a hand back into the cart and helped first Volusia, then Iris out.

Volusia's knees almost buckled as her legs unfolded and her feet hit the solid ground, but she managed to stay upright. She squinted, eyes straining after so long in the near pitch-darkness of the cart. She could see the fire burning and the shadowy form of Ulpius sitting next to it. Her heart leaped into her throat.

Max grabbed her shoulders and pointed her toward the forest. "Run," he whispered.

Volusia broke into an unsteady, shuffling jog, turning her head to make sure Iris was following. A twig cracked beneath her feet, and panic shot through her. She ran faster, fearing that Ulpius had heard the sound and would be in pursuit. Iris's harsh breathing sounded just behind her.

She didn't stop running until a pair of strong arms seized her around the middle. She thrashed for a terrified moment before her senses caught up with her panicked mind. It was just Max.

"Juno's cunt," he said, breathing hard. "I thought you were going to run all the way to Rome."

Volusia glanced anxiously behind him. "Are we safe? Did Ulpius hear?"

"I'd be surprised if he didn't, but he showed no sign of it."

Gratitude rushed through her. Ulpius hadn't seemed eager to carry out Glabrio's orders earlier when he'd been directed to apprehend her. She resolved to make a sacrifice in Ulpius's name to Fortuna, the goddess of luck, once they got back to Rome.

Iris came to stand next to Volusia. "Now what?"

Max shrugged. "We just need to find somewhere to lie low until morning. The legionaries will be on their way, and we'll be free."

He made it sound so simple, but even after what they had suffered tonight, Volusia knew their hardship was only beginning. They still had to survive a long, arduous journey to Rome with no supplies, and likely on foot. And once they got to Rome, she would have to convince the people who mattered that one of the most powerful men in the Roman army had tried to have her murdered.

CHAPTER 14

THEY PASSED THE REST of the night sleeping at the base of a wide tree with sheltering leaves. Or, at least, the women slept. Max stayed awake, both to keep watch for any danger and because he still hummed with anxious energy. His body didn't seem to know that the immediate threat had passed. His muscles were tense, knotted, as if ready for Glabrio to jump out from behind the nearest tree.

Volusia and Iris curled themselves together, and he could tell from the rhythm of their breathing that they eventually fell into a doze. He wished he had a cloak to lay over them, but luckily it was still summer, and they were in no danger of freezing, even at night.

Out of everything terrible that had happened in the last few hours, the worst was that he'd left Elephant behind. Another thing he'd sacrificed for Volusia without a thought. His chest ached, wondering if Elephant was confused by his absence. She would be expecting him soon for her morning brush and treat. He missed her already, her comforting bulk, the way she nudged her head against him when she wanted something.

He would get her back somehow, if it was the last thing he did.

The sun crept over the horizon. As its rays strengthened, Volusia stirred. She sat up with a start, her gaze hopping around frantically until it landed on Max. "It wasn't a dream, was it?"

"I'm afraid not," Max replied.

Her eyes lowered to his arm, and she let out a soft shriek that woke Iris. "Max, your arm!"

He glanced down. His left forearm was covered in sticky dried blood. A thin, shallow slice split his skin. He must have gotten it in the brief fight with Glabrio and the other legionaries, but he didn't even remember feeling a wound, and then it had been too dark to notice the blood. "Oh."

Volusia scrambled to her feet and rushed to his side. She grabbed his arm and inspected the wound, her face paling. This was likely the first time she'd ever seen a wound like this.

Her touch stung, and Max pulled his arm away. "It's nothing. Not even bleeding anymore, see?"

"But—but—" Emotion seemed to stop her words, and her eyes welled with tears. "Oh, Max, you could have died!"

Before Max knew what was happening, Volusia collapsed into his arms, her body shuddering with sobs. She clutched him as if she'd never let go, burying her face against his shoulder. His arms came up to embrace her. Her body felt slight, fragile in his grasp, but he knew the strength beneath her delicate bones. She had stared down a centurion intent on killing her without flinching, and had borne the trials of the previous night without complaint.

Iris, in a rare moment of tact, turned around and began to comb her fingers through her long blond hair, removing a few stray twigs and leaves.

Max held Volusia as she cried. It was good for her to cry, to release all of the fear and anxiety from the past night. Max, too, felt a knot of emotion in the center of his chest, but he couldn't release it, just as he couldn't allow himself to sleep last night. They weren't out of danger yet, and he had to maintain his strength and composure if he wanted to keep Volusia and Iris safe.

Volusia pulled back and gazed up at him with a tear-stained face. "Glabrio is going to tell people in Rome we're dead. Our families…" Her lips quivered, and another tear trickled down her cheek. "My son will think himself an orphan."

A cold realization hit Max at her words. Their parents—and Volusia's son—would be told they were dead. His stomach twisted at the thought of his family's grief, but he couldn't open the door to that now. He fought against the anguish, and forced himself to seize on a rational thought.

"Once we make it to the next town, we'll figure out a way to get horses. We'll steal them if we have to. We can make good time from there. With luck, we'll only be a few days behind the others." Though for his parents, a few days of thinking their son dead would be torture.

Volusia held up a trembling hand. She was still wearing her jewelry, and several gold rings and bracelets flashed in the sun. "I don't think we'll have to steal horses."

Finally, a bit of good news. Max allowed his mouth to stretch into a smile, despite the painful reminder of Elephant's loss. "No, I don't think we will."

Iris cleared her throat. "That plan is all well and good, but what do we do until then? We're in the middle of nowhere with no food or supplies. Who's to say we even make it to the next town?"

She looked so mournfully certain of death that Max rolled his eyes. "First of all, we're not in the middle of nowhere. There is a road, and if we follow it, we'll find a town sooner or later. And we're hardly in a desert. There's a river for water, and with a little effort we can rustle up some food." One useful thing the army had taught him was how to forage, and he'd honed his skills on his country rides with Elephant. The area around Narbo was plentiful with figs, mushrooms, almonds, and apricots, and he bet this area would have a similar bounty.

"If you say so." Iris did not look convinced, but Max ignored her.

There was no reason to delay, so they set off, navigating east in the direction the sun had risen. For now, they'd stay off the road to avoid running into Glabrio and the others.

When they encountered the river once more, Volusia insisted on washing Max's bloodied arm. The wound was not serious, but the sight of it still made her pale and shaky. Nevertheless, she wouldn't let him alone until it was clean and bandaged in a strip torn from her own dress.

Max managed to find some mushrooms of a type he knew were edible, along with a handful of walnuts, which they cracked between two rocks. The sustenance kept them going, but fatigue soon set in, and they stopped to rest in midafternoon. Iris stretched out in a sunny spot with her arm flung over her eyes and instantly fell asleep.

Volusia sat with her back against the tree, shaded by its branches. Max wanted to sit next to her, but instead paced in a tight oval around the small clearing. If he sat down, if he allowed himself to rest, he might never get up again.

The day of walking had brought Elephant's absence into sharp focus. What if he couldn't recover her?

Again, he tried to see reason. Elephant was a valuable horse; Glabrio and the legionaries would take good care of her. But what would become of her once they reached Rome? He let out a tight breath between his teeth. Losing his military career was one thing. Losing Elephant was quite another—intolerable. He refused to contemplate the possibility that she might be gone forever. For now, Volusia was his first priority, but once he had safely delivered her to Rome, he would not rest until Elephant was back at his side.

"Max." Volusia's soft voice cut through his scattered thoughts. "Why don't you sit by me?" She patted a spot on the ground next to her. "Rest a while."

"I need to keep watch." His voice came out gruff and hoarse.

"Over what?" She gestured at their surroundings, empty but for the three of them and a twittering bird in a nearby tree. "You need to rest. I doubt you slept a wink last night."

To placate her, he lowered himself onto the ground beside her. She gave an approving nod. "Now lie down." She patted her thighs as if she meant for him to rest his head in her lap.

"Not necessary."

She narrowed her eyes at him. "Lucius went through a phase where he refused to sleep. You look as stubborn as he did. But I always won in the end." Her voice warmed as she spoke of her son.

He liked the tenderness in her voice. "What strategy did you use?"

"A very simple one. I'll show you." She grabbed his shoulders and drew him down. He resisted for a moment—it was humiliating for a grown man to be handled like a child—but the softness of her touch disarmed him, and he found himself allowing his head to be placed in her lap. Her fingers stroked through his hair, and his eyes fell shut of their own accord.

Her touch had a soothing magic to it, and he found himself unable to open his eyes no matter how much he wanted to. She began to hum, and the resonant vibrations washed over him. Guided by the gentle rhythm of her hand stroking his head, he slipped into sleep.

CHAPTER 15

V OLUSIA'S HEART FELT ABOUT to burst as she looked down at Max's sleeping face in her lap. Her thighs had long gone numb under the heavy weight of his head, but she didn't dare move. He'd been running himself ragged for the past day and a half, all for her sake. He needed to sleep.

She had never imagined that someone would risk so much—and lose it—for her. Of course, Avitus would always have defended her if necessary, but that was a matter of honor. As his wife, she was his to protect. But Max wasn't bound by honor or duty to defend her. In fact, his duty should have compelled him to follow Glabrio's orders and stand aside.

She stroked a gentle finger along the line of his jaw, which was rough with stubble. "Thank you," she whispered.

Max slept for about an hour, then woke in late afternoon. He removed himself from her lap hurriedly, as if embarrassed, and said nothing further. They roused Iris, and resumed their journey until darkness fell.

They walked for another full day, and rejoined the road, knowing the soldiers would be far enough ahead by this point that they'd be safe. The following day, they began to encounter some signs of civilization: fences erected to delineate land allotments, fields planted and animals grazing.

Volusia's legs were heavy with fatigue, and her feet had never hurt so much. The straps of her sandals rubbed her skin raw, and their thin soles were no match for the rugged road. Her body ached from sleeping on the hard ground, and she'd acquired a varied collection of bruises and scrapes all over her skin. Despite her urgency to get back to Rome and reunite with Lucius, at this moment she longed for nothing more than a hot meal and soft bed. And hopefully a bath.

By midday, they entered the gates of a sizable town. Volusia recognized it as Genua, which she'd passed through with Avitus on the journey to Narbo. That journey felt like a lifetime ago, though it was barely two months past.

The first order of business was to convert some of her jewelry into coin so they could pay for food, lodging, and hopefully horses. They passed several shops and finally found one which sold embroidered cloth, jewelry, and some other trinkets.

Volusia had never tried to sell anything before, and wasn't sure exactly how to go about it, but didn't hesitate in removing her ruby and gold bracelet and laying it down on the table behind which the shopkeeper stood. "I would like to sell this, please."

The shopkeeper, a wiry man with shrewd eyes, looked her over with an evaluating gaze which lingered on the incongruity of her dirty clothing and expensive jewelry. His gaze then moved to Max, who loomed at her elbow. Iris stood behind them, arms crossed over her chest.

The shopkeeper picked up the bracelet and inspected it. He laid it on a scale and stacked counterweights on the other side. "May I ask where you came by this piece, lady?"

Likely he thought it was stolen. "It was a gift from my husband, of course."

The shopkeeper's gaze returned to Max. "Is this your husband?"

She shook her head. "I'm a widow." The words sent a pang through her.

Max rested his palms on the counter, leaning forward so his shoulders seemed even broader. "I'm merely responsible for the lady's protection. And to see that she gets a fair price for her jewels."

The shopkeeper finished weighing the bracelet. "My condolences on the loss of your husband, lady. This is a beautiful piece, but these stones are glass. I'll give you thirty denarii for the gold."

Volusia bristled. "Those are rubies, sir."

The shopkeeper shrugged. "I'm sure that's what your husband told you."

He was trying to shortchange her, and she would not allow it. After all she had been through, a shifty shopkeeper would not stand in her way. "Max, give me your knife."

Max removed his short blade from its sheath and handed it to her. She reversed her grip on it and brought the hilt smashing down onto one of the rubies as hard as she could. The table shuddered.

Volusia held up the unharmed bracelet. "If that had been glass, that stone would have shattered. But as you can see, there is not a scratch on it."

The shopkeeper took the bracelet and inspected it, his mouth twisting into a frown.

"My husband paid six hundred for it, but I'm willing to part with it for five hundred, given that we have immediate need of the coin." In truth, she had no idea how much Avitus had paid for the bracelet, but it was a good enough guess. "You can sell it to the right buyer for seven hundred, no doubt." Luckily, Genua was a big enough town with plenty of trade going in and out that there would be a market for expensive goods such as this.

The man gave the bracelet another appraising glance, then a short nod. "All right. Five hundred." He disappeared into a back room for a few moments, emerging with a small wooden box full of coins. He emptied the silver coins onto the scale, weighed them to the correct amount, then swept them into a leather sack, which he handed to Max.

"Wait," Volusia said as Max turned to leave. "I want to sell these as well." She removed the gold and pearl earrings that had somehow survived the ordeal and placed them on the counter.

"We have enough," Max said in a low voice. "There's no need to part with your earrings."

Volusia cast a glance at Iris, lurking by the door to the shop. "I have another use in mind for the money." The events of the past few days had renewed her thoughts of freeing Iris, and she didn't want to send her off empty-handed.

The shopkeeper examined the earrings and this time, gave them a good price without having to haggle.

They took the money, gave him the jewelry, and left the shop.

"Are you sure it's enough?" Volusia asked anxiously. She used to monitor the household accounts, so knew how much wine, food, or fabric cost, but had little concept of what something like a room at an inn or a horse would set them back.

Max hefted the bag of coin. "It will get us a room and some meals. And two decent horses, I'd say. We'll have to take turns walking."

That was enough. Volusia's wrist and ears felt strangely light without the jewelry, but she would have traded the pieces a hundred times over for the certainty of a hot meal and a bed that wasn't rocky dirt.

They found a tavern that looked clean enough, and Max handed over a handful of coins to secure a room upstairs, a vat of hot water for a bath, and a meal for the three of them.

They sat at a rickety table in the cramped dining room. The wooden stool was held together with twine, and the legs were uneven, but sitting on a chair after nothing but rocks and grass felt like the highest luxury.

A few other travelers eyed them curiously, no doubt wondering at their disheveled state. Despite all they had been through, Volusia couldn't suppress a flush of embarrassment at appearing in public like this. She tried to comb her fingers through her hair and rub the dirt from her face. Max, for his part, seemed entirely unbothered, though she noticed that he did position his bulky frame to block her from view of the other travelers as much as possible.

The food that arrived consisted of lumpy porridge topped with a few paltry pieces of gristly, under-seasoned meat, with a pitcher of sour, watery wine on the side. They devoured every bite. The food that Max had foraged on their journey had kept them from starvation, but Volusia still felt as if she hadn't eaten in days.

Once her belly was full, Volusia reached across the table to take Iris's hand. "There's something I've been thinking about these past few days." She took a deep breath. "I don't think you should return to Rome with us, Iris."

Confusion flickered across Iris's face. "What do you mean? Not—" Her mouth dropped open. "Please don't sell me. I know you need the money for another horse, but—"

"Of course I'm not going to sell you!" Volusia squeezed her hand. "No, Iris, I want to *free* you. I know we discussed waiting until we reached Rome, but I'm afraid you'll be dragged into all this mess. More than you already have been. If you return to Rome with me, you'll be questioned once we bring these accusations against Petronax. I don't want to risk that."

Iris's blue eyes darkened with grim understanding. Testimony from a slave was only deemed valid if extracted under torture, so by returning with Iris to Rome, Volusia would be condemning her to abuse of the cruelest kind.

"You've been such a good friend to me—better than I deserved." A rush of emotion tightened Volusia's throat. Iris had been her friend—sometimes her only one—for ten years. She had been there through the early days of marriage to Avitus. She'd held Volusia's hand during childbirth. She'd listened to her frustrations as Avitus spent his nights with others. She'd helped soothe Lucius when he wouldn't stop crying. She had been a constant, reliable, comforting presence.

But letting her go was the right thing to do, if Volusia cared at all for her. Volusia wiped away a tear with the back of her hand. "Maybe one day you'll come back to Rome, and we can be true friends. But until then, you deserve to have your own life back."

Iris squeezed her hand. "Thank you, mistress."

Volusia withdrew the coins from the sale of the earrings and slid them across the table to Iris. "You deserve far more, but I hope these will help you on your journey. You're of course welcome to stay with us for as long as you want. We have the room upstairs to rest in."

Iris closed her fingers around the silver coins. "Thank you, mistress, but I think it's best if I'm on my way. I saw a merchant heading back to Gaul when we were entering the town. If I hurry, I might be able to hitch a ride with him."

"Oh. I see." Volusia couldn't help feeling a bit deflated that Iris was so quick to leave, but Iris was free now, and she owed Volusia nothing. She stood, and gave Iris a quick, tight hug. "May Mercury watch over you on your journey."

Iris returned the embrace, her hands pressing into Volusia's back. "Go with the gods, mistress," she murmured, then pulled away. She tipped her chin at Max. "You. Keep an eye on her."

Max nodded solemnly. "I'll do my best."

A few moments later, Iris was gone. Volusia sat back down at the table and stared mournfully at her empty plate. "I don't think I've gone a day without seeing her since she came to me."

"Since someone bought her for you, you mean," Max said.

She glanced up to meet his gaze. "Iris was better off with me than she would have been anywhere else."

"I don't doubt it," Max said. "But I think you did the right thing by freeing her."

His approval warmed her even more than the food. "I hope her family welcomes her ba—" A jaw-cracking yawn overtook her, and a wave of exhaustion swept over her.

Max pushed his stool back and rose. "Come on, let's find our bed." He wrapped an arm around her shoulders and guided her through the maze of tables and chairs to the rickety staircase in the corner of the room.

Our bed. If she hadn't been so exhausted, those words would have made her blush and shiver, no doubt. But for now, all she wanted to do in a bed with Max was sleep.

CHAPTER 16

MAX EYED THE BED, a lumpy mattress spread with a worn woolen blanket. Volusia had collapsed into it as soon as they'd entered the room, and fallen asleep immediately. Her sprawled form took up almost all of it. They would have to get very cozy tonight, unless Max decided to do the honorable thing and sleep on the floor.

He wished he could fall asleep as easily as Volusia had, but the stress of their journey still had its claws in him. He paced the short length of the room, unable to sit still despite the soreness of his legs and ache in his feet.

His thoughts turned to Elephant once more. Worry squeezed his chest whenever he thought of her. Were Glabrio and his men taking care of her? What if they didn't get the tangles in her mane out and it snagged on a branch? What if they didn't rub her down properly and she caught a chill?

He tried to take a deep breath. Thoughts were racing in his head like bees around a hive. Elephant would be fine. If there was one thing soldiers knew, it was how to take care of a horse.

A knock came at the door, and Max let in two young women carrying a large vat of steaming water. "Thank you," he said as they set it in the middle of the room along with a small bottle of oil and some clean cloths. He handed them a coin, and they nodded and left. The tub wasn't big enough to sit or lie down in, but it was far better than nothing.

Max went to the bed and gently shook Volusia's shoulder. She woke with a start, gazing up at him with unfocused eyes.

"Our bath is here," he said. "I thought you might want to go first."

"That's kind of you." She heaved herself out of bed and went to check the temperature of the water. "Oh, that feels good." She bent to remove her dirt-crusted sandals.

Max turned around, realizing she was about to start undressing. "I could, er, go back downstairs…"

She gave a short laugh. "I'm much too tired to be modest, Max." Fabric flickered in the corner of his gaze.

Instinctively, his head turned to catch the movement. Her dress was in a heap on the ground, and her lithe body was completely bare.

His breath stuck in his throat as he beheld her. Fucking Dis, she was the most beautiful thing he'd ever seen. Her back was to him, but that view was more than enough. His gaze traveled over her slowly, taking in the fine bones of her shoulders, the elegant line of her spine, and the lush curve of her bottom. Her skin was dirty and marred with scrapes and bruises, but nothing detracted from her beauty.

"You're fucking beautiful," he said, his voice a hoarse growl. "I hope you know that."

She tossed a smile at him over her shoulder as she stepped into the tub of water. "Language, Max."

Legs unsteady, he stumbled over to the bed and sat on the edge. Desire welled up in him as his gaze continued to devour the sight of her bare body. His cock hardened inside his braccae, and he curled his hands into fists at his sides as he watched her.

Standing in the calf-high water, she splashed some water over herself, then leaned down to pick up the small vial of oil. The sight of her bending over almost made Max pass out. She poured a small measure of oil into her hand. She rubbed it over her arms, chest, belly, and legs, then scrubbed a damp cloth over her skin to remove it.

"Would you perhaps help me with my back?" she asked.

It took a moment for her words to enter his lust-addled brain. "You...me...help?"

"I can't reach it myself." She turned slightly to hold out the vial of oil, and he glimpsed the curve of her breast, tipped with a pink nipple.

The sight was enough to propel him to his feet. He crossed the distance to her, took the oil, and poured some into his hand. She turned around, sweeping her hair over one shoulder to leave her back completely bare. He could smell the light perfume of the oil, and could see the tiny hairs that covered the back of her neck.

He bit his lip, then touched his hand to her shoulder blade. Gently, he rubbed the oil over her skin. He could feel her bones shifting beneath his hand, but he knew better than to think her fragile.

She leaned into his touch. His hands traveled down her spine, finding the sore spots and trying to soothe them. There was a sensitive spot near her waist that made her gasp and arch her back. Her bottom knocked against his hips, making full contact with his cock, now achingly hard.

He drew in a sharp breath, wondering if she would be scandalized. She was no innocent maiden, after all; she knew what she'd felt. She knew he wanted her.

His oiled hand lingered on her hip. "Do you want me to wipe it off now?" A stack of clean cloths rested on the floor just to the side.

She tipped her head back to rest against his shoulder with a sigh. "I don't want you to stop touching me."

Her quiet words hung in the air. She wanted him—at least in this small way. And he was prepared to give her anything she wanted.

His fingers slid down to grasp a handful of her firm, round bottom. His cock throbbed. "Fuck, Volusia," he growled.

"Language," she whispered.

His other hand moved around to her front, skimming up her stomach and over the ridges of her ribs. He stopped when his thumb brushed the warm underside of her breast, hesitating, hardly able to believe he was really touching her like this. She gave a soft sigh, and he raised his hand to cup her breast. He couldn't hold back the groan that rumbled in his chest at the feel of her breast filling his hand. Her nipple puckered against his fingers, and she shivered when he ran his thumb lightly over it.

Abruptly, she turned toward him, stepping out of the small tub. Water dripped on the floor, and he should have handed her a cloth to dry herself with, but her heated gaze captured him, her hazel eyes reflecting his own desire and longing. She reached for him, and before he knew what was happening, her hands were on his body, grabbing the hem of his tunic and tugging it over his head.

He tossed the filthy tunic to the floor and swept her into a kiss. He reveled in the softness of her mouth, the wet slide of her tongue against his—but broke off in a gasp as her hand closed around his throbbing cock through his braccae.

"Oh, my," she whispered, staring down at the stiffness that filled her hand with an expression that looked something like wonder. Max realized that though she might not be a maiden, the passionless marriage she'd described had likely given her little experience with an aroused male who hungered for her touch.

Her fingers found the ties to his braccae, and with a few deft pulls, she rendered him as bare as she was. The feel of her soft, warm, naked body against his skin was what he imagined Elysium felt like.

They stumbled toward the bed. He meant to lay her down and begin a campaign of pleasuring her thoroughly, but instead she maneuvered to press him down onto the bed and perch at his side, feet tucked delicately beneath her thighs. Her hand found his cock once more, and every muscle in his body shivered against the scratchy blanket as she stroked him, her hand still slippery from the oil. The look on her face was rapt, intent, as she worked her hand up and down.

With painful effort, he summoned the presence of mind to grab her wrist. *He* was supposed to be pleasuring *her*. "Stop, please."

"You don't like it?" Her brow wrinkled.

"Oh, I like it very much," he assured her.

"Then be quiet," she said sternly.

He shut his mouth and surrendered to her touch. She stroked him slowly, almost experimentally, varying her movements as if to gauge his reactions. It was torment, but Max was happy to suffer for her.

The sweet agony built with every ragged breath. His hands clutched fistfuls of the blanket, knuckles straining, until finally pleasure burst over him like a sudden thunderclap. He exploded over her hand, his seed coating her delicate yet very talented fingers. He half-expected her to pull away in disgust, but instead she kept stroking until he reached out to stay her hand as the tremors stopped.

His body relaxed, limp and powerless, into the straw mattress. Volusia leaned over him to brush a kiss onto his forehead. "Thank you," she murmured.

He was fairly sure he was supposed to be thanking her for what just happened, but he wasn't yet capable of speech.

She rose from the bed and fetched a damp cloth to wipe her hand and clean him. Then, she curled herself against his side, resting her head on his chest. He draped an arm over her. For a blissful moment, all of their troubles—the loss of Elephant, the fact that their families would soon think them dead, the revelation of corruption in the highest ranks of the army—seemed miles away. He could even feel a touch of gratitude for Petronax's treachery. Without it, there was no way he'd be here, naked in a bed with Volusia.

He tried to sit up, though his body felt like lead. He needed to show her the pleasure she deserved.

Volusia put a gentle hand on his chest, guiding his body back down to the bed. "Sleep, Max."

"But I want to—"

"I know what you want, and I want it too." She found his hand and twined her fingers through his. "There will be time for that later. For now, sleep."

His eyes fell shut. He wanted to protest more, but a wave of exhaustion was already pulling him under, and he finally allowed himself to succumb.

CHAPTER 17

VOLUSIA FELL ASLEEP CURLED up next to Max's warm, satisfied body. Despite the lumpy mattress and itchy blankets, she could not imagine a better sleeping arrangement.

She woke several hours later. Darkness had fallen, and the bed shifted as Max eased himself out from under her. She squinted groggily at his shadowy form as he went to the tub of water, which now must be cold, and washed himself. A blush rose to her cheeks as she realized she'd accosted him earlier before he'd even had a chance to bathe. From the moment she'd intercepted him staring at her when she undressed, she'd been powerless to resist him.

She had always loved the way he looked at her, even when they were seventeen: hungry yearning tempered with something tender, almost worshipful. He had touched her like that, too. She recalled the clasp of his hand around her breast, undeniably greedy, yet with a reverent softness.

Avitus had only ever regarded her body with mild distaste. Being looked at as Max looked at her, being desired as Max desired her was intoxicating. His reaction to her touch thrilled her. She had never felt so powerful as when he was shuddering and gasping beneath her hand.

The embers of desire that had been suppressed by exhaustion now burst back into flame. Volusia sat up in bed.

At her movement, Max looked up from scrubbing his hands. "Sorry, didn't mean to wake you."

"It's all right." She ran a hand through her hair, combing out the tangles.

His gaze lingered on her. She wondered how much of her he could see in the darkness. "Sorry if I crowded you in the bed. I meant to offer to sleep on the floor earlier," he said as he finished washing. "That would have been the polite thing."

She arched an eyebrow. "Surely it's clear by now that I don't want politeness. I want you, Max."

He dropped the cloths he'd been using to dry himself and came to the bed. His knees sank into the mattress as he climbed toward where she sat in the middle. Her gaze traveled down his long body. Gods, she hadn't even touched him yet and his cock was already thickening. Was it truly possible for someone to want her that much?

An answering heat swelled between her legs. She rested a hand on his strong, warm shoulder, then slid her hand up to twine her fingers in his hair.

"I've wanted you since I was seventeen," he said in a rough whisper, and lowered his head to capture her mouth in a long kiss.

"Then have me." She allowed her body to relax beneath him, stretching out on the bed. His weight covered her, solid and heavy, reassuring rather than oppressive.

"Just one thing," she breathed when his mouth finally broke from hers. "I don't want to risk a child."

"Understood," he said, "but there's some ground to cover before that becomes relevant." He raised himself off of her and began to move down her body, dropping kisses on her collarbone, breasts, and stomach as he went.

"Ground...to cover?" Her voice rose to a squeak as his fingers delved between her legs. She was well-acquainted with the pleasures to be found there; nearly ten years of a solitary marriage had taught her not to rely on another for her own satisfaction.

But the stroke and tease of Max's big, capable hands was like nothing she had ever felt. He touched her as delicately as if she was made of the thinnest glass, but every movement still sparked a rush of pleasure.

He explored her with his fingers for several blissful minutes. She gave an involuntary moan of disappointment when he took his hand away—only to break off in a gasp as he replaced it with his warm mouth. She had never imagined this as something a man might do to a woman, but Max's imagination was clearly more expansive.

Her back arched, pressing herself closer to him, needing the slide of his wet tongue, the gentle suction of his lips on her most sensitive place. He slipped his hands beneath her hips, tilting her toward him as he buried his face between her legs.

Her thighs tightened around his head. She flung a hand down to grab his hair, using the pull of her fingers to encourage him in the movements and rhythm she liked. The pleasure built, and she gasped his name. His abbreviated name was better suited than most to cry in the throes of pleasure—one syllable, easy to choke out amid ragged, frantic breaths. She said it over and over again as the flick of his tongue and clasp of his lips urged her on to greater heights.

When she finally exploded, he growled against her in satisfaction. As the tremors subsided, she collapsed back onto the bed, every muscle weak and sated. Her thighs released their grip on his head, and he wiped the back of his hand across his mouth with an appreciative grin.

"I always wondered what ambrosia tasted like," he said. "Now I know."

Her cheeks, still flushed, heated even more. He lay down next to her, stretching his body alongside hers, and pulled her into his arms. Little shocks of pleasure sparked where he touched her. His arousal bumped her hip, and she reached down to take hold of it.

The rhythm of his breathing stuttered. She loved this effect she had on him, able to make him quiver with the lightest touch. She rolled onto her side, facing him, and lifted her knee to rest atop his thigh, opening herself to him.

"We can just go back to sleep if you like," he whispered in her ear. "You must be tired still."

She gave a light chuckle. "If you think I'm letting you go back to sleep at this moment, you're sorely mistaken." She gave him a long, lingering stroke.

In a fluid but forceful movement, he rolled her flat on her back and pinned her beneath him. Her thighs parted once more, her feet tracing a line up the back of his calves. He reached down to align their bodies. His cock pressed against her entrance, then his hips canted forward, and her slick folds welcomed him, offering no resistance as he buried himself deep. Her eyes fluttered closed as he filled her, her mind overwhelmed with the warm pleasure of him inside her.

He let out a low moan and lowered his head to rest in the curve of her neck and shoulder. He muttered something, almost certainly an obscenity, but his mouth was muffled against her body.

She drew her knees up and tilted her hips, urging him deeper. He braced his arms on either side of her head and began to thrust. His movements were slow and gentle, and she could tell he was holding back, afraid of hurting her.

She wrapped her legs around his waist. "Harder, Max," she whispered. "Fuck me like you've been waiting ten years to do it."

He let out an incoherent groan and obliged. By the gods, he obliged. The hard, fast thrusts drove every thought from her mind. Nothing remained but the feel of his body on top of her, inside her, and the rasp of his breath against her skin.

She even forgot about her request for him to take precautions—but he remembered. He withdrew from her and spilled himself over her stomach with a grunt. Then he collapsed on his back next to her, chest heaving, a glimmer of sweat on his forehead.

On unsteady legs, she raised herself out of bed and tottered over to grab a damp cloth, which she used to clean both of them. Then, she tossed it away and climbed back into bed, pulling the blanket up over both of them. He gathered her to his chest, and she let out a contented sigh.

Moments later, Max had fallen back to sleep, his arms slackening around her. She closed her eyes. A slight tug of melancholy pulled at her. This coupling with Max had laid bare the feelings that had been simmering under the surface since they were seventeen, but their future was so uncertain. They had the rest of their journey to spend with each other, yes, but what would happen once they reached Rome?

Her priorities needed to be bringing Petronax to justice and caring for her son, which would likely require making a strategic marriage to give him an influential stepfather. Max, for all his virtues, was not the sort of man who had the connections or influence to set Lucius up for a successful public career, and she had a feeling he wouldn't relish the responsibilities that a life with her entailed. He sought a life of freedom, of adventure, and wouldn't want to be tethered to Rome and its politics, or a stepchild.

Nevertheless, her heart ached as she thought of what he'd sacrificed for her. His military career, his beloved horse, and nearly his life. She vowed that if she was successful in bringing down Petronax, she'd ensure that Max was reinstated to his position in the army. That, at least, would begin to repay some of what she owed him.

CHAPTER 18

M AX WOKE WITH HIS face buried in Volusia's golden hair. Sunlight streamed into the room, and the sounds of early morning echoed from the tavern downstairs: murmurs of conversation, stools and tables scraping as they were pushed back to sweep the floor, footsteps on the stairs.

He sat up, gently disentangling himself from the sleeping woman beside him. Volusia was sleeping on her stomach, one slender arm raised to pillow her face, the ivory skin of her back left bare by the blanket.

His memories of last night were hazy, and he questioned if they were real, but his cock throbbed as he looked at her. It clearly remembered what being inside her had felt like.

Volusia stirred and rolled over, which exposed her beautiful tits to the sunlight. Unable to resist, he allowed his hand to cup one, his finger coaxing her pink nipple to harden.

She shivered and opened her eyes, giving him a shy smile. "Good morning."

"It's a *very* good morning so far." He gave her nipple a playful pinch, which caused her to yelp and slap his hand away with a giggle.

He wanted nothing more than to stretch his body over hers and sink into her once more, but the morning light made him remember their responsibilities. Now that they were fed, rested, and had some coin to their name, they had to return to Rome as fast as possible, so their families would know they weren't dead.

Volusia seemed to be of the same mind, for she swung her legs out of bed and crossed to where they'd dumped their clothes yesterday. She lifted her filthy dress with a frown. "We need new clothes."

Max nodded. "Agreed. Let me see what I can do." He threw on his stained and ripped tunic, grabbed a few silver coins, and headed downstairs.

An hour later, he'd bartered for a spare tunic and dress from the tavern keeper and his wife, and had also secured them breakfast, two mediocre horses, and a small supply of food for the journey.

By midmorning, they were off. "How long do you think it will take us to reach Rome?" Volusia asked as he guided the horses down the road away from Genua. Since Volusia wasn't an experienced rider, Max kept hold of a lead attached to her horse. The brown gelding he rode was stocky, with a lumbering gait—nothing compared to Elephant's graceful, fluid movements, but he would have to do.

"A little over a week, I think," Max said. "Maybe eight or nine days. With luck, we'll only be a few days behind Glabrio."

"Good," she murmured. He knew she must be thinking of her son, who would soon believe himself to be an orphan.

Max didn't know what to say, so he spurred the horses into a canter, which removed their ability to speak.

When the light faded at the end of the day, they made camp in a grassy area a little ways off the road. Max built a fire while Volusia portioned out some of the bread, cheese, and dried apricots they'd packed.

The stars brightened the darkening sky as night fell. While they ate, he became entranced with the way the firelight flickered over the curves of her face, casting shadows across the hollows of her throat and collarbone. Despite wanting to reach Rome as soon as possible, he relished these few days that remained with Volusia. Their paths would diverge once they reached Rome. Volusia would return to her family, and Max to his—and more importantly, he'd set out to get Elephant back.

These could be the last days he'd ever spend with her, and he would savor every moment.

Volusia finished her last bite of bread and washed it down with a swig from the wineskin. She turned her head to meet his gaze, catching him in the act of scrutinizing her. He glanced away, embarrassed, but her finger caught his chin, turning his face back toward her.

She leaned over and brushed her lips against his. Desire sparked instantly at her touch. He slid a hand to cradle the back of her head, pressing their faces closer. Her mouth opened for him, and his tongue delved inside to meet hers.

He eased himself backward to lie on the hard ground, bringing her over him. He didn't want her to be uncomfortable on the uneven ground. Indeed, a twig immediately dug into his back, but he didn't care.

"You want me like this?" she whispered as she rubbed herself over his already aching cock.

He groaned. His hands closed around her hips, pressing her even tighter against him. "I want you every way I can have you."

Their hands grasped at each other's clothes, tugging and bunching and shifting, and a few gasping breaths later, she sank down onto him. He closed his eyes in bliss as her tight warmth enveloped him. His hips angled upward, finding a deeper seat inside her. She braced her hands on his chest and wiggled her hips to settle herself more fully onto him. The movement made him gasp. She grinned and did it again, then struck up a gentle, rolling motion of her hips.

Max reached up to caress her breasts. She was still wearing her dress, bunched around her thighs. He tugged it off her shoulders, needing to see the play of firelight over all of her. The dress slid down easily, as the tavern-keeper's wife had been stockier than Volusia, and soon her breasts were bare. The dancing shadows from the fire made her look otherworldly, like a forest nymph taking her pleasure from an unsuspecting traveler.

He tried to keep his wits about him as his lust mounted. She wasn't a forest nymph; she was Volusia, and she'd made it clear she didn't want to risk any consequences from their coupling. He grasped her hips to slow her movements, and slid a hand between her legs, where their bodies joined. She arched her back, pressing into his hand, as he rubbed the spot that gave her pleasure.

Doing this while he was inside her was novel and thrilling. He could feel every twitch and stir of her body, the tiny shocks and quivers that grew stronger as her climax approached. When she finally gave herself over to the tide of pleasure, the clenches of her body around him almost undid him, but he rode it out with her. He drank in the sight of her body bowing and shuddering on top of him, the sound of her gasping cries in the empty forest.

When it finally left her, he gathered her to his chest, their bodies still connected. She was warm and limp and breathless.

"Don't stop," she whispered. She kissed his neck, drawing a groan from his lips.

He renewed his grip on her hips, his fingers digging into her plush bottom. He thrust upward into her in short, hard strokes. She moaned in his ear, her voice husky and rough.

When the pleasure became too great to withstand, he pulled her off of him, his hand replacing the clasp of her body. Exhilarating spasms wracked him, and he exploded over his stomach.

Volusia curled up against his side, heedless of the twigs and leaves that must be beneath her, and stroked his chest. He turned his head to kiss her, his mind fuzzy and reeling. He'd known pleasure with a woman before, and had picked up some useful tricks from past encounters that Volusia seemed to appreciate. But those encounters seemed the barest shadow compared to what he felt with Volusia. She was everything he could ever want, but he knew their time together was running out.

They made good time on the rest of their journey. Volusia enjoyed traveling with Max more than she had any right to, especially under their fraught circumstances. He was easygoing and confident, always ready with an amusing anecdote to take her mind off her worries.

As they proceeded south down the Italian coast, farms and villages appeared with more frequency, and they had a better chance of spending the night at an inn or in a kind farmer's barn as opposed to camping by the road. Max asked anyone they encountered if a band of soldiers had passed through recently. At first, the answers indicated Glabrio and his men were four days ahead of them. As the days passed, the time decreased to three days, then two. Max and Volusia could make better time on their horses than the soldiers could, burdened with more supplies. Even so, there was no way they'd beat Glabrio to Rome.

"I think we'll reach the city gates by midday tomorrow," Max said as they sat in a hayloft. They'd paid a farmer for a meal and the use of his barn for the evening, and their horses were munching happily on hay in an empty stall below. It smelled of manure, but the shelter was welcome.

Anticipation swelled within Volusia, tempered by a guilty reluctance to part from Max. "That's good."

"I'll take you to your parents' house first. Then I'll go to mine." He toyed with a stray piece of hay. "What are you going to do about Petronax?"

Volusia had spent much of their journey strategizing how to approach the matter, and she had the rough outline of a plan. "I will convince my stepfather to take my evidence before the consuls. He has influence, as a former consul. They'll have to take him seriously." The outlandish accusations of a grief-stricken widow would be too easy to dismiss. She needed her stepfather's voice, and she knew Rufus would be outraged at the danger she'd faced. "Your testimony will be useful as well."

He nodded. "I'll do whatever you need. And if you're successful in bringing Petronax to justice? What then?"

"Of course I will do everything in my power to reinstate you in the army. You could get back everything you've lost."

His gaze remained on the piece of hay he was twirling between his fingers. "And what of yourself?"

She swallowed hard. Talking of the future was more difficult than it should be. "I don't know," she said quietly. "I only know I'll do whatever I must to secure Lucius's future. Avitus wanted our son to follow in his footsteps. I'll make sure he carries on his father's legacy. I owe it to Avitus."

At that, Max glanced up, his eyes narrowing. "You don't owe anything to him."

"Of course I do," Volusia said, surprised at his gruff tone. "He was my husband, and the father of my child."

"He wasn't a good husband to you." Max snapped the strand of hay, crushing it in his grip.

"He never mistreated me."

"Just because he didn't beat you doesn't make him a good husband," Max said. "He didn't love you. You said as much yourself."

"He was honest with me from the start." Volusia's chest tightened. She didn't know where this argument had come from. There hadn't been so much as a sharp word between them this whole time, and now they were arguing about her dead husband, of all things?

"He should never have married you. Not if he couldn't love you as you deserve to be loved."

"If he hadn't married me, someone else would have. Either way it wouldn't have been you." The words came out more cutting than she intended, and she bit her lip, but didn't take them back.

His jaw clenched, a muscle pulsing. "I'm well aware I wasn't good enough for you." In a surge of motion, he rose to his feet and paced to the opposite side of the hayloft, the boards creaking beneath him.

"Max, that's not what I meant." She followed him and put a hand on his arm. This was not how she wanted to spend their last night together. "We weren't right for each other back then. You wanted to join the army. I wanted to make a good marriage and raise a family."

He turned to face her, his eyes dark and serious. "And now? Are we right for each other?"

She took a sharp breath. She knew the answer in her bones, and it pained her. No, they still weren't right for each other. They wanted different things. Max didn't want to live in Rome, and if he managed to rejoin the army, he'd be forbidden from marrying anyway.

He must have seen the answer in her eyes, or maybe he felt it too, for his shoulders slumped.

But she couldn't let him go, not yet. She reached up and caressed his cheek. "I only know about tonight, and tonight, I think we're right for each other." She stood on her tiptoes and brushed her lips against his.

His arm encircled her waist, drawing her against his body. His other hand tilted her chin up, claiming her mouth with his. Desire surged within her. She angled her hips against his, feeling the ridge of his cock, already hard. The responsiveness of his body never failed to thrill her.

Together, they stumbled over to the makeshift bed, a few blankets atop a pile of straw. She sank to the floor first, hiking her dress up to bare her thighs. Max shucked off his tunic and braccae, then joined her. His body settled over her. One forearm braced against the straw as his other hand slid down to explore between her legs. She arched her back and opened herself to him.

His fingers brushed over her, slipping in the wetness that had quickly gathered. He pressed one finger inside her gently, while his thumb circled her most sensitive spot. "Fuck, Volusia," he whispered against her neck. "I love how wet you get for me."

She clung to his shoulders. He had learned her body well over the past week, and knew exactly how to touch her to make her senseless to anything but pleasure.

"It is for me, isn't it?" he continued, his voice growing rougher, his breath hot on her skin. "Tell me it's for me." His fingers quickened, his gentleness giving way to a firm, demanding rhythm.

"It's for you, Max," she gasped. The muscles of her stomach contracted as a tight ball of yearning gathered in her core.

He lowered his head to take her nipple into his mouth, and the swipe of his tongue sent her over the edge, careening into an abyss of pleasure. Her nails dug into his shoulders, and she buried her moans against his chest, though no one was around to hear but some sheep and a few horses.

He pressed her thighs open and slid his cock inside her as she was still quivering. His entrance caused a wave of renewed sensation that was almost painful in its intensity, but she welcomed it. She wanted to wring every last bit of passion from this final encounter.

He hooked a hand behind the crook of her knee and eased her leg forward, so he could push even deeper into her. She curled her other leg around his thigh, anchoring their bodies together. Slowly, he began to thrust, sinking into her over and over again with a delicious rhythm.

Too soon, he withdrew with a grunt and rolled onto his back. She grabbed his hand before it could close around his cock. "Wait," she murmured.

"Volusia, I'm so close," he groaned.

"I know." She positioned herself over him. There was something she'd been wanting to try, but she'd been too shy until now. But there was no point holding back anymore.

She lowered her head until her lips brushed his straining cock.

A shudder ran through him. "Fuck," he whispered.

She closed her lips around him and took him in, sliding her mouth down as far as she could. She wasn't entirely sure how to go about this, but she'd heard enough salacious jokes from her married friends back in Rome that she understood the basics. She tried to replicate the rhythm he struck when he was inside her, hoping that would bring him pleasure.

His hand cupped the back of her head, his fingers sliding into her hair. His breathing grew harsh and shallow, with another gasped obscenity as she swept her tongue along his length.

"Volusia, if you don't stop, I'm going to—oh, fuck," he moaned as she tightened her mouth around him.

She didn't stop. He'd been so careful, so thoughtful in their couplings over the past week, always interrupting his pleasure to ensure they wouldn't risk conception, even when she'd abandoned herself to the throes of desire. At least once, she wanted to let him lose himself inside her.

His fingers curled around the back of her head. His hips bucked, pushing himself deeper into her mouth, and he let out a rough grunt. Her mouth filled with warm, salty liquid. She swallowed quickly, then when he released her head, reached for the water skin to wash it down.

He lay against their makeshift bed, eyes half-closed and a dazed look on his face. She curled herself next to him, stretching an arm across his chest. His arm came up to cradle her back, brushing down her spine in a soothing rhythm. "Volusia, that was…" He shook his head, seemingly at a loss for words.

She smiled, pleased with herself, and rested her head on his chest.

They were silent after that. Slowly, his breathing deepened, and she knew he'd fallen asleep. She savored the sound of his breathing, the warm solidity of his body beneath her, around her. She tried to commit everything to memory. Soon, these memories would be all she'd have left.

CHAPTER 19

T HE SUN BEAT DOWN as Max and Volusia made their way through the city gates of Rome. A steady flow of people proceeded through the gates, mostly farmers, craftsmen, and merchants come to sell their wares to the urban population. Max and Volusia blended into the crowd.

Max's jaw tensed as soon as the walls of the city were behind them. He'd grown up in the city, yes, but ever since he'd experienced the fresh air and expanse of the countryside, merely stepping foot in the city made him feel trapped and suffocated.

Max dismounted, then helped Volusia down. They'd need to walk the horses through the busy, twisting city streets.

Volusia was quiet as they walked through the city, proceeding from the outskirts to the more central neighborhood where her family lived. He guessed she was bracing herself for the reunion that was about to come, and all the emotions it would entail.

He didn't speak, but kept a gentle hand on her elbow, guiding her around potholes and piles of refuse in the streets. Most well-bred Roman ladies traveled solely by litter, so he doubted she had ever actually walked the streets of the city in which she lived.

They passed several blocks teeming with over-crowded apartment buildings that always seemed at risk of toppling—similar to where Max had grown up—and crossed into the more fashionable neighborhood on the Caelian Hill where Volusia's family lived. The streets were wide and quiet, swept clean in front of each house by household slaves.

When they reached her family's house, Volusia stopped short. Leafy cypress branches, just beginning to brown, were nailed to the door, a sign that death had visited this family.

Max secured the horses' reins to a post outside. Volusia reached out a trembling hand and knocked on the door. A moment later, a slat in the door slid back, revealing the face of a young man. He stared at Volusia, blinking, for several moments, as befuddlement spread across his face.

She smiled uncertainly. "Hello, Orion."

The young man finally found his voice. "My lady! Is it really you? We thought—"

"Yes, I'm afraid there was a misunderstanding. I'm not dead, as you can see. Now, may I please come in?"

"Of course, lady." Orion's face disappeared from the small window, and there was a scraping sound as he unbarred the door. It swung open, and Max followed Volusia into the shadowy antechamber.

Memories of the last time he'd been here flooded back: the night she'd kissed him and he'd subsequently been thrown out by her stepfather, Rufus. So much had changed since then. His adolescent infatuation with Volusia had been tempered over their decade apart, like molten metal hardening into a finished object, but it had never left him. Now, after all they had been through, all he had sacrificed for her, his love for her was stronger than ever. The pain of their imminent parting already sliced at him, mingling in a bittersweet jumble with the satisfaction of bringing her safely home.

Orion ran off to fetch Volusia's parents. Max and Volusia crossed into the atrium. Max eyed a column on the other side of the room. Behind that column was the spot they'd first kissed, ten long years ago.

Hurried footsteps sounded, and Volusia's stepfather burst into the atrium, closely followed by her mother, Sabina. Rufus's scrawny frame seemed to have become even thinner since Max had last seen him, and dark shadows hovered beneath his eyes. Despite Max's deep dislike for Rufus, he couldn't help feeling a twinge of sympathy for how the news of Volusia's apparent death had affected him.

Sabina, too, looked pale and exhausted. She stopped short, and a small cry flew from her mouth at the sight of Volusia. She faltered for a moment, and Rufus caught her elbow. His gaze lit on Max with incomprehension, then passed over him to fasten on Volusia.

Volusia launched herself forward, and both parents swept her into an embrace. Max hung back, trying to fade into the shadows of the atrium. A flurry of weeping and half-gasped questions sounded from the cluster of people. Volusia answered, explaining an abbreviated version of the events which had led them here.

"They will pay for this," Rufus growled, still clinging to Volusia. "To treat the wife of a governor thus—" His eyes, usually so cold and ruthless, shone with tears, and Max felt another unwilling stab of compassion for the man.

Another figure entered the room, a small boy who had to be Volusia's son, Lucius. He had Avitus's gray eyes and dark hair, but Volusia's fair complexion and slender build. He blinked at the scene before him. "What's going on? You've interrupted my lesson."

Rufus and Sabina released Volusia, who turned to see her son. "Oh, my darling," she whispered, her voice shaking.

"Mama?" He stared at her. "Grandfather said you were in Hades. Did you escape? Did you see Cerberus? Does he really have three heads?"

Volusia's lips twitched in a smile even as a tear trickled down her cheek. "There was a mistake, my love. I wasn't in Hades. Just Gaul."

"Oh." The child looked a trifle disappointed for a moment, then ran to Volusia and hugged her tight. She dropped to her knees and wrapped him in her arms. Her frame shook gently with sobs.

Lucius pulled back from the embrace, his eyes lighting with excitement. "Does this mean Papa isn't in Hades either? Is he coming back too?"

Volusia kissed him on the forehead. "No, my darling. I'm very sorry, but Papa's not coming back."

"Oh." His lips trembled, and he sniffled. Volusia folded him into her arms once more.

Max's throat tightened at Volusia's reunion with her son. Watching them together, he suddenly felt out of place. He was intruding on a moment that didn't belong to him. No one seemed to notice him; Volusia's entire focus was Lucius, and Rufus was holding Sabina, who was sobbing against his chest.

It was time to leave. He had fulfilled his mission of bringing her home. She was back with her family, and she no longer needed him.

Max slipped out of the atrium and nodded to Orion, who had resumed his post by the front door. "Please tell her I returned to my family. She can reach me there if she needs me," Max said.

Orion bowed his head and hauled open the front door. "Yes, sir."

Max left the house, and untied the horses' reins from the post outside. He felt strangely bereft as he led the animals through the streets. Volusia had been by his side day and night for so many days, through so much hardship and uncertainty. He hardly knew what to do with himself without her.

But the sight of her son brought one fact into clear focus: Volusia had more important things to worry about now than whatever fragile thing was between her and Max. Lucius would always be first in her mind, as the boy should be, and every decision she made would be for him.

Max crossed the city to the neighborhood on the Esquiline Hill where his adoptive family lived. It was a less ostentatious area than where Volusia's family lived, filled with respectable but smaller homes.

His pace slowed as the door to the house came into view. It, too, was adorned with a cypress branch to signify mourning. His chest constricted, but he took a deep breath and walked up to knock on the door.

Paris, one of the household slaves, speechlessly let him in. Max strode into the atrium. He stopped short at the sight of Gaia, his grandmother, sitting in a sunny spot in the atrium weaving. Memories rushed over him. As a child, he used to sit on the floor and watch her weave—one of the few times he sat still. He remembered the soothing motion of the shuttle through the warp threads, the rhythmic sweep of the loom.

Her head turned toward him. Her graying hair now bore streaks of silver, which hadn't been there the last time he'd seen her.

The wooden shuttle dropped from her hand and clattered to the stone floor. She shot to her feet, her golden skin blanching. "Max," she whispered. "Is it…is it really…" She wavered.

In several long strides, he closed the distance between them and grasped her shoulders to steady her. "It's me," he said, his voice suddenly raspy.

She gave a little cry and collapsed into his arms, clutching him with desperate fingers. He embraced her gently. Gaia had always been slight, but she felt thinner, more fragile since the last time he'd hugged her upon leaving for Gaul.

Paris must have fetched Aelius and Crispina, for they stumbled into the atrium a few moments later.

"Max," Crispina gasped. She gripped Aelius's hand, knuckles white. Aelius was struck dumb. He was thirteen years older than Crispina, and right now Max could see every one of his fifty-two years. Lines were etched around his eyes and mouth, and a sprinkling of gray lightened his hair.

"They told us you were dead!" Crispina hissed.

"I'm sorry I couldn't send word," Max said. "It's a long story. But I'm not dead, as you can see."

Gaia disentangled herself from Max to make room for Aelius and Crispina, and a moment later he was sagging under the weight of his adoptive parents' embrace.

"How could this happen?" Crispina demanded. "They said you and Rufus's daughter had drowned in an accident on your way back to Rome."

Max tried to explain as concisely as he could. "Volusia was planning to accuse the legion's commander of murdering her husband. So he gave orders for her to be killed on the journey. I…" He hesitated. "I defended her, and we made it look like we'd been swept away by a river."

"Gods below," Crispina swore.

A smile wavered on Aelius's lips, and he spoke for the first time. "You did say you wanted adventure when you joined the army."

Max grinned. "I did, didn't I?" Then he sobered. "I'm afraid that sort of adventure is done for me. I disobeyed and attacked a commanding officer. I'll be lucky to escape a trial for mutiny."

"We won't let anything of the sort happen to you," Crispina said, her voice ringing with determination. "Besides, Rufus will no doubt pull every string he can to seek justice for his daughter. That must clear your name, as well."

Max nodded. "That's the plan." His stomach gave a loud growl.

"You poor thing, you must be starving." Gaia stepped forward to take his arm. "Let's see about some food."

"Thank you, Grandmother." He couldn't resist a smirk. Gaia had always hated when he called her Grandmother.

She shot him a good-natured glare. "I shall forgive that one, seeing as you've only recently returned from the dead."

"I wonder what else I can get away with." He chuckled, and followed her in the direction of the kitchen.

An hour later, Max had been fed, dressed in fresh clothes, and thoroughly questioned. His family wanted to know every detail about what had transpired on the journey to Rome. He told them everything except what had happened between him and Volusia, claiming that his defense of her had been motivated purely by honor. He sensed a touch of suspicion in Crispina's gaze, but she didn't challenge him.

After a hearty meal, he left the house to head to the closest baths. Finally, he'd get truly clean after weeks of hard travel.

Max entered the grand, columned building which housed the baths, paid the entrance fee, and stripped in the changing room, stowing his clothes in a cubby. He took a towel with him into the next room, which contained a round, steaming pool. Lamps were mounted on the walls, but the room was almost completely dark otherwise. There was only one other person soaking at the other side of the pool. Max was grateful the baths weren't crowded; he didn't feel like socializing.

He laid his towel on a bench and stepped into the hot water. The heat washed over him in a rush. He closed his eyes and leaned back against the marble edge of the pool, submerging himself up to his neck. Sweat broke out on his face in the dark, stifling room. The muscles of his neck and shoulders finally relaxed, letting go of the stress that had gripped him for so long.

He had succeeded in bringing Volusia home. She was safe, reunited with her family. Their families no longer thought they were dead. Everything, for a moment at least, was all right.

Two things still nagged at him. Firstly, there was the matter of Elephant. He needed to find his horse. If he were Glabrio, and found himself with an extra horse, what would he do?

Sell her was the likely answer. Anxiety swelled in his chest at the thought of Elephant being thrust into unknown hands. If he was lucky, Glabrio had waited until they reached Rome to sell her, rather than passing her off somewhere along the journey. Max would have to visit every horse dealer he could find and ask if they'd seen her. Luckily, Elephant was a fine horse, and would have fetched a good price. The dealers would remember her.

He felt better once he'd made a plan to find Elephant, but the other thing that bothered him was not so easy to resolve. His feelings for Volusia had become impossible to ignore, and he could no longer tell himself it had just been a childhood infatuation. He had to hope his feelings would fade once they were no longer bound together by danger.

But the ache under his ribs made him fear she wouldn't be so easy to leave behind. Despite the stress of their journey, he missed the nights they'd spent together snuggled in an uncomfortable bed at an inn or a pile of straw in a barn. He already missed her constant presence at his side.

He wondered if she had spared him a thought after returning home. No doubt she was entirely focused on her son, as she should be. He should do the same, and set his feelings for her aside.

Water splashed as the man on the other side of the pool climbed out. Max glanced over. Lamplight caught the man's face, and Max squinted. He looked uncannily like…

"Silvanus?" Max's voice echoed around the room.

The man grabbed his towel, threw it around his waist, and hurried from the room. Max settled back into the pool. His eyes were playing tricks on him in the dim light. Avitus's secretary had stayed in Narbo. His mind was too full with thoughts of Volusia.

Once his skin was pink with heat, he rose out of the bath, wrapping a towel around his waist, and moved into the next room, the frigidarium. A dome rose over the large, deep pool, and windows high in the walls let in shafts of light, shimmering on the water. He tossed the towel onto a bench, held his breath, and plunged into the freezing water.

The shock of the cold consumed him for an exhilarating instant. He rose, gasping, and slicked back his hair, wishing the water could wash away his fruitless longing for Volusia.

CHAPTER 20

VOLUSIA WOKE IN A soft bed. For the first time in weeks, there was no smell of a campfire or snuffling of animals or hard ground beneath her…or Max's arms around her. The bed linens smelled of lavender, and the house was blissfully quiet.

For a moment, she was disoriented, thinking herself back in her house in Narbo. Then, as she sat up and squinted around the half-lit room, she remembered. Max had brought her home yesterday.

It was strange to wake alone after so long by his side. She felt a tug of longing for the steady comfort of his presence, but shook it off. She could dwell on her feelings for him later, but for now, she had a mission.

She swung her legs out of bed and wrapped a shawl around her shoulders. Her trunk rested against the wall of her bedroom. Glabrio's men had delivered it when bringing the news of Volusia's apparent death, and her parents had stowed it in her old bedroom without touching it.

She unfastened the metal clasp and heaved the lid open. She sifted through layers of clothes, shoes, hair ornaments, cosmetics, and other personal effects, which all now seemed like relics of another life.

In the middle, wrapped in a square of fabric, she found the tablet with her only evidence against Petronax. She remembered giving this to Iris when they were packing to leave Narbo. Another pang of bittersweet sadness passed through her. She missed Iris, but hoped she'd found a new life for herself with her family in Gaul.

She opened the tablet to ensure it hadn't been damaged in the journey, then laid it on her bed while she dressed and brushed her hair, braiding it as best she could. She would need to find another maid soon, but she feared no one could replace Iris.

Volusia took the tablet and went to her stepfather's study. He often woke early to handle correspondence before breakfast.

As she expected, Rufus was seated behind his desk, stylus poised over a tablet. He glanced up when she crossed the threshold, his face brightening into a smile. "My dear, you look rested. Are you hungry? I can send for some breakfast."

"Soon, Father, but there's something I wanted to discuss with you first." She sat in the chair opposite his desk and slid the tablet toward him. "This tablet contains evidence of Avitus's suspicions against Petronax. That he was overtaxing the population and pocketing the province's income for his own gain."

Rufus frowned and picked up the tablet, squinting at the barely-there words. "I see."

"Yesterday you said you wanted to see the men who did this brought to justice. Will you help me bring this evidence against Petronax?"

His frown deepened. "Certainly I'll see the centurion and those who followed his orders dismissed from the army in disgrace. But bringing charges of murdering a governor against a legionary commander is quite a different matter. There is still a civil war going on. Petronax has a whole legion of men loyal to him. If he decided to take up arms against the Republic and join Sextus Pompeius, it could go very badly."

Volusia leaned forward. "But I have evidence of his treachery."

Rufus set the tablet down. "You have some partially-erased speculation. I'm afraid this will not be seen as solid proof."

Volusia clasped her hands together, fingers twisting. "Isn't the fact that Petronax ordered me killed proof that he was up to something?"

Her stepfather's lips tightened. "Petronax will deny giving such an order. The centurion will take the blame."

In a surge of frustration, she rose to her feet and paced the small length of the study. "So you're saying I have nothing. My husband was murdered, and you think I should let the killer get away with it?"

Rufus raised his hands in a conciliatory gesture. "I'm saying you should be grateful to be alive, and turn your focus to the future, rather than the past."

She clenched her fists. "Lucius is my future, and he deserves justice for his father's death. Please, Father, you have influence. You can bring these charges before the consuls, and they'll listen to you. Won't you help me?"

His gaze shifted away from her, guilt flashing briefly. "I'm afraid it's not that simple, my dear. You see, I plan to mount another campaign for consul in the next election."

"Another consulship? Are you sure that's wise, in times like these?"

He waved a hand. "The civil war could take years to resolve. Octavius's army still has to take Sicily from Sextus Pompeius. While they are slaughtering each other, someone needs to do the real work of governing. And if I want another consulship, I can't go around accusing legionary commanders of murder, based on nothing but scribbles."

Volusia took a sharp breath. "So you're choosing your political ambitions over your daughter. I don't know why I expected anything less." Rufus had always been ambitious to a fault, but she'd thought that in this, of all things, he would side with her.

She meant her words to rile him, but he remained calm, the only disturbance a flush of red rising to his pale cheeks. "I am choosing to extend the influence and reputation of our family. Not tear it down by bringing what will be seen as baseless accusations against a powerful man." He rose to his feet and clasped her shoulders. "My dear, you've been through a great deal in the past few weeks, more than any young woman should suffer. Just take a while to let it settle. Soon, you'll be able to put it all behind you." He kissed her forehead.

She allowed the gesture, but her body hummed with frustration. If her own stepfather wouldn't support her, how was she to bring Petronax to justice? Maybe she should take his advice. Pretend Avitus really had died of an illness and move on. Focus on Lucius, his future.

No, she decided. Avitus deserved justice, and Petronax couldn't be allowed to continually bleed the province dry. She would find a way, whether she could convince Rufus to help her or not.

The day after his return, Max visited the markets just outside the city walls where horse dealers did their business. He kept an eagle eye out for flashes of dappled gray among the clusters of chestnut, black, and white horses, but he knew there was little chance Elephant was still here.

He approached every dealer he came across and asked if they'd seen an elegant gray mare pass through the markets in the last few days. Some hadn't seen any horse matching that description. Others had seen a gray mare, but didn't recall where or to whom she'd been sold.

Finally, as the sun rose to its midday height, he found someone who not only had seen Elephant, but remembered the name of the dealer who'd sold her, a man called Burrus.

Excitement quickened his pace as he followed the directions given. He found a balding man leaning against a fence post, supervising a paddock containing three horses. Max gave them a cursory scan, but Elephant was not among them.

Max raised a hand in greeting. "Are you Burrus?"

The man glanced over him, gaze lingering on the purse of coin hanging from Max's belt. "I am. You're in search of a horse? I have three beauties here." He waved an expansive hand at the horses in the paddock.

"I am in search of a horse, but not one of those." Max stepped closer. "Someone told me you sold a gray mare a few days back. I want to know who bought her."

Burrus frowned. "Yes, I remember the mare."

"So, where is she?" Max pressed.

The man raised his chin. "I'm not in the habit of giving out my clients' personal information. Besides, why do you want to know?"

"That horse is stolen property," Max said. "She was stolen from me and sold unlawfully. You bought her from a centurion, didn't you?"

Burrus's eyes narrowed. "Not my problem. I paid honest money for her."

"It will be your problem if you get a reputation for selling stolen horses," Max growled. "Isn't any good dealer responsible for ensuring the legality of his sales?"

"What are you, a lawyer?" Burrus snapped.

Max was the furthest thing from a lawyer, but before setting out this morning, Aelius had given him some pointers on laws surrounding stolen property. But in any case, threatening Burrus with legal trouble likely wasn't going to get him the result he wanted at this moment. He took a deep breath and tried another angle. "All I need is a name and a location, and I'll trouble you no further." He dipped a hand into his purse and withdrew a bronze coin.

Burrus took the coin, considered for a moment, and pocketed it. "She went to an estate east of the city. Near Tibur. I did business with an agent of the landowner, not the man himself. Don't remember the landowner's name. His agent paid six hundred sestertii for her."

Tibur was only a few hours' ride away. He could be there and back by dusk.

Max handed Burrus another coin for good measure, thanked him, and left. He fetched one of the horses he and Volusia had ridden to Rome on, obtained more money from the coffers at home, and set off on the eastern road. He pushed the horse as fast as he dared, but the gelding didn't have Elephant's graceful, exhilarating speed.

He passed through miles of rolling vineyards and farmland. Soon, sprawling villas dotted the landscape, each grander than the last and surrounded by fields, vineyards, and orchards. He paused several times to ask slaves working the fields if any of their masters had purchased a gray horse recently.

At the fourth estate, someone said yes. "A pretty one, too," the young man said, leaning on his scythe.

Hope sparked in Max's chest. He smiled and handed the laborer a coin. "Yes, she is. Where are the stables?"

The young man pointed, and Max set off. Around a bend from the fields, a grassy pasture sat before a cluster of stable buildings. A flash of gray caught his eye on the other side of the pasture, and his stomach flip-flopped. It was her. Her slender neck was bent to the ground, tail swishing as she cropped some grass.

He drew his gelding to an abrupt stop, leaped off, and threw the reins over one of the fence posts. Then, he vaulted the fence, aware that he was trespassing but unable to bring himself to care. "Elephant!" he called as he landed on his feet inside the pasture.

She raised her head, ears twitching. Then, her powerful body was in motion, cantering toward him, her graceful legs eating up the distance between them.

She drew to a halt, prancing before him. He lifted a hand to pat her nose, and she snorted, jerking her head away from his touch. She must be irritated with him for abandoning her. "I'm sorry," he murmured.

She let out a soft whuffle and lowered her head, pressing her nose against his chest. His arms curved around her, stroking her cheek. For a long moment, his entire being was centered on the big, warm mass of horse in his arms.

"Hey!" A shout split the air. "You can't be in there."

Max turned to see a red-faced man gesticulating on the opposite side of the fence. Max released Elephant and walked toward the man. "Are you in charge here? I'd like to buy this horse."

The man blinked. "I'm in charge of the stables. We only just bought this mare. The master won't want to sell her. Be off with you now, and stop wasting our time."

"This horse is stolen property," Max said. "Legally, she belongs to me."

The man let out a short bark of laughter. "Stolen property? Are you fucking with me? Get out of here before I call our guards to drag you out."

This irritating man was now the only thing standing between Max and Elephant, and Max wanted nothing more than to punch him in the mouth and ride off on Elephant.

But he forced himself to go about things the right way. He adopted a relaxed posture, leaning his forearms against the fence. "I have plenty of witnesses who will swear under oath that I've owned her since she was a filly. You may have bought her in good faith, but she wasn't free to be sold. And if your master doesn't sell her back to me, I'll take this to the courts. I doubt that will please your master. If you would be so good as to fetch him, we can sort this out between us."

The stablemaster glared at him. A muscle in his jaw pulsed, and he let out a grunt of defeat. "I will see if he will speak with you. Come with me." He beckoned Max to follow him.

Max gave Elephant one last glance, reluctant to leave her again even for a moment, but followed the stablemaster to the villa. Max waited in the atrium as instructed. The stablemaster lurked in the background.

Max surveyed his surroundings. A cluster of portrait busts, depicting the family's ancestors, sat near the center of the atrium, along with several fancy-looking vases, no doubt expensive antiques. Max had once smashed an antique vase the day Crispina had first brought him home, which had almost caused Aelius to throw him out. But Crispina had stood up for him, and he'd been a part of their family from that day forward.

A paunchy, gray-haired man entered the atrium, frowning at Max. "I'm told you want to buy my horse."

"She's my horse, in fact," Max said. "She was stolen from me, but I'm willing to buy her back from you. I'll match the price you paid for her."

The man's brows drew together. "This is ridiculous. I purchased the mare in an honest sale."

"She was not free to be sold." Max crossed his arms. "I can easily prove to a court that she's been mine since I was seventeen. Now, either you can accept my generous offer of payment, or I can ride back to Rome and find a lawyer. Eleph—the mare will be repossessed once my ownership is proven, and you'll have no payment. At least I offer you a good price." He held out his purse, stuffed with coin.

The man glowered hotly at him for a long moment. Finally, good sense won out, and he snatched the purse. "Now get off my property. You—" He snapped his fingers at the stablemaster, who stood at attention. "Make sure he leaves."

The stablemaster nodded. "Yes, sir." He beckoned to Max with a sour look on his face. "This way."

Max returned to the pasture where Elephant waited. While the stablemaster fetched a rope halter and lead, Max inspected Elephant for any sign of injury or mistreatment. To his relief, she seemed in perfect health. Her mane and tail had been kept free of tangles, her hooves had been properly cleaned, and her coat brushed to its usual soft sheen.

She snuffled at his hair once he finished his inspection. "Yes, we're going home," he said. "Quite the adventure we've both had, isn't it?"

She snorted and tossed her head.

A few moments later, Max was leading Elephant out of the pasture, with a triumphant bounce to his step. She was his once more. The grief and anxiety that had been simmering in him since their parting finally eased.

He brought Elephant to where the gelding waited. Elephant looked the other horse over with a critically tilted ear. Max switched the saddle and bridle from the gelding to Elephant, and put the rope halter on the gelding, keeping the lead in his hand.

He mounted Elephant. She gave a little prance as his weight settled into the saddle. A broad grin stretched across his face. He tensed his legs for a moment, and she eased into a walk. The motion of her gentle, familiar gait soothed something deep within him. Finally, he was back where he belonged.

Max's stomach growled as he rode away from the estate, and he realized he hadn't eaten since breakfast, which had only consisted of a couple hard-boiled eggs and some of yesterday's porridge. He turned Elephant toward the road to Tibur, planning to grab a bite to eat before making the trek back to Rome. The gelding followed, marching stolidly by Elephant's side.

Once he entered the town of Tibur, he dismounted from Elephant and led both horses through the streets, making his way toward the center of the town. The narrow streets soon opened up into a small market square, lined with stalls selling various wares and most importantly, food.

He found a small boy lurking in the shadows between buildings, and gave him a bronze coin to mind the horses on the edge of the square. He cast a glance at the boy's skinny frame. Max remembered the days when luck, theft, or doing odd jobs for strangers had been his only shot at going to bed with a full stomach.

At the market, he surveyed the food stalls, and chose one selling chickpea fritters. Chickpea fritters would forever remind him of that afternoon he and Volusia had spent in Narbo together, sharing a snack in an alleyway. He purchased two fritters, crispy and dripping in oil—one for himself, and one for the boy—and then became tempted by the adjacent stall, selling wheels of sheep's milk cheese. His family would enjoy some fresh cheese, so he pulled out a coin. "One, please."

The older woman behind the stall glanced up at him as she wrapped the cheese, then froze as her eyes landed on his face. "Quintus," she breathed.

That name—one he hadn't heard since he was a child—sent a shiver down his spine, but he didn't let himself pause to examine it. "You have me mistaken for someone else." He laid the coin down on the wooden surface. "The cheese, please."

Her hand flashed out to grasp his. She wore a loose dress of linen, dyed a pale blue, and no jewelry or other adornments. Her skin was tanned, and a few streaks of gray lightened her hair. Her eyes searched his face with an intensity he found disquieting. There was something familiar about her face…

"It *is* you," she breathed. "You don't know me?" she asked, her voice taking on a plaintive edge. "You really don't?"

He stared at her once more, his mind trying to resolve the thread of familiarity he found in her face. But there was nothing. He didn't know anyone in Tibur, after all. Likely she was confused, though she didn't look old enough to fall prey to the befuddlement that often afflicted elders. "I need to go." Gently, but firmly, he tried to tug his arm from her grasp.

"Quintus." She didn't release him, her grip growing tighter. "I'm your mother."

CHAPTER 21

MAX STARED AT THE woman before him uncomprehendingly. The noise of the market around him faded. *Mother.*

He hadn't seen his mother, Maia, in twenty years, since he left home as a child, preferring to take his chances on the street rather than suffer his father's temper. He remembered little about his childhood—only the constant, aching fear that plagued his early years. And he remembered his mother standing by as his father took out his anger on Max, her face blank and frozen.

Max yanked his arm out of her grip so roughly she stumbled, catching herself on the wooden table between them. "No," he said.

"It's true," the woman insisted. "I know you, Quintus."

"That's not my name." It was, though. Or it had been. He had been born with the name Quintus, and as a child he'd been obsessed with stories of the famous general Quintus Fabius Maximus, who had faced off against Hannibal a century and a half ago. The fact that they had the same given name made him feel a sense of kinship with the great man.

When Max ran away from home, he'd appropriated the name, insisting that he be called Maximus. It made him feel brave, even though he couldn't claim any of the noble deeds that would ordinarily bestow the name Maximus upon someone. Crispina, recognizing that it was a ridiculous name for a child, had compromised and called him Max, and the name had stuck.

Max turned away from the woman, but she shot out from behind the stall and blocked his path, her voice rising in desperation. "I've thought of you every day." Her voice shook. "I never knew what happened to you. I have prayed and sacrificed and begged the gods to bring you back to me. And now it's finally happened." Her eyes glistened, and a tear rolled down her weathered cheek. "Things are better now. I live outside Tibur now with your sister. She married a farmer, and they made a good life for themselves."

He blinked, befuddled. "Sister?"

Maia nodded. "I was with child when you…when you left."

Left. More like *escaped.* "What of…" He cleared his throat. "…my father?"

Her eyes darkened. "Bastard got himself killed in a tavern brawl years ago. That was when we left the city, and Furia found herself a husband."

"Oh." Max wasn't sure what to say. He felt nothing at the news that his father had died an ignoble death, not even relief.

"Come home with me," Maia said. "Meet your sister. You have a little niece and nephew, too. They'll be so pleased to know their uncle. We're your family."

For a moment, he was tempted at the prospect of having a family that was truly his own. But he did have a family—Aelius and Crispina and Gaia. They had done more for him than his mother ever had. Without their kindness, he would have had nothing. He probably wouldn't have survived a year on the streets. He never would have had Elephant, or joined the cavalry, or met Volusia. Going with his mother, even for a visit, would mean turning his back on everything they had done for him.

He stepped away, putting an arm's length between them. "I can't. I need to be back in Rome before dark."

Her face fell, but he couldn't let himself feel anything in response. He pushed past her and headed for where the two horses waited on the edge of the square.

"Quintus!" she called after him, her voice high and beseeching. "Will you come back?"

He didn't answer.

The hours-long ride back to Rome passed in a blur. Max let Elephant take the lead, following the road west. The gelding trudged beside them.

His mind whirled, going back over every detail of his unexpected encounter with his mother. Half-remembered flashes of his childhood resurfaced, none of them happy. He couldn't let go of the resentment he felt toward his mother, even though he knew she'd likely been powerless to stop his father.

All the same, the prospect of a sister tempted him. She must be no more than twenty years old, yet she'd already married and made a family for herself. He felt unaccountably jealous.

Her future was secure, while his was anything but. He still had no idea what he should do with his life if he was unable to rejoin the army. Even if he was allowed to return to the army, his experience with Petronax and Glabrio made him question if he wanted to. Petronax had used his power to exploit those beneath him. And Glabrio had followed orders so blindly he'd been ready to murder two innocent women.

Was that all the army held for him—grasping for power and blindly following orders?

The walls of Rome appeared on the horizon, casting long shadows on the rolling hills. The sun was setting behind the city, and Max squinted in the rays of golden light.

He desperately wanted to tell someone what had happened today, what he had learned, but he hesitated to bring it up to his family. He didn't want them to think that he cared more about his birth family than them. As far as Max was concerned, Crispina, Aelius, and Gaia were his real family. It had just taken him a bit longer to find them.

But there was one person he knew he could speak frankly to, without fear. Once he entered the city, he dismounted and turned the two horses toward the Caelian Hill.

He knocked on the door of Volusia's house. The small hatch in the front door slid back, revealing the face of Orion, the same slave who had greeted them two days ago.

"I would like to speak with Volusia," Max said. "I think you know me—I'm Maximus Herminius."

Orion hesitated. "The lady is not receiving visitors, sir."

"Tell her it's me, please. I think she'll want to speak with me."

Orion chewed his lip, but disappeared from the window to slide back the bolt and haul the front door open. "Please come in, sir. I'll send someone out to watch your horses."

"Thank you." For the second time in as many days, Max entered the atrium of the house he'd been banned from ten years ago. He leaned against a column and waited while Orion went to fetch Volusia.

Footsteps sounded, and Max straightened up quicky. Excitement bloomed in his chest. It had only been two days, but he couldn't wait to see Volusia again.

The figure that entered the atrium, however, was not Volusia, but her scowling stepfather. Max felt his shoulders curl into a defensive slouch as soon as Rufus came into view.

Rufus stopped a short distance away and raised his chin at Max, eyes narrowed. "I thought you were aware you were not welcome in this house."

"You didn't turn me away when I was bringing your daughter back from the dead."

Rufus's beady eyes flashed. "That, of course, was an anomaly."

"So you're going to turn away the person who saved your daughter's life? Without me, she'd be lying in a Gallic ditch with her throat cut. You could show a bit of gratitude."

Rufus flinched. For all his faults, the man really did love Volusia. "If it's compensation you seek, I will ensure that you are appropriately rewarded."

"I don't want your money." Max crossed his arms over his chest. "I want you to thank me for saving her life. Preferably on your knees."

"The years have not made you any less insolent, I see," Rufus hissed.

"The years have not taken the stick out of your ass either," Max shot back.

Rufus's pale face reddened. With his eyes narrowed and mouth pinched, he looked even more like a weasel than usual. It was a good thing Volusia wasn't his blood daughter, or else she might have inherited his weaselly look. But if anyone would be a pretty weasel, it was Volusia.

"You will leave this house immediately, or I will have you removed," Rufus declared.

"I want to speak with Volusia."

"You have no further business with her."

"I suggest you ask her if she wants to speak with me. If she doesn't, I'll leave."

Rufus opened his mouth, no doubt to summon a burly slave to throw Max out, but before he could speak, Volusia herself entered the atrium.

"I thought I heard voices—oh, Max!" Her face brightened into a smile. "What are you doing here?"

Max cast a smug grin at Rufus, who glowered hotly enough to melt metal. "I was—"

"He was just leaving," Rufus said. "He didn't mean to disturb you."

Max ignored him. "I wanted to speak with you about something."

"He is not allowed in this house!" Rufus shouted.

"Father." Volusia's voice took on a note of steel. "It's been ten years. You need to set this feud aside." She crossed to Max and put a hand on his arm, which made Rufus sputter with rage. "Max saved my life and brought me back to you. The least you could do is not be rude to him. And you certainly have no right to prevent me speaking with him."

Her words seemed to deflate Rufus's rage a touch, but the color in his cheeks didn't fade. "This is my house—"

"Then let us go outside." Without waiting for a response, she headed for the front door. Max followed her, casting one more smirk back at a speechless Rufus.

Outside, Volusia let out a cry of delight as she saw Elephant. "You found her!" She hurried over to Elephant and allowed the horse to snuffle at her face and hair.

"I just returned from bringing her back." Max dismissed the slave who'd been watching the horses. He wanted to be alone with Volusia, if only for a moment.

He told Volusia the story of how he'd discovered Elephant and bargained for her return, while Volusia stroked Elephant's neck. Then, he told her of the encounter with his mother in the market square, the revelation of a sister he never knew he had.

Volusia listened with wide eyes. "I'm so sorry that your father is dead," she said quietly when he finished.

"Don't be," Max said. "He was a bastard."

She ran her fingers through Elephant's mane. "Do you think you can find it in yourself to forgive your mother?"

Of course Volusia's first instinct was forgiveness; she was the most forgiving person he had ever met. She'd even befriended her husband's lover.

The memory of the Silvanus lookalike at the baths briefly surfaced, but Max was focused on Volusia's question. He leaned his shoulder against Elephant's solid body, facing Volusia. "On one hand, no. On the other hand, if my parents hadn't been so terrible, I'd never have found Aelius and Crispina. My life would have looked very different." Even if his birth parents were paragons of familial love, they still lived in poverty. He would have faced a life of labor and struggle, if he hadn't been driven to escape.

Her gaze softened. "Well, whatever you feel about your mother, perhaps don't deprive yourself of a sister. If I had a long-lost brother, I'd be desperate to meet him."

Part of him still balked at the thought of reopening the door to his past, though he was undeniably tempted to meet this mysterious sister. He'd think it over more later, but for now, he didn't want to dwell on it any further. "And you? How have you been?"

She smiled. "It's only been two days since you last saw me."

"Feels like a year," he admitted.

Her smile widened, then faded. "It has been rather strange to return home, after all that happened to us. I tried to convince my father to take my evidence to the consuls, but he refused." Her lips tightened. "He didn't want to risk making enemies, as he's eying another consulship soon."

"Selfish prick."

She gave him a reproving glance. "Don't be rude. I think he does mean well. He wants me to put the past behind me and focus on the future. But I don't think it will be that easy. I can't just forget what Petronax did to Avitus. He needs to be brought to justice."

Max nodded in agreement. "What are you going to do?"

She sighed. "I don't know what I can do. My father's support would have been useful in getting people to listen to me."

"Useful, but not essential," Max said. "To Dis with your father. You can go to the consuls yourself."

"They won't listen to me. A grieving widow spouting accusations against a legionary commander?" Her shoulders slumped.

"*Make* them listen." He hated seeing her like this, unsure of
herself, downhearted and silenced. Her stepfather should have
raised her up, bolstered her confidence. Instead he had stifled her.
"I know you can do it."

"Am I supposed to march up to one of their houses, bang on
the door, and demand an audience?"

Her tone was joking, but Max didn't laugh. "Why not? You're
a citizen of the republic they've sworn to protect. You deserve to
be heard."

"It sounds so simple when you say it like that." She stepped
closer to him, resting a hand atop Elephant's saddle. "Do you remember how simple things used to be when we were seventeen?
All I worried about was if my husband would be handsome and
buy me nice gifts."

"And I only cared about the horse my parents had promised
me, and whether or not I'd be able to make you laugh at the next
dinner party." He laid his hand on top of hers. Elephant's bulk hid
them from view of the house, so he didn't hesitate to slide an arm
around her waist and pull her close. It felt so right to have her in
his arms again that all he wanted to do was savor the feel of her
body.

But desire soon heated his blood. He tightened his arm around
her, and lowered his head to kiss her.

She turned away with a shy giggle, so his lips met her cheek.
"Max, anyone could see!"

The street was quiet at the moment, but Volusia was right,
anyone could wander by. He wasn't prepared to give up his

chance at a kiss, so he pulled her into the narrow alley between her house and the neighboring building. Shadows cloaked them. He took her in his arms once more, and she didn't push him away as he pressed his mouth to hers.

She kissed him back enthusiastically, and slid her hands over his chest to anchor on his shoulders. His hand tangled in her hair, tilting her face up to take possession of her mouth. They stumbled back, until her body pressed against the outer wall of her house. Lust spiked, scrambling his thoughts and reducing everything to heated gasps and groping hands.

She hooked one leg around his, and let out a purr as his rapidly stiffening cock nudged against her thigh. His breathing stuttered as her hand grazed over him through his tunic.

He grasped her thigh, hiking her leg up to open her to him. "I could take you like this," he murmured, his voice hoarse with desire, "if you'd let me."

She put a hand on his chest. "I would certainly not," she said, looking adorably indignant. "I will not be taken in an alley!" She giggled and pushed him away.

He released her and stepped back, taking a deep breath to clear his mind of the lust still muddling his thoughts. Taking her in an alley had been a stupid idea, and she'd been right to refuse, but her rejection threw even more light on the differences between them. In moments like this, Max was more than willing to let everything else fall away, to focus solely on the pleasure they could find with each other.

But Volusia deserved better. She deserved a man who could think beyond the present moment, who could help her build a future for herself and her son.

"I will always desire you, Max," she said, her voice soft. "But…"

"I know." He didn't want to hear her say it, to hear out loud that he wasn't the right man for her. He kissed her on the forehead, one last time. "It's almost dusk. I should see to the horses and then get home."

She nodded. They left the alley, and Volusia disappeared inside. Max untied the reins of the two horses, and headed for home.

CHAPTER 22

After Max left, Volusia requested dinner for her and Lucius to be brought to her room. She didn't want to see her stepfather after how he had treated Max. Instead, she ate with Lucius, listening to him spout facts about the reigns of ancient kings and the battles they'd fought. He was such an intelligent boy, with a vast ability to understand and retain information from his tutors' lessons and the books he devoured. He had a particular aptitude for numbers, and loved nothing more than to work out complicated sums on his abacus. Great things awaited him, if she could give him the right opportunities.

Once they finished eating, she put Lucius to bed and returned to her room. She sat at her dressing table, painstakingly removing the threads that secured her hairstyle. She could have summoned a maid to do it, but without Iris she preferred to be alone.

A knock disturbed her as she brushed out her hair. "Who is it?"

A throat cleared. "Your father."

Volusia set down her brush. Usually, when Rufus wanted to see someone, they were summoned to him—even his wife and stepdaughter. "Come in."

The door swung open, and Rufus entered, hands clasped before him. "Your absence at dinner impressed upon me that I may have upset you earlier. Your mother suggested I may owe you an apology."

Volusia turned toward him but didn't rise from her chair. "You were extremely rude to Max."

Rufus's lips tightened. "He is insolent and coarse."

"He saved my life. Even if he hadn't, you had no right to try to dictate whom I may or may not speak to. I'm my own woman now, Father." Thanks to Avitus's will, she was emancipated from guardianship and in control of his entire estate, to keep in trust for Lucius until he came of age.

"Yes," he admitted. "But might I still have the privilege of advising you?"

"Let me guess. You want me never to speak to Max again and pretend he doesn't exist." Rufus would never see the loyal, brave, fearless man Max had become. It pained her for Max to be so misunderstood.

Rufus fixed her with a steady gaze. "I would be pleased if you came to that decision, I won't lie. Setting aside my vehement dislike, I know you were fond of him once. And now, after he has so gallantly saved your life, and with the time that you spent together on the road, it would not surprise me if that fondness had resurfaced." He watched her face carefully.

Volusia suddenly found the carvings on her ivory comb fascinating. She said nothing. Anything she could say would only confirm his suspicions.

"And now that you are your own woman, as you say, you might think there can be no harm in pursuing that fondness," he continued. "I certainly can't stop you, so I wish only to caution you against destroying Lucius's prospects and throwing your life away."

Her throat grew tight. "You think it would be throwing my life away to spend it with Max?"

"He is a disgraced solider without influence or prospects. He can do nothing for you, or for our family."

To hear it said so plainly made her chest ache. Max was not right for her. But that didn't stop her from wanting him so much it hurt. Even today, she'd been only a breath away from letting him take her in the alley, an arm's length from her family's house. Only the most tenuous grasp on propriety had saved her.

She could write off their couplings on the journey as a need for comfort. Now that she was back in Rome, back to her real life, she had to put Max behind her.

She gave a shaky nod. "I understand."

His gaze softened. "Good. I'll leave you to rest." He turned for the door, then hesitated. He crossed the room to her, brushed a soft kiss onto her forehead. She closed her eyes. Max had kissed her forehead today, too, and the memory of it overwhelmed her for a moment. When she opened her eyes, Rufus was gone.

In the morning, Volusia found papyrus and a pen, and drafted a letter. She had taken Max's advice to heart, and planned to go over her stepfather's head to reach out to the consuls directly. She had only a passing acquaintance with one of the two consuls, Titus Annius Ligur. The other consul, Aulus Licinius Hortensius, had been a contender for her hand before she'd married Avitus. She recalled him as a kind, patient man with a shrewd mind. He'd been quite taken with her back then, and she hoped she could use that old fondness to her advantage.

Rufus would be furious if he found out what she'd done. Depending on how far word spread, it had the potential to damage his plans to campaign for reelection. Every politician was an army veteran, and a candidate's daughter accusing a high-ranking commander of murder and corruption would not be taken kindly. But she would deal with him at the appropriate time. For now, she had to make her voice heard.

Volusia hoped the papyrus would show the seriousness of her words, rather than using an everyday wax tablet. She opened the letter with some niceties, then laid out the events that had taken place in Narbo and on the road to Rome. She closed with a request for an audience to discuss further and determine the correct actions. She sealed the letter with a glob of wax, and gave it to a trusted messenger with instructions to deliver it into Hortensius's hands only. Writing everything out so plainly was a risk, but it was better to give him all the information she had and let him think about it, rather than chance him cutting her off or her forgetting something crucial when they spoke. Now, she had only to wait for a response.

CHAPTER 23

MAX SQUINTED INTO THE rising sun as he took the eastern road out of Rome. He'd told Aelius and Crispina he was going to visit an army friend outside the city, and had gotten an early start, as the ride to Tibur would take several hours.

He had decided to take Volusia's advice and visit his sister and her family. He had no desire to see his mother, but knew he might not have a choice. He couldn't ignore the prospect of a sister. He wanted to meet her, to see if they were anything alike or if his upbringing with Aelius and Crispina had changed him too much.

The long, flat stretch of road ahead was empty at this early hour. He urged Elephant into a gallop, and let out a whoop as her hooves ate up the distance. Wind whipped through his hair, and his chest lightened. Even if today was a disaster, getting a chance to ride Elephant would still be worth it.

As he approached Tibur, he paused to ask anyone he passed if they knew where Furia and her husband lived. Someone pointed him north of the town, so he headed in that direction.

He slowed as an obstruction on the road ahead came into view. A farmer had gotten his turnip-filled cart stuck in a muddy rut, and was trying to push it free without much success. A donkey watched dispassionately.

Max drew Elephant to a halt and dismounted. "Can I give you a hand with that?"

The man stood back from the cart and wiped his forehead beneath the wide-brimmed straw hat he wore. "Much appreciated."

Max set his shoulder against the cart, and together, they heaved until the cart rolled free.

"Thank you kindly." The farmer gestured to the pile of dirt-crusted turnips in the back of the cart. "Help yourself, if you like. Finest in the Republic." He grabbed one and held it out.

Max eyed the grubby vegetable. "Thanks, but perhaps you could give me directions instead. I'm looking for the farm where a woman named Furia lives."

The man dropped the turnip, mouth falling open in surprise. He stepped back, squinting at Max with new suspicion. "What business do you have with my wife?"

His wife? Max raised his hands in a conciliatory gesture. "She's my—" He swallowed hard, fighting the strangeness of the words. "My sister."

The man's eyes widened. "You're the long-lost brother?"

"I guess so." It still felt strange to think of himself as someone's brother. "I'm Maximus."

A smile spread across the other man's face. "Well, the gods must have arranged it for us to meet like this! I'll take you home straightaway. It's just around the bend. Furia will be overjoyed. Maia didn't say anything about you coming to visit—were we expecting you? I'm Appius, by the way. Fine horse you have there."

Max grinned. The man's gregariousness was endearing, and anyone who recognized Elephant's superiority was sure to be a friend. "Thank you. The visit was a surprise. I hope that doesn't cause any problems."

Appius shook his head. "Only that her mother—your mother, I mean—is out grazing the sheep until dusk. I can send someone to fetch her."

"No need," Max said quickly. "I came to see Furia."

Appius gave him a sidelong look but said nothing. He hitched the cart back to the donkey and pointed up the road. "Our farmhouse is just up ahead. No more than a quarter of an hour. You can ride ahead, if you want."

"I'll walk with you," Max said. He took Elephant's reins in hand and walked with Appius, next to the slowly moving cart. Elephant huffed in impatience, but Max patted her neck soothingly. "I hear you have children?"

Appius nodded, his face lighting up with pride. "A boy, Tullus Appius, four years old. A true terror, mark my words, but Furia keeps him in line. And a little girl, born last winter. Are you married? Children?"

The image of Volusia flashed into his mind. "No."

"Ah, well, plenty of time for all that."

Max changed the subject. "What crops do you grow?"

The rest of the short journey passed with an enthusiastic description of the best growing conditions for turnips, and which sacrifices to which gods tended to yield the best harvests.

Soon, a small farmhouse came into view, surrounded by fruit trees and a pasture in which another donkey and a pair of oxen grazed. In front of the house, a young woman held a chicken in both hands, apparently in the middle of scolding it. A baby was strapped to her chest. On the other side of the yard, a young boy chased the rest of the chickens, laughing uproariously.

The young woman's face brightened at the sight of her husband. "Appius! You're back early. Who's your friend?" She was tall for a woman, with curly, sun-bronzed hair—a similar shade to Max's own—spilling over her shoulders.

Appius clapped a hand on Max's shoulder. "This, my love, is none other than your long-lost brother, Maximus."

Furia dropped the chicken in a flurry of feathers and squawking. She stared at Max. "Fucking Dis."

Yes, they were definitely related.

Max smiled uncertainly. "I'm sorry for the surprise."

She stepped closer to him, her sharp brown eyes scanning him from head to toe. "Your name is supposed to be Quintus."

"I go by Maximus now," he explained. "Or Max, if you prefer."

"Mother didn't say you were coming. In fact, she said you were quite rude to her when you met."

Her gaze appraised him like a centurion sizing up a new recruit. Max couldn't help jumping to defend himself. "It was a shock. I wasn't going to come at all, but…I was curious to meet you."

"Mother talked of you all the time," she said. "Still does. All these years later, she still prays to see you again every time we go to the temple. I guess the gods finally decided to listen."

Her words should have made him feel sympathy toward his mother, but he couldn't summon any warm feelings just yet. "I don't want to see her," he said in a low voice. "I only came to see you."

"She's changed, you know," Furia said. "Everything changed after Father died."

Max was saved from having to reply by the arrival of the young boy, who must be Tullus. He ran between Furia and Max, and stared up at Max curiously. "Who's that?"

Appius swung the boy into his arms. "This is your uncle, Maximus."

The boy squirmed in his father's grasp. "What's an uncle?"

"He's my brother," Furia explained. "Just like you're Appia's brother."

Tullus paid no attention to her explanation, as he'd noticed Elephant. "Horsey! I want to see the horsey!"

"You can pet her, if you like," Max said. "As long as you show the proper respect."

Appius set Tullus down, and the boy ran toward Elephant, stopping a few paces in front of her. He held out a hand solemnly, waiting for her to sniff.

Elephant bypassed the outstretched hand and snuffled at the boy's hair. Tullus squealed in delight. "It tickles!"

"She does enjoy a good head of hair," Max said.

Furia stepped forward to stroke Elephant's neck. "You rode all the way from Rome?"

Max nodded. "We made good time."

"You both must be hungry. Appius, see to some water and hay for the horse, and I'll take Maximus inside for some lunch. Tullus, go with your father."

Max couldn't help grinning at the way Furia ordered around her husband and son. He gave Elephant's reins to Appius with thanks, then followed Furia inside. The farmhouse consisted of one room with a loft upstairs, accessible by a ladder. It was clean and cozy, if not luxurious.

Max sat at the central table. Furia placed a half loaf of bread in front of him, along with some cheese and a few hard-boiled eggs. She poured him a cup of well-watered wine. Her manner was polite, but she kept shooting him sidelong glances heavy with doubtfulness. He couldn't blame her—it must be a shock to have a long-lost sibling show up on her doorstep, and she deserved some time to warm up to the idea of him.

"Thank you," he said as she slid the cup of wine toward him.

Furia untied the baby from her chest, set the child in a cradle, and sat opposite him. "I know this probably isn't the sort of food you're used to, living in Rome and all. It seems you've done well for yourself."

"I got lucky," he said. "And I have simple tastes. Some of the best meals I've ever had have been eaten around a campfire on campaign."

"You're in the army, are you? You do have the look of a soldier."

He nodded, and told her an abbreviated version of the major events in his life: his adoption by Aelius and Crispina, his up-bringing, and his time serving in Gaul.

"So what brings you back to Italy?" she asked. "Are you on leave?"

"Not exactly." He hesitated. "My centurion thinks I'm dead. If he didn't, I'd be on trial for mutiny and insubordination."

Furia's eyebrows shot up, and she leaned forward. "Now that sounds interesting."

"Believe me, I wish it weren't." He told her what had happened with Glabrio and Volusia—but left out his feelings for Volusia. It was rather nice to speak to someone unbiased, someone who was interested in the drama of the tale but not consumed with shock or outrage as his family had been. Furia had a quiet, contemplative way of listening that made her easy to talk to. "So I'm stuck for the moment," he finished. "If Volusia can prove that Petronax had her husband murdered, then I have a chance of being reinstated in the army."

"Is that what you want?"

The question cut deep. Since his adoption, he'd been trying to fit into the life that Aelius and Crispina wanted for him, to repay their kindness by living up to their expectations. They would have been thrilled if he'd followed in Aelius's footsteps and made a name for himself in politics, but he'd been atrocious at his lessons and barely knew the difference between an aedile and a praetor.

Joining the army had been a compromise. His parents hoped one day he'd command a legion and gain reputation for himself that way. To Max, the army had represented freedom, adventure, a chance to see new lands and spend his days on horseback, away from the confines of Rome. But now, he'd seen what the army really was: bureaucracy, blind loyalty, and corruption. He was less certain by the day that he wanted any part of it.

"I don't know," he muttered.

His sister watched him, sympathy in her dark eyes. "I know nothing about such things, so I have no advice, but I will pray that everything turns out as it should."

"Thank you." He changed the subject, not wanting to dwell on his own issues anymore. "It seems as if you've done well for yourself, too."

She nodded. "A humble sort of well, I think, but it suits me. Our fortunes are dependent on the harvest, and we've had a few hard years, but I've been blessed with a loving husband and two healthy children." She glanced at the cradle where Appia had fallen asleep, and smiled. "I could not ask for more." Her smile grew sly. "If you'll let me be nosy, is there a lady in your life? The girls must be all over a handsome soldier."

Despite himself, a blush heated his cheeks. "Nothing serious." To his surprise, he found that he actually wanted to confide in Furia, to tell her all about Volusia and his decade-old, doomed infatuation. But he'd only known Furia for an hour—too soon to get into matters of the heart.

She chuckled.

At that moment, Tullus burst into the cottage. The boy marched straight up to Max. "Can I ride your horse, please?" he asked plaintively. "Papa said if I asked nicely, you might let me."

"Do you know how to ride?" Max asked.

"Yes," Tullus said, chest puffed out.

"He does not," Furia said. "And I won't have my only son break his neck falling off a horse."

"Tell you what, why don't we go for a ride together?" Max said. "You can sit in front of me and hold the reins. Only if your mother agrees."

The boy's eyes lit up, and he turned to his mother. "Mama, please? Can I?"

"It will be perfectly safe," Max assured Furia.

She gave a nod. "All right."

Max took Tullus outside. He mounted Elephant with Tullus wedged safely in front of him, and showed him how to use the reins. Max could direct Elephant well enough with just his legs, so the reins were mostly superfluous in any case.

The boy crowed in delight as Elephant trotted around the pasture. Max kept an arm wrapped securely around Tullus's middle. They finished a few laps around the pasture, and then Max showed Tullus how to make Elephant stop by gently tugging the reins. He handed the boy down to Furia, and dismounted.

Tullus jumped up and down. "I want to go again!"

"Maybe next time," Furia said. She glanced at Max. "That is, if there is a next time."

He recognized the invitation in her words. She was saying that she accepted him—at least enough to invite him back. "Yes, I'd like to pay another visit." The prospect of forging a relationship with his birth family, watching Tullus and baby Appia grow up, brought a strange warmth, a feeling of satisfaction.

Furia gave a short nod. "Good."

An hour later, he said a reluctant goodbye, needing to get on the road before it got dark. As he rode, his mind lingered on the cozy, tidy farmhouse, the happy children and his sister's contentment with her simple life. He wanted something like that. A quiet life, a family. Two things the army could not give him.

But every time he tried to picture that life, Volusia was there, tending a fire, sweeping a dirt floor, cuddling a baby. That was not the sort of life she had been born to, nor was it what she wanted. She needed to stay in Rome, to raise her son to take advantage of the power and opportunity that his birth afforded him. She was not destined to be a country farmer's wife. Any path he took—rejoining the army or seeking a simpler life—would lead him away from her.

CHAPTER 24

WHEN MAX ARRIVED HOME at twilight, a note waited for him, placed on the table next to his bed. His heart leaped when he opened it and saw that it was from Volusia. She wrote to say that she'd reached out to one of the consuls, and he'd agreed to meet with her tomorrow at noon. She asked Max to come with her to share his side of the story.

Max pilfered a blank wax tablet from Aelius's study and scrawled a quick reply—*"I'll be there"*—then asked Paris to deliver it before darkness fell.

At noon the next day, Max traveled to the address Volusia had given him. In an attempt to look like someone whose word could be trusted, he wore a tunic borrowed from Aelius, pale green with blue embroidery edging the sleeves and hem. It was a bit tight in the shoulders, but Crispina had been confident that he looked trustworthy and respectable. The civilian clothes felt strange, much too light without the weight of chainmail armor on his shoulders or a sword strapped to his waist.

Just as Max arrived outside the stately home, a litter borne by four burly men pulled up on the street. The slaves set the litter down carefully, and one of them extended a hand to help the lady within.

Volusia descended from the litter, a vision in crimson fabric. Max caught his breath. She looked like a lady of Rome through and through. A gossamer-thin palla was secured to her hair with pearl-tipped pins, flowing down her back from the top of her head to her ankles. Beneath, she wore a red stola which left her arms bare. It was belted at the waist, drawing attention to the curves of her breasts and hips. The stola was traditionally only worn by married women, not widows, and Max saw the message in her clothing choice. Today, she was Avitus's wife, come to seek justice for her husband.

Max ran a hand over his chin, feeling a few pricks of stubble. He wished he'd paid more attention shaving this morning. Despite his fine clothes, he suddenly felt scruffy and unkempt in comparison to her.

Volusia smiled when she saw him, but it wasn't her usual smile, full of warmth and light. A veneer of dignity, like just-formed ice on a lake, veiled her features. "Thank you for coming."

"Of course," he said. "I promised I'd help you, however I can."

One of the litter bearers had gone ahead to knock on the door and announce their presence. The door opened, and a slave within conducted them into the atrium. A huge collection of at least a dozen portrait heads—ancestors of the family—dominated the space. Based on their number, they must have gone back centuries.

A man in his early forties entered the atrium. He wore a long tunic that reached his ankles, and several gold and silver bangles weighed down his arms. He shared the same wide forehead and weak chin of the portrait heads in the center of the atrium, so Max surmised that this was the man they'd come to meet, the consul Hortensius.

"Volusia, how lovely to"—Hortensius broke off when he saw Max, standing at Volusia's elbow, but recovered smoothly—"see you again. I didn't realize we'd have company." He took her hand and kissed it.

"This is Maximus Herminius, the legionary I spoke of in my letter," Volusia said. "Max, please meet Aulus Licinius Hortensius."

Max clasped arms with Hortensius, muttering a polite greeting. Volusia and Hortensius clearly knew each other already, which she hadn't mentioned.

"My condolences on your husband's death," Hortensius said. "Despite my fierce jealousy of him, Rome lost a great man."

The pieces started to come together in Max's mind. Volusia and Hortensius knew each other, and Hortensius admitted jealousy of Volusia's husband. Hortensius must be a past suitor.

And now Volusia was free to marry again, and would be in search of an influential husband just like the weak-chinned man standing before them.

Jealousy knotted in Max's stomach. He drew himself up, straightening his shoulders inside the too-tight tunic. He was taller than Hortensius, and he doubted the consul could even lift a sword with the bangles weighing down his scrawny arms.

Volusia and Hortensius were talking, and as they moved toward another room, Max hurried to follow. His jealous fantasies had distracted him.

"Your letter was most concerning," Hortensius said. "I hope you don't mind, but I did some asking around yesterday, and I made contact with the centurion you spoke of."

"You spoke with Glabrio?" Volusia asked.

Hortensius drew them toward a door off the atrium that must be his study. "Yes, and I—"

Volusia stopped short as she entered the doorway, and Max almost ran into her from behind. She drew in a sharp breath.

"—invited him here to sort out this matter," Hortensius finished.

Next to Hortensius's desk, Glabrio stood, beefy arms crossed over his chest. His customary glower deepened as his gaze moved from Volusia to Max.

Old habit made Max's arm twitch as if to salute, but he forced his arm to remain by his side. He was no longer Glabrio's subordinate.

Volusia's small hands clenched into fists. "Hortensius, he tried to kill me! How can you think it a good idea for him to be here? I don't feel safe."

Hortensius seated himself behind his desk. "As consul, I'm accustomed to hearing both sides of a matter before I come to a decision."

"I mean you no harm, lady," Glabrio said, his voice gravelly. "On my honor as a soldier."

Max didn't like having Glabrio here any more than Volusia did, but to leave would show weakness or a lack of conviction in what they had to say. He leaned down to murmur in her ear, "It will be all right. Just ignore him and speak to Hortensius."

She took a long breath and nodded. "Fine."

There was only one chair opposite Hortensius's desk, so Volusia seated herself while Max and Glabrio remained standing, glaring at each other.

"Surprised to see us?" Max said.

Glabrio scowled. "I'll see you dragged before a tribunal if it's the last thing I do."

Volusia fixed him with an icy stare. "You'll do no such thing."

Hortensius raised his hands. "We're not here for this sort of talk. Volusia, you claim that Glabrio attempted to kill you on orders from Petronax, the commander of the legion stationed in Narbo. Glabrio, what do you have to say to that?"

Glabrio stepped forward. "It's true, sir. I was carrying out a direct order from my commanding officer."

Hortensius's thin eyebrows rose. "Did you know why Petronax gave this order?"

Glabrio shook his head. "I did not, sir. It's not my place to question orders. My duty is to obey."

"You're a sheep with a sword," Max said. "How much did your last shearing yield?"

Volusia bit her lip, and Max recognized the expression on her face from long-ago dinner parties: she was trying not to laugh.

"Silence, legionary!" Glabrio roared. "You will not address me with such insolence."

"I'm not your legionary anymore," Max said. "You have no more authority over me than any citizen."

"Let us not raise our voices in front of the lady," Hortensius interjected sternly.

Volusia inclined her head in dignified gratitude, but Max caught a glimpse of the smile twitching at her lips.

Hortensius addressed Glabrio once more. "So you do not deny attempting to take Volusia's life, but you would swear before a court and the gods that you were acting on an order from Petronax?"

Glabrio nodded. "I'll make any oath required. I was merely carrying out my duty."

The centurion's indifference was disgusting. Max murmured a soft "ba-aa" which made Volusia snort with laughter. She parlayed the sound into a cough, pressing a hand delicately to her mouth.

Glabrio's face purpled. Hortensius glanced at Volusia with concern. "Are you well, lady? Should I have some wine brought?"

"No, thank you," Volusia said, her voice steady. "Just a momentary tickle." She turned her head to cast Max a reproving look.

"I have another question." Hortensius rested his elbows on the desk and steepled his fingertips. "There were several other legionaries as part of the escort, correct? Were they given the same order by Petronax?"

Glabrio shook his head. "Petronax gave the order to me directly."

"So you"—Hortensius fixed his gaze on Max—"were the only one who saw fit to disobey. Why was that?"

Max opened his mouth, but Glabrio spoke first. "It was plain as day. There was an inappropriate attachment between the two of them." He waved a disdainful hand at Max and Volusia. "Always skulking around the horses in the evening, and sitting close around the campfire."

Hortensius's brows drew together, and he looked at Volusia. "Is that so?"

"We're childhood friends," she hurried to say. "Of course Max didn't want to see any harm come to me. Frankly, I was offended that none of the other soldiers stood up against such a blatant transgression. It's disgraceful."

Hortensius turned to Max. "Your answer? Why were you the only one to stand against your centurion?"

The smart reply would have been to agree with Volusia. She wasn't wrong, after all. But the truth rose to his lips before he could stop it, rushing out in a torrent of careless words.

"Because I l—"

"Legionary Maximus's motives for defending me are irrelevant," Volusia said sharply. Her gaze lingered on him, much softer than her words. In that moment, Max knew: she understood what he'd been so foolishly about to confess.

Because I love her.

He allowed himself to sink into the depths of her hazel eyes, to forget Hortensius, Glabrio, even the threat of a tribunal. It was the truth: the painful, aching truth.

Volusia drew her gaze back to the consul and the centurion. "All that matters is that I was put at risk because Petronax was afraid of what I knew about my husband's death."

"That brings us to the actual manner of your husband's death." Hortensius's face assumed an expression that was likely supposed to be sympathetic but instead made him look like a pouting child. "I know such things are difficult to speak of, but your letter made no mention of any proof that Avitus was murdered. Did you find poison in the kitchen? Or speak with a slave who had been bribed to spike his wine?"

Volusia bit her lip, this time in dismay. "No, I...I admit I have no idea how he could have been poisoned. We ate from the same platters, drank wine poured from the same jug." Her shoulders slumped.

"Unfortunately, if you have no proof that foul play was involved in Avitus's death, then it will be very difficult to move forward here," Hortensius said.

"But I told you about the wax tablet I found," Volusia insisted. "Clearly Petronax was involved in something unsavory."

"The tablet was just your husband's musings. There's not even a clear connection to Petronax." Hortensius's voice was slow and gentle, as if trying to placate a child on the verge of a tantrum. His tone infuriated Max, but he bit his tongue. Picking a fight with a consul was not going to help their situation.

Volusia pointed an accusatory finger at Glabrio. "It's been established that Petronax tried to have me killed. Surely that warrants investigation on its own."

Hortensius glanced at Glabrio. "Perhaps it does. I'll draft a letter to Petronax to inquire why he gave that order."

"A letter?" Volusia's tone sounded as disbelieving as if Hortensius had suggested she grow wings and fly to Gaul to ask Petronax herself. "It will take weeks to arrive, and he will just ignore it and pretend it got lost on the way. A letter will not see justice done for my husband. Or restore the position that Max lost by defending me."

Hortensius waved a hand. "As for that, I'm sure there's a legion in Syria or Egypt that could use a legionary. He can easily be reassigned." The consul spoke of Max as if he weren't there. "As for Petronax, he has been a capable commander for many years.

Such men are rare, and it's inadvisable to make enemies of them, especially during these troubled times." He leaned forward, his gaze earnest. "Without firm proof, this is all I can do. Quite frankly, it's more than I should do, but I do want to help you, Volusia, if I can."

Volusia let out a tight sigh. "I understand."

Was she really going to give up that easily? Max waited for her to come up with something else, but she was silent. He itched to protest, but forced himself to stay quiet. This was Volusia's battle to fight, and she understood these political machinations better than he did.

Glabrio stepped toward the door. "If my work here is done, I will return to my other duties." He glared at Max. "You're very lucky you have friends in high places, legionary, or else I'd have you dragged straight from here to a tribunal."

Max rolled his eyes.

Hortensius rose from behind his desk. "I'm sure we'll have your word that nothing of the sort will occur, centurion. The legionary acted honorably, even if he did disobey your orders."

Glabrio gave a reluctant nod. Hortensius moved to escort him out of the study and back into the atrium. Max started to follow, but Volusia hung back, lingering in the doorway to the study.

"Max," she whispered, gazing up at him. "What you said...were about to say..."

He let out a deep, shuddering breath. The words came back to him, still on the tip of his tongue after she'd interrupted him earlier. "I love you." His heart gave a painful clench at finally admitting it. "I loved you when I was seventeen. I loved you when I stepped in front of Glabrio's sword. And I love you still, Volusia."

Consternation flickered across her face, and she opened her mouth. His stomach knotted, unsure of what she'd say. But before she could speak, Hortensius returned, having seen Glabrio off.

"I was wondering if I might have a word before you leave," the consul said, then glanced pointedly at Max. "A *private* word."

"I don't think we have anything more to say, Hortensius," Volusia said. "You've made your position quite clear."

He reached for her hand, which made Max's teeth grind together. "You must understand, Volusia, I was speaking as Hortensius the consul earlier. I have a responsibility to hear all sides of a matter, and as much as I sympathize with your efforts, I can't act unilaterally without proof."

Volusia lowered her gaze. Max wished she would yank her hand back, but she allowed him to keep touching her. "I understand. I appreciate your sense of duty."

"Now, if we could speak further…" He cast another significant glance at Max.

"Max, would you wait for me outside?" Volusia asked. "I'm sure this will just be a moment."

Max narrowed his eyes. He had no intention of leaving Volusia alone with Hortensius. "I'll wait in the atrium." He took a few steps out of the study and planted himself in front of a column, where he still had a clear view of the two where they stood inside the study.

Hortensius gave an irritated sigh and lowered his voice, but Max could hear clearly. "As I said, before I was speaking as

Hortensius the consul. But if you might permit me to speak as Hortensius the man, who has always held you in high regard…"

Max's fingers clenched into fists.

"I would be remiss if I did not offer whatever assistance I can, as a simple citizen rather than a consul. I know widowhood can be a fraught position for a woman."

"Thank you, but Avitus's estate has left me quite secure," Volusia said.

"That is good to hear. But I know you have a son, and he will no doubt feel the loss of his father keenly in the coming years. You'll recall that my own wife died without blessing me with any children. I have always desired a family, and given my respect for your late husband it would be an honor to contribute to his son's upbringing."

Max stared in disbelief. Was this bastard really proposing marriage, after setting Volusia up to face the man who'd tried to kill her, and refusing to take action on her accusations?

Max willed Volusia to slap Hortensius. If she didn't, he was more than happy to step in and deck the consul.

But Volusia showed no outrage. She smiled sweetly. "Your offer is kind, and well-received. I'm sure you'll understand that with my husband so recently deceased, I'll need to take some time to sort out his affairs and determine what path is best for me and my son."

"Of course, of course." Hortensius placed a hand on Volusia's shoulder, and Max's jaw clenched so hard he expected to crack a tooth. "You know where to find me if you have need of me."

Volusia gave a dignified nod, and allowed Hortensius to conduct her out of the study. Max fell into step behind her. He gave

Hortensius one last glare before they passed through the front door and back out onto the street.

The heavy door swung closed behind them. Max turned to Volusia, anger simmering over every inch of his skin. "The nerve of that bastard," he growled.

She glanced up at him. "Hortensius? I thought he was quite respectful."

"He wants to fuck you."

"Language. And he's just an old friend."

"An old friend who wants to fuck you."

She arched an eyebrow. "Sound familiar?"

He had no rebuttal to that, so he changed strategy. "He set you up by inviting Glabrio there. The man who tried to kill you."

She let out a long sigh. "Yes, that was rather unpleasant of him, but he was right that he needs to hear all sides of something. His fair-minded approach is why he was elected consul."

"So are you going to marry him then?" It was not a prudent question, nor a polite one, but it was out of Max's mouth before he could stop it.

"Maybe," she said evenly. "I want a father for my son. And I want a husband for myself, someone who's there for me every day. Anything less would be little better than what I had with Avitus. But before I think of such things, I have to resolve this business about Petronax." She kneaded a hand against her temple. "I keep trying to go back to that night, that dinner where he must have consumed the poison. I must have missed something. I wish I'd spoken to Silvanus more about it. Maybe he would have remembered something that I missed."

The mention of Silvanus sparked Max's recollection of his uncertain sighting at the baths. "Are you sure he stayed in Narbo?" Max asked. "It's just that I was almost sure I saw him at the baths the other day."

She frowned and shook her head. "Silvanus in Rome? I don't think so."

Max shrugged. "Maybe it wasn't him, but I could have sworn it was."

"That's odd," she said. "If he's already back in Rome, he must have left right after we did. I offered for him to travel with us, but he said he'd accepted a permanent position in the province. He doesn't even have any family in Rome."

"I guess he changed his mind," Max said.

"I'll have someone find him—if he is here, that is," Volusia said. "If he could remember something that proves Avitus was murdered, then Hortensius will have to listen to me." She put a hand on his arm. "Thank you, Max. For everything."

He helped her into the waiting litter, and stepped back as the four litter-bearers prepared to lift it.

"Wait," Volusia called, and they stilled. She beckoned Max closer, leaning out of the litter to speak in a soft voice. "About what you said earlier... I won't be able to stop thinking of it for some time. Max, I love you too, but..."

He could think of several conclusions to that sentence.

I love you...but my stepfather hates you.

But I love my son more.

But not enough.

He'd known since he was seventeen that his love for her was doomed. The past few weeks had only made that clearer. There were too many obstacles: Rufus's hatred of him, her son's need for an influential stepfather, even the fact that she'd want to live in Rome while he couldn't stand the city.

"I know," he said, his voice suddenly hoarse. "I still love you, though." The words might have been the most futile he'd ever spoken, but at least he could hear how they sounded as they hung in the air, and see the warmth that spread across her face, mixed with uncertainty. Speaking them aloud turned his decade-old longing into something real, something he could grasp onto even if Volusia would never be his.

And hearing from her lips that she loved him, too—well, that could be enough to sustain him until the end of his days.

He stepped back from the litter. The litter-bearers bent and lifted the litter in a smooth motion, then set off down the street. Max watched the litter disappear around the corner.

He needed to seriously consider Hortensius's offer of joining a far-off legion in Syria or Egypt. The military life was the only thing he knew, after all. If not the army, what would he do with himself? Maybe, if he traveled east, the hot desert sun would finally burn away thoughts of Volusia.

CHAPTER 25

VOLUSIA RETURNED HOME, HER mind reeling from Max's confession, Hortensius's proposal, and the question of Silvanus.

She focused on the last one, as it was most pertinent to her current situation. Once she brought about justice for Avitus, she could focus on her future—whether that included Max, Hortensius, or someone else entirely.

If Max was right, why had Silvanus seemingly come back to Rome when he'd told her he planned to stay in Narbo? Maybe he'd taken their conversation to heart and started asking questions about Petronax. Maybe the commander had gotten wind of it, and Silvanus had decided it was safer to retreat to Rome.

Whatever the reason, Silvanus seemed her only lead to possibly uncover the proof that Hortensius required.

The problem now was that she had no idea where to find Silvanus. If he even was in Rome.

When she reached home, she asked Orion to do some investigating. He could ask the slaves at the baths where Max had spotted Silvanus. Perhaps someone would remember him and knew where to find him. If that didn't work, there were plenty of taverns and gathering spots in that neighborhood he might frequent. If enough people were asked—and enough coin offered as motivation—someone would know him.

Orion accepted the mission with a nod. Volusia handed him a purse of coin with which to make his questions welcome, and he set off.

It could take days to locate Silvanus, if Orion was even successful. Volusia didn't know how to occupy herself. If she tried to pass the time at weaving, as she was often accustomed, she knew her mind would wander to Max. For now, it was safer not to think of him.

She went in search of Lucius and found him in the peristyle sitting with one of his tutors. The private garden at the back of the house was often a favorite spot for lessons on sunny days. She'd taken Lucius out of school shortly before leaving for Narbo; his intelligence irritated the other students, and after finding out that he'd become the target of bullies, she'd swiftly arranged private tutelage.

The tutor rose to his feet when Volusia appeared and greeted her with a respectful nod. "Good afternoon, lady."

Lucius jumped up, barely catching a scroll as it rolled off his lap. "Mama! I'm learning about the Punic Wars. Did you know they fought with elephants?"

Her mind immediately jumped to Max and his beloved horse. "I did know that. Quite strange to think of, isn't it?"

"How many elephants did Hannibal try to cross the Alps with?" the tutor asked Lucius.

"Thirty-seven," Lucius answered promptly, and the tutor nodded. Lucius had the ability to retain all sorts of information, but numbers especially seemed to stick in his mind like honey to a spoon.

Volusia smiled. "Is he doing well?" she asked the tutor.

"He's the smartest boy I've ever taught of his age, lady," the tutor said. "His memory is prodigious, as is his skill with arithmetic."

"I'm sure you say that to all the mothers."

"I assure you, I do not, lady," he said. "You are welcome to stay and see for yourself, if you like."

Watching Lucius learn about long-ago wars seemed a safe way to occupy her mind, so she nodded. "Thank you." She took a seat on a bench opposite them.

The tutor quizzed Lucius on dates of various battles and names of commanders, all of which he answered correctly. The tutor then explained a certain point about the military strategy used by one of those commanders, which Volusia barely followed, and asked Lucius how that strategy differed from previous battles. Lucius gave a clear, concise answer, which pleased the tutor.

Listening to this lesson reaffirmed Volusia's belief that Lucius had great things ahead of him, if she could only provide him the right opportunities. Aligning with a man like Hortensius, a patrician and a consul at that, could open many doors.

But as soon as she thought of Hortensius, Max's words echoed in her mind. *"I loved you when I was seventeen. I loved you when I stepped in front of Glabrio's sword. And I love you still, Volusia."* She had spent ten years in a loveless, if cordial, marriage. Could she enter another marriage for reasons that had nothing to do with love, even if it was best for her son?

Regardless of what she wanted, Max had his own life to live. He didn't enjoy living in Rome, preferring the expanse of the countryside and the comparative wilderness of the provinces. He was not the sort of man who would be happy hosting dinner parties every night to foster social connections. Besides, now that he'd been offered a position in a distant legion, he might leave and she'd never see him again.

An icy hand squeezed around her heart at the thought. She wished she hadn't told him she loved him—even though it was the truth. It was a pointless, irrelevant love, and it would only hold both of them back.

Elephant cantered down the road to Tibur as Max traveled to visit Furia and her family again. His mind had been awhirl in the days since the audience with Hortensius and the ensuing conversation with Volusia. He needed to decide if he was going to accept Hortensius's offer of a position in another legion. Ordinarily, the thought of joining a legion somewhere as distant as Syria or Egypt would have thrilled him, promising new adventures and maybe another shot at that pesky promotion, if he found himself under a less unpleasant centurion. But now, uncertainty turned his thoughts into a jumble.

He'd spent ten years in the army, hoping for glory and adventure. There had been a few moments of adventure—some exhilarating battles, the excitement of seeing new lands—but mostly, it had been drudgery like collecting taxes and repairing buildings.

As for glory, his experience with Petronax and Glabrio had disabused him of that notion. The army didn't reward bravery. It rewarded corruption, in Petronax's case, and the ability to blindly follow orders, in Glabrio's.

That wasn't want he wanted, but what else was there?

He needed open space and fresh air to properly think. He couldn't concentrate in the city, even at home. The walls might block some of the street noise, but he still felt confined.

He also couldn't tell Aelius and Crispina he was thinking of rejoining the army—not yet, at least. They would support whatever he chose, but lately Crispina had been dropping lots of hints about introducing him to some eligible young women so he could start a family and settle down. They would not be excited to send him off to the furthest corner of the Republic, even if they didn't stop him.

Furia, though, might be able to hear his musings with a more impartial ear. He had enjoyed speaking with her at his last visit, and he had promised to visit again so Tullus could have another ride on Elephant.

He found the farmhouse easily this time, and hopped down from Elephant. He saw a figure out in the turnip fields that looked like Appius, and waved. Appius waved back.

Max removed Elephant's tack and led her to the small pasture at the front of the farmhouse, where she could frolic, graze, and drink from the trough of water. Then, he headed toward the cottage. The door was ajar, and a woman's voice emanated from within, cooing to a child. It must be Furia and Appia. Max grinned and pushed open the door. "Surprise, I thought I'd—"

He stopped short as the woman on the other side of the one-room cottage turned to face him, the baby in her arms. It wasn't Furia, but his mother.

"Quintus!" Maia gasped, her shocked expression quickly giving way to delight. "Come in, sit down. Let me get you something to eat."

The sight of his mother standing by a hearth fire dredged up a long-buried memory. It rose in his chest, choking at his throat like a grasping hand.

He backed out of the house and slammed the door behind him. He made it to the pasture on stiff, unsteady legs, and braced his hands on the slats of the wooden fence.

His head spun as the memory washed over him. He remembered his mother, belly swollen, standing by the fire while his father berated her. Max didn't remember the words, but he remembered the bellowing. It had made him put his hands over his ears.

His mother had shot back a remark, her voice just as angry. Father had grabbed a ceramic jug and flung it at her. It smashed into the wall behind her.

That was when Max had started to cry. A poor choice, as it drew the attention of both his parents.

"Can't you shut up?" his mother had said, her voice sharp with irritation.

His father started toward him, thick fingers balling into fists. By now, Max knew what awaited him if his father got his hands on him. Instinct took over. Before his father could reach him, Max dove for the door to their ramshackle second-floor apartment. He threw himself down the stairs that led to the ground floor, falling down most of them, and raced through the courtyard into the street.

No one followed him.

That was the last time he'd seen any of his family, until now. He'd braved the streets, stealing food and shelter where he could, until his luck turned and he'd met Crispina. His life had never been the same since.

Now, twenty years later, his heart hammered in his chest as fast as it had when he'd run out the door. The memory of that day had been hazy until now. It all came back to him in a dizzying wave—the terror, the helplessness, the overwhelming urge to escape.

Something warm pressed against him, and he opened his eyes to see that Elephant had crossed the pasture without being called. She nudged her head into his shoulder on the other side of the fence. Max stroked her neck, inhaling deeply. As always, her presence and earthy scent grounded him. She whuffled into his ear.

Footsteps rustled behind him, and he whipped around, his hand going to the empty spot on his hip where his sword should be.

It was only Furia. She eyed him with concern. "I was out back with Tullus. Mother said you'd shown up."

How was he supposed to explain what had come over him the instant he saw his mother? "I…I didn't expect to see her."

"You knew she lived here." Furia's brows drew together. "If you're going to be rude to her, there's no point in you visiting."

"I didn't mean to be rude. I just…" Max shook his head. "Seeing her makes me remember things."

Furia's gaze softened. She stepped closer to him and leaned against the fence. Elephant snuffled at her curly hair, which Furia permitted. "Lucky you were able to forget things in the first place."

A pang of guilt hit him. What might she have endured, that he'd avoided with his escape? "Sorry," he said, his voice little better than a grunt.

"Oh, Max." She put her hand on his arm. "I wish you wouldn't blame our mother for what our father did. She was as scared of him as we were."

Max didn't remember his mother being scared. He remembered her being curt, dismissive, and scornful. Now, he realized that might have been her only way to hide her fear.

"Everything improved after he got himself killed," Furia continued. "We left the city, moved out here, and I was lucky enough to meet Appius. Now that I've become a mother twice over, I understand why she acted the way she did. If Appius woke up one day with a mind to yell and beat me, gods forbid, I would do whatever it took to protect my children. Even if it meant staying with a horrible man who put a roof over my head and food on the table rather than being cast into the streets with nothing, or standing up to him and getting myself killed, leaving my children without a mother."

Max nodded, mulling over her words. "I wish I'd known about you. I could have gone back for you. You could have had a better life."

She grinned. "I have no patience for the sort of hoity toity life you found."

"I didn't either, most of the time." He managed a chuckle. He had put Aelius and Crispina through many trials as they tried to civilize and educate him. "I think I made at least four tutors quit."

Furia chuckled. "Don't feel guilty about me. This"—she gestured at the peaceful farm—"is all I've ever wanted. And try to forgive our mother, if you can."

Max heaved a deep sigh. He thought of Volusia, capable of forgiving her husband for dishonoring their marriage, even capable of befriending her husband's lover. If he could be just a little bit like her, maybe he could find enough compassion to start to forgive his mother. "I will try."

"Good. Will you come back inside now?"

He nodded, and allowed Furia to lead him back inside. In the cottage, Appius was sitting and talking with Max's mother near the fire. Maia looked up when she saw them enter, but Appius kept talking, his back to them, describing the day's harvest. Furia went to check on baby Appia, asleep in her cradle on the other side of the room. Max took a seat next to Appius, who fell silent.

Max had no idea what to say to his mother—not yet—so he turned to Appius. "The harvest was good today?"

Appius nodded and resumed talking with a careful glance between Max and his mother. From across the room, Furia caught Max's eye and gave him a nod.

Max said nothing directly to his mother, nor did she try to speak to him again, but the family passed a pleasant enough afternoon and evening. He spent the night, as it was too far to ride back to Rome. He'd told Aelius and Crispina that he might be gone overnight, so they wouldn't worry.

In the morning, Max woke early and tiptoed out of the cottage to check on Elephant. She'd passed the night in the pasture, with oxen, sheep, and a donkey for company and a full supply of grain.

A blanket of fog settled over the landscape, and dew sparkled on the grass. A chill wind, heralding autumn, made him shiver. Max took a deep breath of the crisp, fresh air. It smelled of manure and hearth-smoke, but the air was still fresher than any breath he could take in Rome.

Elephant trotted over to the fence and extended her nose in greeting. He stroked her, wondering what the air in Egypt smelled like. There was probably sand in it.

The door to the cottage opened and closed, and Furia emerged, Appia squirming in her arms. Furia smiled in greeting as she approached. "Usually Appia is the first to wake. I half-expected you to sleep 'til noon. Isn't that what the posh Romans do?"

Max grinned. "Not anyone who's ever been in the army."

"Will you be rejoining your legion soon? The last time we spoke, you said you weren't sure if you'd be able to, given all that happened."

His smile faded as he remembered the reason he'd come to visit his sister in the first place. "I've been offered the opportunity to join a legion in the east. Syria, or Egypt. Somewhere like that."

She shifted Appia in her arms. "So you've come to tell me that you're leaving. Well, I'm sad to hear it, especially after we've just gotten to know each other, but you must do what's best for you."

Max let out a long breath. "That's just it. I'm not sure if the army is the best choice, after what happened. I used to think it was. It seemed to be the only thing I was good at. And I have no idea what else to do with myself."

"You're not going to follow in your adopted father's footsteps and become a politician?"

"Fuck, no," he said, which made her laugh.

Furia sat Appia on the fence, an arm securely around her middle. The little girl reached out a chubby hand toward Elephant, who allowed her nose to be clumsily patted. "I don't know if this would interest you, but I heard the other day about a parcel of land near here that's going up for sale soon. It's undeveloped, but a good size. You could clear it and build a nice house and have plenty of room for a few fields. Appius could help advise on the planting."

"I don't know if I'm cut out to be a farmer," Max said. But the idea of owning land out here in the country intrigued him. He imagined a little piece of countryside that was all his own, far away from the noise and crowds of the city. A cottage just like Furia's. He closed his eyes for a moment to imagine it. The image of Volusia, tending the hearth and sweeping the floor, rose in his mind.

No, that was nonsense. Volusia was not meant to be a rustic country wife.

"What about horses, then?" Furia asked. "You could breed them. Maybe even set up a riding school. There are plenty of wealthy families with country estates out here whose sons are headed for the army and need to learn how to handle a horse."

Horses. The idea struck him with a visceral sense of rightness that took his breath away for a moment. He could spend his days out in the country surrounded by horses, putting his skills and passion to good use. He would be his own master, and wouldn't have to follow anyone else's orders.

Furia must have seen his reaction on his face, for she smiled. "It would be nice to have you close."

"Do you know the price of this land?" Max asked. That could easily be an insurmountable obstacle. He had some money saved from his army salary, but he doubted it would be enough to buy land, clear it, and build. Perhaps he could ask Aelius for a loan, an advance on his inheritance.

She shook her head. "I don't. But I'll give your name to the seller and have him write to you. I should warn you though"—her eyebrows wiggled jokingly—"the land borders that of a farmer with no less than three unmarried daughters. I guarantee you'd have some *very* friendly neighbors."

"I'd have to build a wall," he muttered.

"Well, if you're going to settle down, you'll need a wife at some point to look after you. Appius was lost before he found me."

"I don't want a wife." The words came out sharper than intended, but they were true. He only wanted Volusia, and she was lost to him.

Furia's smile faded. "Has some girl broken your heart?"

"No—yes—I don't know. It's complicated."

Understanding lit in her eyes. "Is that why you were considering going all the way to Egypt? You want to run away from someone."

"Yes," he admitted. "Sort of." He hadn't spoken of his feelings for Volusia to anyone, and the hopelessness of it all weighed on him. In a few words, he told Furia all about Volusia. Their childhood infatuation, her stepfather's hatred, the circumstances that had brought them together once again, and the differing paths that would tear them apart.

Furia listened closely. When he finished, she gathered Appia into her arms. "So you were willing to save her from an assassin and lose your position in the army for her, but now you're about to give her up because she wants to live in Rome and you don't?"

"It's more complicated than that," Max muttered. "And saving her life was the work of a moment. This is the rest of our lives."

"If you love her, and she loves you back, don't let her go so easily," Furia said. "Such a love is hard to come by. Don't throw it away."

The prospect of a life without Volusia was bleak and joyless, and his sister's words kindled a tiny spark of hope. Now that he had the idea, even if implausible, of buying land in the country instead of returning to the army, maybe there was a way to craft a life that would please both him and Volusia. A life that would satisfy him while still fostering Volusia's ambitions for her son.

He had no idea how, of course, but fresh determination to try filled him. After all they had been through, he had to try *something* to keep Volusia at his side.

CHAPTER 26

T HE LITTER SWAYED TO a stop and gently lowered until it rested on the street. Volusia brushed the curtains back and peered out into the street. She frowned. "Are you sure this is the right address?" she asked Triton, the closest litter bearer.

"Yes, lady," he said. "This is the address that Orion gave us."

After a few days of searching, Orion had succeeded in finding someone who knew Silvanus and where he lived, for which Volusia had rewarded him handsomely. Today, Volusia had set off to speak with Silvanus. She'd taken a risk by arriving unannounced, but she feared that he'd ignore her letter if she sent a message first. They hadn't parted on the best terms in Narbo.

She'd expected to find Silvanus living in a humble home on the outskirts of Rome, or maybe in an apartment building somewhere. But this street was barely a few blocks from where her family lived, filled with grand homes. A senator lived around the corner. How had a former secretary come by such a prime location?

Triton walked up to the front door and knocked, then announced Volusia's presence to the slave who answered the door. Volusia waited inside the litter as the slave went to alert Silvanus of her arrival. She wondered if he'd pretend not to be home.

But a few moments later, the door opened once more, and she was invited inside. Triton helped her down from the litter, and the four litter-bearers waited on the street as she entered the house.

"Please wait here, lady," the slave said as she entered the atrium. "The master will be with you shortly."

"Thank you." Volusia adjusted her palla as she glanced around the atrium. It was large and bare. No statues of ancestors adorned the space. The floor tiles had been half-chiseled off in one corner, perhaps to make room for a mosaic. The walls looked like they'd recently been given a fresh coat of paint. A few crates sat in the corner, likely belongings waiting to be unpacked.

Her list of questions for Silvanus was growing. A seed of suspicion took root. Why had he lied about staying in Narbo? Why had he come to Rome, where he had no family? And now, how could he afford a house like this in a prime neighborhood?

Silvanus entered the atrium. He no longer had the gaunt, exhausted look of the last time she'd seen him, and he'd exchanged his sober gray tunic for an embroidered blue one. A golden bangle adorned his slim wrist. She'd never seen him wear jewelry before.

His lips pulled down in a frown as he surveyed her. "Volusia. What are you doing here?"

She smiled despite the rude greeting. "Forgive me for the surprise. I heard that you'd returned to Rome, and I thought it would be nice to pay a visit."

"*Nice*," he repeated unenthusiastically.

"This is such a lovely home," she said. "I didn't realize you had connections in the city."

"I don't." He stared at her in cold silence for a few long moments.

She realized he was trying to make this encounter awkward enough that she'd leave, but she would not be put off so easily. "Might I presume upon you for a cool beverage? It's rather hot outside."

He huffed. "I was just sitting down to lunch. I suppose you could join me." He spoke the words as reluctantly as if he was suggesting she shave him bald.

"Oh, that would be lovely." She summoned another bright, simpering smile, and followed him to the dining room on the other side of the atrium.

He had changed. As long as she'd known him, he'd always been courteous and even deferential to her. They had both seemed to have a tacit agreement to be civil to each other, to pretend for Avitus's sake that they were well-disposed toward each other. Was this unpleasant, cold man the real Silvanus? Had the quiet, accommodating, competent secretary been just a façade?

They entered the dining room. A strange feeling came over Volusia as she saw the plates laid out on the low table, the jug of wine in the center. For a moment, she was back in their dining room in Narbo, back at the dinner where Avitus had taken ill. Her head spun with the force of the memory, and she had to reach for the wall to steady herself.

Silvanus spoke, his voice questioning, but the words didn't penetrate her mind. She had thought back to that dinner a thousand times, had scoured her brain to pull out every detail.

She had assured herself that all three of them—herself, Avitus, and Silvanus—had taken food from the same platter and drank wine from the same jug. She remembered Silvanus comment-ing on how well-seasoned the duck was as he freshened Avi-tus's goblet of wine. Then, he'd warned her that her palla had come unpinned on one side, and she'd turned away to fix it.

The room spun. A conclusion to her earlier questions about Silvanus came into sickening focus.

A hand touched her arm, and she pulled away jerkily. The contact brought her back to the present. She took a stumbling step away from Silvanus. "Excuse me, I have to"—her mind raced—"speak with my litter-bearers."

"Your litter-bearers?"

She nodded, a half-plausible explanation jumping to her lips. "I forgot to tell them that they were supposed to collect my mother from visiting someone nearby, and bring her home before returning here to wait for me. Excuse me, I'll just be a moment."

Volusia hurried from the dining room and returned out-side, where the four litter-bearers waited on the street. They straightened up when they saw her.

"Done already, lady?" Triton asked.

"I—" She broke off, her mind whirling as she tried to figure out what to do. Should she leave, gather herself, and then decide on a course of action?

No, she was on the verge of untangling this whole mess. She couldn't leave without getting to the bottom of this.

Max's face rose in her mind. He'd been in this with her since the beginning. She had to tell him what she'd realized. He could come and bear witness to Silvanus's guilt, if indeed she was right.

"I need you to take a message for me, quickly," she said to Triton. Max would come as soon as he received it, she had no doubt.

She gave the message to Triton, then returned inside. She paused a moment to compose herself in the empty atrium. She would have to tread very carefully, and she didn't know how Silvanus would react. She might be putting herself in danger, but she'd survived worse. Silvanus couldn't pose more of a threat than Glabrio and his soldiers.

Before she could convince herself to leave, she rejoined Silvanus in the dining room. He was already seated with a plate of food before him, and did not rise to greet her. Two slaves stood against the wall holding jugs of water and wine.

She smiled apologetically. "Forgive me for my absent-mindedness. I knew I was forgetting something."

He shrugged and waved a laconic hand at the empty couch beside him. Volusia sat and served herself from the platter of vegetables and cold meat, though she had no appetite. The two slaves stepped forward to fill her goblet with a mixture of water and wine, and she murmured thanks.

"Tell me why you're really here," Silvanus said. "I don't think you're stupid enough to believe that we're actually friends."

"There's no need to be rude." She decided to play the conversation as she'd originally planned it, as if her horrible realization hadn't taken place. "I came to speak to you about Avitus. About how he died." She watched his face.

Silvanus let out a weary sigh and reached for a piece of cheese. "This again? Volusia, it's time to move on. He got sick, he died. It happens."

"I don't believe that's what happened to Avitus. Maybe if I never discovered his suspicions about Petronax, I could believe that. But I went to see one of the consuls, to discuss my concerns—"

Silvanus cast her a sidelong glance. "You spoke to a consul about this?"

She nodded. "He refused to take any action without proof that Avitus was murdered."

"Proof you will never find, because it didn't happen." He spoke carelessly, then tossed back a gulp of wine.

His nonchalance infuriated her. He wasn't even nervous. He showed no guilt when discussing the death of a man who had cared for him, maybe even loved him. He'd left her a widow and her son fatherless, and all for what—some money? A fancy house in a posh neighborhood?

Rage unfurled in her chest, and words rose unbidden to her tongue. She'd intended to wait for Max's arrival before broaching this, but she couldn't hold back anymore. "I know you did it, Silvanus."

She hoped to shock him, to shatter his icy composure, but he met her gaze evenly. He snapped his fingers, and the two slaves immediately left the room, closing the door behind them.

Silvanus turned back to her, an eyebrow arching. "Do you?"

She swallowed hard. This was it, the moment she'd lay it all out before her. Justice for Avitus—and for her son—was within her grasp. "You murdered the man who loved you."

"Loved!" He scoffed. "Avitus didn't love me. He only valued me for what I could do for him. I was a good secretary and a better fuck. Or maybe it was the other way around."

His crudeness made her lips tighten. "Why did you do it?"

"Do you even have to ask?" He made an expansive gesture at the room around them. "I was born in a tiny village in the middle of nowhere with nothing but a life of labor and hardship in front of me. I wasn't brave or strong, and I was useless with a sword, so I couldn't seek glory in the army. But I was determined, and there was nothing I wouldn't do if it got me out of that village. I worked my way up until I got that position on your husband's staff. I thought that was as high as I could climb. Being the secretary to the governor of a wealthy province is a position of influence. Especially after he took more of a...*personal*...interest in me, I thought I had it made."

"I was right about you," Volusia said through gritted teeth. "At the beginning I thought all you wanted with Avitus was his position." She had allowed Silvanus's façade of meekness and humility to fool her, to lull her into overlooking his ambition. How could she have been so stupid?

He ignored her. "After we got to Narbo, Avitus started noticing things he wasn't meant to. Accounts not adding up, missing tax revenue, that sort of thing. We both realized Petronax was stealing from the province. I tried to warn Avitus away from pursuing it. I knew making an enemy of Petronax could jeopardize everything. Avitus would have profited from the scheme as well. But he was stubborn."

"He was doing the right thing," Volusia said. "He was a man of honor. Unlike yourself."

Silvanus shrugged. "Well, one of us is in a grand house with ten slaves to wait on his every need, and the other one of us is nothing but ashes in an urn."

Volusia flinched.

"He kept poking at it," Silvanus continued. "And I realized I was chained to a sinking ship. I started to make plans to leave, but then one of Petronax's men approached me. He offered money in exchange for poisoning Avitus. Of course I negotiated the price up as much as I could. I had nothing to lose—I knew that if I refused, I'd have disappeared within the week because of what I knew, and someone else would have done away with Avitus anyway. So yes, I did it. I had no choice, but now I have enough coin to buy a magistracy in the next election. From there, who knows?"

Volusia drew in a breath as she absorbed everything Silvanus had said. That must have been how Petronax came to know of her suspicions. The only person she'd told was Silvanus, and he must have relayed it to Petronax, who had ordered Glabrio to silence her.

One last question occurred to her. "W-Why are you telling me this?" He had, after all, just confessed to murder. Her breathing stuttered as the danger of her situation washed over her. Max wasn't here yet. She had no one to protect her. Her litter-bearers were outside—but due to her lie, Silvanus thought she'd sent them away on another errand. She could scream, but no one would hear her.

He fixed her with a steady, cool stare. "Because you sealed your own fate the moment that accusation left your lips, Volusia. If you think I'm going to let a stubborn little widow ruin everything I've built for myself..." His hand closed around the handle of a dinner knife.

Volusia had started gathering her legs under her as soon as he'd begun speaking. Her muscles tensed, and she made to bolt for the door.

But Silvanus anticipated her movement. He lunged toward her, the knife outstretched, pointing straight at her throat.

She scrambled backward, still on the low dining couch. Her foot kicked out, making contact with Silvanus's chest. The force thrust him back for a moment, long enough for her to sweep an arm over the dining table, sending plates, cutlery, and cups crashing over the couch between them. Glass and pottery shattered as it hit the floor, and metal platters clanged, the noise deafening. She hoped desperately that the cacophony would alert someone—but then again, she was in Silvanus's house, and his servants wouldn't dare interfere.

The cascade of dinnerware stymied Silvanus for only a moment, and Volusia couldn't find her feet fast enough. Silvanus lunged at her once more. Volusia twisted desperately. The knife sank into the cushion of the couch next to her ear. Silvanus swore.

His body had landed half over hers, his weight stifling even though he was not a large man. Volusia jerked her knee up and caught him in the stomach. She grasped for the knife, yanking it out of the couch. Silvanus grabbed her wrist. Instead of letting him take the knife from her, she flung it wide. It clattered away, out of reach for both of them.

"You are determined to make things difficult for yourself, aren't you?" he growled. His hands closed around her throat.

Panic seized her. She writhed and twisted, tearing at any part of him she could reach with her nails. But the pressure didn't ease. She wheezed, frantically seeking any scrap of air.

Relief didn't come. Black spots popped in her vision. She was going to die like this. Her son would be an orphan, and Max...Max would never know how much she loved him. His face was the last thing she saw as darkness swallowed her.

CHAPTER 27

MAX RETURNED TO ROME in the early afternoon. He rubbed Elephant down and saw her safely returned to a cozy stable stall, then headed home. He planned to grab some lunch and then head to the baths to wash away the grime from his travel.

As he was going to the kitchen to see what could be rustled up for lunch, Paris came to find him. "Sir, there's a messenger for you in the atrium. Says he has a message from the lady Volusia."

Max's interest piqued. "Thanks. I'll see what it is." He turned away from the kitchen and went to the atrium.

A broad-shouldered man waited, hands clasped in front of him. Max thought he recognized him as one of Volusia's litter-bearers. "You have a message for me from Volusia?"

The man nodded. "Yes, sir. She said it was urgent. She said to tell you 'Silvanus did it.' And she asked you to meet her at his house, right away."

Max frowned. "His house? You mean—"

"She's visiting the gentleman named Silvanus, sir. That's where I came from."

Max's stomach gave a horrible lurch as he realized the significance of her message. Silvanus did it. Silvanus had killed Avitus. How was that possible?

He couldn't stop to think about it. Volusia was at Silvanus's home, alone, likely on the verge of confronting him about his crime. He prayed she would wait for him before doing anything reckless. But what if Silvanus realized she knew? What if he—

"Juno's cunt." He grabbed the messenger's arm. "How far is Silvanus's house from here?"

"No more than a quarter mile, sir."

"Take me there straightaway." Volusia was in grave danger, and he had to get to her.

Max stumbled up to the front door of Silvanus's house, breathing hard. He and the messenger had run the short distance as fast as they could. He felt the lack of a weapon at his hip keenly. He didn't know what he was about to walk into, but he'd have to face it unarmed.

Max banged on the front door. "Silvanus! Open up!"

Silence within. Max realized too late that banging on the door like a madman was not the way to get whatever slave who manned the entrance to admit him.

Max backed up a few paces, then threw his shoulder against the door. It didn't budge. He cast a desperate glance back at Volusia's four litter bearers, who were watching him in shock. "Help me with this."

The man who had served as the messenger eyed the sturdy door doubtfully. "It will take a battering ram to get through that door, sir."

Max clenched and unclenched his fists, frantic energy pulsing through his veins. Volusia was in there, and she was in danger. He had to get to her.

He bolted from the front of the house to the side, into the narrow alley that separated it from the neighboring house. His gaze alit on a small door hiding in the shadows. It must lead into the kitchens and back storage rooms.

This time, Max didn't bother knocking. He charged at the door, ramming his shoulder into it. It burst open, wood splintering around the handle.

Twin shrieks sounded from the two women in the kitchen when he barged in. One clutched a bowl of vegetable peelings, and the other was elbow-deep in disemboweling a rabbit.

"Sorry," Max said reflexively. The women stared at him.

A scream and the sound of crashing and shattering echoed from elsewhere in the house, and Max took off running toward the noise. He followed it, veering crazily through the corridors, until he burst into the dining room.

His soldier's brain immediately took stock of the scene before him and propelled his body into motion, before the rest of his mind could catch up. Silvanus and Volusia were on the dining couch, a wreckage of plates and food around them. Silvanus's hands were wrapped tight around Volusia's throat as she struggled.

Silvanus looked up as he entered, shock spreading across his face. Max crossed the room in several long strides. He bent and grabbed a heavy metal pitcher, his body moving without conscious thought. Silvanus's mouth opened. Max brought the pitcher down hard on Silvanus's head. The man went limp, and slumped off the couch to the floor.

Volusia lay on the couch, unmoving.

Now that the immediate threat had been vanquished, terror set in. Max dropped to his knees next to the couch. His shaking fingers brushed her cheek. He called her name, and jostled her shoulder. Her head lolled.

He bent his head close to her face, trying to see if he could hear or feel her breathing, but his own heart was pounding too hard. He thought he felt a wisp of breath against his cheek. He called her name again, louder.

A tiny motion caught his eye—an almost imperceptible movement of her chest. Thank all the gods, she was alive.

"Volusia," he gasped. "Volusia, come back to me."

Her eyelids fluttered open. Her gaze, at first hazy and unfocused, settled on him. Her mouth opened and her lips moved, but no sound came out.

He laid a hand, still trembling, on her shoulder. "Don't try to talk. It's all right. You're safe now."

A noise behind him caught his attention. Silvanus was stirring. With brisk movements, Max unfastened his belt where it cinched his tunic and kicked Silvanus onto his stomach. He bound the man's hands behind him, then dragged him over to slump against the wall.

Several pairs of footsteps sounded, and Max grabbed a knife from the pile of fallen dining implements. Had the servants come to defend their master?

Two of Volusia's litter-bearers entered the dining room. They must have followed Max in through the kitchen entrance. Their mouths fell open as they beheld the scene.

Volusia struggled into a sitting position, a hand massaging her throat.

"Lady, are you injured?" one of the litter-bearers asked.

She opened her mouth again, but only a breathy croak came out. She shook her head.

"I think she'll be all right," Max said. "We need to deal with him." He gestured to Silvanus, now groaning and wriggling as he slowly returned to consciousness. "Go to the home of the consul Hortensius. Tell him we have the proof he required, nearly at the expense of Volusia's life." He knew the consul cared for Volusia, and any hint of a threat to her would make him come right away to ensure her safety.

The litter-bearers nodded and left. As they departed, Max glimpsed another figure in the corridor behind them. One of Silvanus's slaves, a young man, was staring wide-eyed at the bound and half-conscious figure of his master. He flinched when Max caught his eye.

"You all should leave now, while you can," Max said to the slave. "Tell the others." There would likely be an investigation, and if Silvanus was convicted, his slaves would be confiscated as part of his estate. There was also the unpleasant fact that the slaves would probably be questioned in any investigation, and testimony from a slave was only considered valid if extracted under torture.

The young man met his gaze, nodded quickly, then ran. Max returned to Volusia's side. She was sitting upright, and some color had returned to her cheeks. He sat next to her and wrapped an arm around her shoulders. "Are you all right?"

She nodded, and tried to speak once more, but couldn't summon any sound. She grasped his hand and squeezed it.

He squeezed back. He had come so close to losing her, and now, all he wanted to do was pour his heart out to her. He might lose her still, in a different way, but he had to try. This likely wasn't the best time, with Volusia nearly strangled and a half-conscious murderer tied up on the other side of the room, but he couldn't stand to wait a single moment more.

"I know you can't talk right now, but I have something to say that can't wait." He slid off the couch, coming to kneel before her. One knee brushed a fragment of broken pottery, and his foot landed in a puddle of spilled wine, but he didn't care. "You already know that I love you. I thought I had to give you up because I wasn't good enough for you, and I couldn't give you the life you needed. But I realized there's more for me than the army life. I want to buy land in the country and breed horses, away from the city. I may not be able to teach Lucius how to give a speech or introduce him to a bunch of senators, but I can teach him how to ride a horse and throw a punch. You know all of my flaws. I'm not well-spoken or cultured or even particularly intelligent. But I swear to you, by Mars's hairy ballsack..."

She smothered a grin even as her eyes welled with tears.

He renewed his clasp of her hand. "I'll make up for all of my faults tenfold with how much I love you."

She gazed down at him. A tear spilled down her cheek. She traced her fingertips down his face, a gentle caress. She opened her mouth and her lips moved. Max leaned closer to hear the barely-there whisper. "Pluto…and Proserpina."

Max blinked at her, befuddled. Had she hit her head in the fight? For a moment, he couldn't figure out what the king and queen of the underworld had to do with this.

Then, he realized her meaning. Proserpina spent six months in the underworld with her husband, and six months in the land of the living. Volusia was suggesting she spend half the year in the countryside with him, and the other half in Rome, where she could foster her ambitions for her son.

Max shook his head vehemently. "No. I won't spend six months apart from you. I don't even want to spend another fucking hour apart from you ever again, Volusia."

She held up a finger. "Not…apart. Six months…Rome. Six months…country."

He understood her full meaning. She was suggesting a compromise, that they split their time between Rome and the countryside. Max could have six months to spend with his horses, and Volusia would have six months to participate in the social scene and engage the best tutors for her son.

That meant that Max would have to spend half the year in crowded, noisy, smelly Rome. Ordinarily, the thought would have made him shudder, but if it meant he could have Volusia at his side, he would gladly pay that price.

He nodded. "Agreed."

She looked at him questioningly. "Army?"

"I don't want that anymore," Max said. "I joined the army because I wanted adventure and freedom. Adventure I found in some measure, I suppose, but there's no freedom to be had in taking orders." He grasped her hand. "Instead, I want to be free to love you. And loving you has already been an adventure, hasn't it?"

A smile spread across her face. She leaned close, as if to kiss him, but drew back hastily at the sound of footsteps coming closer. Max rose to his feet as Hortensius swept in, followed by the twelve burly lictors that served as his bodyguard.

The consul's gaze snapped to Volusia, lingering on the livid bruises that were now blooming on her throat. "What in the name of Dis happened here?" He crossed the room to stand before Volusia, concern darkening his eyes.

Max stepped forward. "She's all right. She just can't talk." He gestured to Silvanus. "This was his doing."

Hortensius pointed a commanding finger at Silvanus. "Secure him."

Two of the lictors jumped forward and hauled the groggy Silvanus to his feet, keeping a firm grip on his arms.

Hortensius approached him. "Why did you attack the lady Volusia?"

Silvanus squinted at him, his gaze hazy. "Because the bitch was going to ruin everything."

Hortensius made a quick gesture, and one of the lictors struck Silvanus in the face, bloodying his lip.

Volusia cast Max a distressed look. Trust her to be so softhearted that she didn't even want to see the man who'd just tried to kill her beaten.

Max, for one, didn't mind if Hortensius's men wanted to give Silvanus a couple more whacks for good measure, but he cleared his throat, hoping to change the direction of the conversation. "I can tell you what I know, but Volusia will have to share the full story when she's able to speak. Volusia figured out that Silvanus, Avitus's secretary, poisoned him back in Narbo, on Petronax's orders. It seems he tried to attack her to keep her quiet." He didn't know how Silvanus had been convinced to murder Avitus, but judging by this giant house, money must have been involved.

Hortensius surveyed Silvanus dispassionately. "Will you confess to the murder of Avitus under oath?"

Silvanus's lip curled. "Why would I condemn myself?"

"We have the testimony of a respected lady," Hortensius said. He turned to Volusia. "Will you testify to what you know under oath?"

She nodded.

Silvanus glared at her. "So then you'll have me killed anyway. I won't confess."

Volusia raised a hand, drawing everyone's attention. "Mercy," she whispered.

Hortensius gave her a look of incomprehension. "You're asking for mercy for the man who was a moment away from killing you?"

For once, Max agreed with the consul. Even Silvanus looked skeptical.

Volusia cleared her throat. "He had...no choice. Impossible situation."

Max understood: if Silvanus had refused to carry out Petronax's bidding, he would have met a similar fate as Avitus.

Hortensius considered for a moment, then turned back to Silvanus. "If you give a full confession, including information on Petronax, who must have put you up to this, then I will see that you receive a sentence of exile. You'll keep your head, though you'll never set foot in the Republic again."

Silvanus's jaw tensed. "Fine. I'll talk."

Hortensius gave another signal to the lictors, and they dragged Silvanus away. Hortensius approached Volusia. "Can my men escort you home?"

Volusia opened her mouth and glanced at Max.

Max folded his arms over his chest. "*I'll* see her home."

Volusia smiled at Hortensius and nodded.

The consul's lips tightened. "As you wish."

He turned to leave, but Volusia raised a hand and cleared her throat. "Pet...ronax," she whispered.

"I think she wants to know what will happen to Petronax," Max clarified.

Hortensius shot him an icy glare. "Obviously." He returned his attention to Volusia. "Assuming Silvanus gives us satisfactory information that confirms Petronax's guilt, I will send a small force to Narbo. Petronax will be quietly done away with...much as he did away with Avitus."

"You're going to have him assassinated, rather than bring him to trial publicly?" Max asked.

Hortensius's lips thinned even further. He did not deign to look at Max, but kept his focus on Volusia. "Learning of the corruption of a celebrated commander would destabilize the Republic more than it already has been due to the civil war. Publicizing Petronax's treachery would not be a prudent decision."

Volusia nodded. "Understood," she whispered.

"If that is all, I must return to other matters." Hortensius inclined his head to Volusia. "I'll send a messenger tomorrow to ensure that you're recovering well."

He left, followed by the remaining lictors. Max helped Volusia to her feet. "Come on, let's get you home."

She held up a hand. "One thing...first." She stood on her tiptoes and tilted her face up to kiss him, picking up where they'd left off before Hortensius interrupted them.

Joy swept over him in a heady rush. He cradled her face in his hands as he kissed her back, careful of her bruises.

"I love you, Max," she murmured against his cheek, her voice gaining strength. "City, country...wherever we go, I'll love you."

He couldn't speak, but he hugged her as tight as he dared, enfolding her in his arms. She was everything he had ever wanted. For the first time in a while, he could see the rest of his life spread before him, bright with hope.

There was only one thing that could stain his delight. He drew back gently from the embrace. "Your stepfather still hates me." What if Rufus tried to prevent them from getting married?

"Yes." She gave a raspy sigh. "He may never like you, but I think I can convince him to tolerate you."

He grinned. Where Rufus was concerned, toleration would have to be enough. He put an arm around her shoulders and led her from the empty house, into the sunlight outside.

CHAPTER 28

"**A**BSOLUTELY NOT." RUFUS GLOWERED at Max from across his desk.

Volusia sighed. She'd been afraid that her stepfather would be stubborn about their betrothal. She'd tried to convince Max to let her put forward the proposal on her own, knowing that Max's presence tended to inflame Rufus, but he'd insisted that the honorable thing to do was to ask for her hand himself.

Max wasn't making any efforts to endear himself to Rufus, though. He was sprawling languidly in a chair, his long legs stretched out before him and his hands clasped loosely over his stomach. She wished he could try to look a little more deferential.

Rufus continued. "I will not consent to my stepdaughter marrying this, this—"

Max straightened up. "Man who saved her life not once, but twice?" He cast a meaningful glance at the bruises on Volusia's neck, now faded to shadows after a week. "What more could you want in a son-in-law?"

Volusia cleared her throat. "Father, allow me to remind you that I don't need your consent to marry Max. According to the terms of Avitus's will, I am emancipated, free to do what I wish."

Rufus's eyes darkened. She could tell that he knew it was true, knew that he couldn't stand in her way, and he hated it.

She softened her voice. "But I do want your blessing, because I love you, and I want us all to be a family. I love Max, and I know he's the right man for me."

Max grinned smugly.

Rufus leaned forward, his gaze intent upon her face. She recognized the posture as the one he used when he was trying to negotiate, to broker a deal, to convince a fellow politician of something. "My dear, are you sure there are no better options you wish to consider? I heard that the consul Hortensius had expressed interest. He's a fine man, with excellent prospects. Think of all the doors he could open for Lucius."

"Yes, but I don't love him," she replied. "I spent ten years married to a man who never truly loved me, nor I him. I want something different for the rest of my life. I want to love and be loved without restraint, without condition." Tears rose to her eyes. That would work in her favor—Rufus hated seeing her cry.

Max reached over to gently brush away a tear as it rolled down her cheek. "I hope this is the only time you'll cry on my account."

She caught his hand and held it. "These are happy tears, my love."

Rufus grimaced and made a noise of disgust. "Fine," he ground out. "You have my blessing. On two conditions."

Volusia had risen to her feet to hug him, but paused. "Yes?"

"First, you must wait the customary ten months after your first husband's death to remarry."

"Ten months?" Max exclaimed. "That's an eternity."

Volusia shot him a quelling look. It was a reasonable condition, after all. "It's already been nearly two months since Avitus died. So it's only eight months."

He grumbled but said nothing.

"The second condition?" Volusia asked.

"Lucius must agree to this as well," Rufus said. "I don't want my grandson to be saddled with a stepfather he dislikes."

Volusia nodded. "That's fair." It could present a problem, as Max and Lucius were different as could be—Max gregarious and irreverent, Lucius studious and disciplined. But she felt certain that if she could show Lucius why she loved Max, he'd grow to love Max too.

"Then I suppose we are agreed," Rufus said reluctantly.

Volusia walked around the desk to hug him. "Thank you, Father. This means a great deal to me."

He kissed her forehead. "You know you will always have a place here if—or when—you tire of your choice."

"I'm sure I won't, but thank you." She kissed him on the cheek. Despite his high-handed ways, she knew her stepfather had only her best interests at heart. He and Max were more alike than they knew, and she hoped one day, they'd grow to realize that.

The next day, Max made his way to Volusia's house once more, this time leading Elephant with him. The sun had never shone so brightly, and every step felt buoyant with joy. He'd never imagined that he would actually be engaged to Volusia. And in eight months, she would be his wife.

If her son agreed. His mission for today, and for however long it took, was to endear himself to Lucius. He had little experience with children, much less trying to get one to consent to him marrying its mother, but he remembered how delighted his nephew Tullus had been by Elephant. He figured all boys liked horses, so his plan was to introduce Lucius to Elephant and hopefully impress him that way.

"I don't like horses," Lucius informed Max when Volusia brought him outside.

Max blinked. "You don't like horses?" He had not accounted for this possibility.

"They're big and they smell and they could trample me." Lucius shrank back, clutching a handful of Volusia's dress.

Volusia patted his shoulder. "It's all right, dear. Max's horse is very gentle. I've ridden her myself." She gave him a little push. "Why don't you go pat her nose?"

He resisted, planting his feet stubbornly. "I don't want to."

Max suppressed a sigh of frustration. This was not going well. Lucius's eyes were wide, and his slim shoulders were tense. He was clearly terrified.

"I can't do much about the smell, but I can show you that she'll never trample you." He walked several paces away and laid down flat on the ground, then clicked his tongue in the signal for Elephant to come to him.

She trotted toward him, then stopped as she reached him, her hooves a handspan from his ear. She lowered her head and nudged his shoulder, as if asking what in the world he was doing down there.

Max grinned and got to his feet, brushing dirt from his tunic. "See? No trampling."

Lucius still looked unconvinced, but this time, he allowed Volusia to gently propel him toward Elephant. He reached out a trembling hand and allowed Elephant to sniff his fingers, though he took a hurried step back when Elephant snorted and tossed her head.

"It's all right," Max said. "She won't hurt you."

Lucius crossed his arms over his chest and set his jaw. At least he wasn't running back into the house, so Max decided to make the most of the moment. "Her name is Elephant."

Lucius's nose wrinkled. "Elephant? That's a stupid name for a horse. Though I suppose she was already named that when you got her, and you had to keep the name?"

"No, I named her that myself," Max said, trying not to be defensive. "After Hannibal and his war elephants."

"Hannibal was an enemy of Rome," Lucius said staunchly.

"Yes, but he was a great general."

"Alexander the Great had a horse named Bucephalus. That's a good name for a horse. Why couldn't you have named her something like that?"

Max rolled his eyes. This child was somehow equally irksome and endearing. "I liked the name Elephant."

"Hmph." Lucius gave Elephant's nose another tentative pat. "Did you know Hannibal had thirty-seven war elephants when he crossed the Alps? But not many of them survived the crossing. Do you know how many elephants he had at the battle of Zama?"

"No, but I assume you're going to tell me," Max said dryly.

"Eighty."

"That's a lot of elephants."

Lucius nodded in solemn agreement. They were silent for a moment. Max noticed that Volusia had slipped inside the house, leaving him alone with Lucius.

As the silence stretched, Max wasn't sure what else to say. He was on the verge of asking Lucius if he knew any more facts about elephants when the boy spoke.

"Is it true you're in the army?"

"Yes," Max said, then corrected himself. "I was. For almost ten years."

Lucius glanced at Max, something hiding in his gaze, then looked back at Elephant. "Mother says I will have to join the army when I'm grown, if I want to be a consul one day, or a governor like my father."

Max nodded. Ten years of military service were required before running for any political office. "That's true."

Lucius lowered his hand from Elephant's nose. "Were you scared when you joined the army?"

Max leaned against Elephant's side, stretching an arm over her warm back. "I was too stupid to be scared." He realized what was behind Lucius's question. "Given that you seem to be much smarter than me, I wouldn't be surprised if you were scared."

Lucius shrugged and said nothing.

"Listen, that's a long way off. By the time you're seventeen or eighteen, I bet you'll feel differently. You'll be excited to leave Rome and see different lands. You'll make new friends and have some adventures. Besides, maybe you'll decide that you don't even want to go into politics. Then you won't have to join the army."

Lucius shook his head. "Mother wants me to become a great man like my father."

"There's more than one way to do that. You don't have to be a politician or a statesman." Max hesitated. Volusia might not thank him for undermining her ambitions for her son. But Lucius should understand that he had options. Max had only joined the army because he thought it was his only option to make something of himself, and it hadn't exactly ended well. "You could become a man of trade, or be a great writer or historian. With a good education, which you seem to have, you can do anything."

Lucius gave Max a searching, considering stare, then a small nod.

Two weeks later, after a series of similar visits, Lucius had grown confident enough around Elephant to feed her apple slices without shrinking away in fear. He'd become more talkative around Max, too, and Max was starting to find Lucius's endless stream of obscure facts charming. Max even borrowed one of Lucius's books on the history of the Punic Wars so he could quiz the little boy on long-ago battle tactics and generals. He tried his best to stump Lucius, but the boy answered every question flawlessly.

One sunny afternoon, Max enjoyed lunch with Volusia and Lucius at a small table in the atrium of her family's house. Rufus was out for the day on business—as he always was when Max visited—and Volusia's mother was visiting a friend, so it was just the three of them. This was how it would be once they were married, Max realized with a surge of warmth in his chest. He wanted nothing more than the chance to enjoy a sun-filled lunch with Volusia and her son.

"Darling, you're not eating your plum," Volusia said to Lucius. "Is it underripe?"

Lucius had gone to the trouble of carefully slicing his plum into sections, but had piled them in the corner of his plate instead of eating them. "I'm saving them for Elephant," he announced. "May we go see her after lunch?"

A broad grin spread across Max's face at the fact that Lucius had reserved a portion of his own lunch for Elephant. "Soon she's going to like you more than me if you keep spoiling her."

Volusia wrapped her arm around Lucius's slim shoulders and pulled him close to kiss the top of his head. "Of course you may go visit Elephant with Max. Do you think you'd like it if you could see her every day?"

Lucius's face brightened. "Yes!"

"Then I have something very important to ask you, darling." Volusia reached across the table to clasp Max's hand. "Max would like to marry me, and become your stepfather. Do you think you would like that?"

Lucius glanced from Max to his mother. Max never imagined he'd feel so nervous about the judgment of a nine-year-old.

"I suppose that would be all right," Lucius said.

A ringing endorsement if there ever was one.

"He's not very good at naming horses, though," Lucius continued.

Max grinned. "Tell you what, you can name the next horse I buy. Deal?"

Lucius nodded solemnly. "Agreed."

Volusia hugged her son and kissed him on the forehead. "Thank you, darling. If you're finished with your lunch, run along and fetch a cloak to go visit Elephant."

Lucius ran off. Volusia rose from her chair and crossed around the table to Max, settling herself in his lap. "Are you ready to be a stepfather?"

Max wrapped his hands around her hips, savoring her weight and warmth on top of him. "He's too smart for his own good, but I think we'll get along."

Volusia laughed and looped her arms around his neck. "I can only hope you'll be a good influence on each other. But *please* don't teach him to swear. At least not until he's older."

"Until he's older," Max promised.

"We've fulfilled one of my father's conditions. Now we only must wait eight months, and we can be married."

"Eight months." Max groaned. "That's an eternity."

"We spent ten years apart, and we have a lifetime ahead of us." She touched his cheek, bringing his face close to hers, and brushed her lips over his. His mind buzzed with the pleasure of her touch. "A few months is nothing. I'll be your wife before you know it."

CHAPTER 29

EIGHT MONTHS LATER, Max reclined in the dining room of his family's home, his wife beside him. They had been married earlier that day at Volusia's house, and then had journeyed in a merry parade to the wedding feast here.

The dining couches were crowded with people, including both of Max's families. He'd finally told Aelius and Crispina about his reconnection with his mother and sister, and they had been overjoyed to meet Max's birth family.

Now, Aelius was chatting amiably with Appius, while Rufus looked on and occasionally butted in with a self-important comment. Gaia and Volusia's mother Sabina were cheerfully battling over who got to hold baby Appia, and Crispina was seated between Furia and Max's mother. Lucius entertained little Tullus with the dutiful air of an older brother.

Max and Volusia were at the center of it all. He gazed at Volusia, resplendent in her white and saffron-yellow wedding finery. Like the other women, she didn't recline, but perched upright beside him, feet tucked delicately beneath her body. He still struggled to believe that she was really his wife. A gold ring sparkled on her left hand, where she'd once worn Avitus's ring. Now, she was his.

And he was irrevocably hers, as he always had been. He didn't need a ring to signify it. Every breath that filled his lungs, every pump of blood through his veins, it was all for her.

They had received word a few months ago that Petronax had fallen victim to an unfortunate riding accident. Hortensius had replaced both him and the province's governor with men he trusted, and promised to review regular reports of the province's finances to ensure that no further corruption was festering. Silvanus had disappeared into exile, and Max was happy never to see the man again.

Max's mother rose from her seat and came toward the central wing of the table where Max and Volusia sat. Maia clasped her hands, fingers twisting tentatively.

Max stiffened at her approach. He still wasn't entirely comfortable around her yet, though they had reached a careful, bland cordiality where they could exchange small talk without awkwardness. Volusia laid a hand on his arm, which instantly made him relax.

"Quin—I mean, Maximus," his mother said, flushing as she stumbled over his name. "I just wanted to say how honored I am to be here today, to see you married. And to such a fine lady." She offered Volusia a cautious smile.

Max opened his mouth, but no words came out. He often found himself tongue-tied around his mother, stuck between the scared little boy he'd once been and the man he was now.

Volusia gracefully interceded. "We are very happy to have you here. It's a blessing to be surrounded by family on a day like this."

Maia inclined her head to Volusia, then returned her attention to Max. "I know…I know I wasn't the mother you needed. But it brings me more joy than you know—more than I deserve—to see the man you've become."

In their prior, surface-level conversations, his mother had never acknowledged their past. Now, the words eased something tight in Max's chest, a knot of long-held anger and resentment. It didn't disappear entirely, but it loosened enough for Max to summon a small smile. "Thank you," he said quietly.

Maia nodded to them both, then resumed her seat next to Crispina. His adoptive mother had been watching the exchange, and her gaze caught Max's. Crispina gave him a small nod of approval before returning her attention to the meal.

Max let out a breath. Volusia's hand was still on his arm, and he lifted it to his lips, pressing a kiss to the back of her fingers. She gave him a dazzling smile, and the warmth in her eyes cleared his mind of everything but his desire for her.

The past eight months had been as tortuous as he expected. Max had kept himself busy, the only way to stave off his longing for Volusia. He'd bought the land near Furia and Appius, and he hadn't even had to ask Aelius for a loan. Volusia had inherited all of Avitus's wealth, and it was more than enough to purchase the land, clear it, and build a cozy house.

With his savings, he'd acquired a few healthy young mares and a selection of stallions from which to breed his first generation. By this time next year, he would have a few foals if all went well. The stallions had been offered to Elephant, but she'd turned her nose up at all of them. She was past her most fertile years anyway, and Max was happy to keep her all to himself.

But tonight, his focus was on the other most important lady in his life. Volusia was his now, forever. They'd said the words, eaten spelt cake blessed by a priest, and Volusia had lit the sacred fire at his family's home. There was only one more wedding tradition to complete, and Max had been aching for it for eight months.

Max leaned over to whisper in Volusia's ear. "I've eaten enough." He raised his eyebrows significantly.

She blushed and hid her grin behind her wine cup. "As have I."

His mouth went dry with anticipation. He rose to his feet and extended a hand to help her up. As they stood, cheers and laughter sounded from their guests. Rufus, however, was scowling, scrawny arms crossed tight over his chest. His greatest fear was that Max would defile his stepdaughter, and now it was about to happen. Rufus just didn't need to know that it had already happened several times over.

For good measure, Max seized Volusia around the waist and pulled her into a deep kiss, to resounding whoops from the guests. Bowls of candied nuts had been strategically placed on the table, and as they broke apart from their kiss, everyone began pelting them with the nuts, meant to ensure their fertility.

Volusia, laughing, clung to Max as they tried to dodge the hail of nuts. Max grabbed her and put her behind him, shielding her with his body as if from enemy bombardment as they made their way toward the door of the dining room. On their way, Max snatched a handful of nuts from an unused bowl and hurled it back at the guests, giving way to a new round of raucous laughter.

Finally, they made it out the door, into the empty hallway. Max slammed it shut behind them. Volusia was breathless with giggles, her face red and her flower crown askew. She looked more beautiful than ever.

Silence fell between them as they walked down the hallway to Max's bedroom. A sudden spell of nervousness seized him. Apart from a few stolen kisses, he hadn't touched her since they'd slept together on their journey back from Gaul. Those encounters on their journey had been hasty, desperate, full of fear that they'd soon be separated. Now, they had the rest of their lives ahead of them. Max wanted to savor this night, but he worried his desire would get the better of him.

In the bedroom, Volusia glanced around. A small smile curved her lips. "It's so funny to think that after all we've been through, this is the first time I'm seeing your bedroom."

"Does it meet your approval?"

She reached up and rested her arms atop his shoulders. "It could have three walls and a dirt floor and I'd still be happy to be here, right now."

He kissed her, and the desire he'd been carefully keeping tethered for the last eight months came surging back in full force. Before his brain caught up to his body, he had pushed Volusia against the wall and was kissing her as if her mouth was the only thing that could keep him alive.

His hand lowered to the knotted belt cinched at her waist. It was tied in a complicated knot that was traditionally supposed to make things difficult for the bridegroom on his wedding night. Max grabbed an end and yanked.

"Be gentle," Volusia chided breathlessly. "I had my mother knot it loosely this morning, so it wouldn't give you too much trouble."

Max worked at it with his fingers, but his hands were clumsy with urgent desire. However loosely Sabina had tied it, Max didn't have the presence of mind to untangle all of the loops and knots. He gave up quickly. "Fuck this." He grabbed a handful of her skirt and began to lift it over her knees.

Volusia pushed his hands away. "Max, slow down!" She replaced her dress, shaking out the folds. "I will not be taken against the wall on my wedding night." She shoved him gently, so he took a few steps back, then she took hold of the knotted belt. Her deft fingers worked through the knot. With a few strategic pulls, it loosened and dropped to the floor.

Next, she unpinned the crown of flowers and the long yellow veil from her head, and set them gently atop a chest of drawers. She bent to untie her sandals and kicked them off.

Her sleeveless white dress was the only thing remaining. Max stepped forward, ready to shuck it off her, but she held up a hand. "Easy, soldier. Attend to your own garments and wait until I give the order to advance."

Despite his ardor, Max rather liked this commanding wife of his. He fell back, and wrestled himself out of his unwieldy toga and tunic. He balled up the heap of clothing and kicked it into a corner out of the way.

She gave his body an appreciative glance, her gaze lingering on his cock.

"Does this meet your approval as well?" he asked, his voice suddenly hoarse.

"I think I need to inspect at closer range." She moved closer to him and trailed a hand over his chest, down his taut stomach, until her fingers circled his cock. "Mm," she whispered. "Yes, it does indeed."

Max let out a groan as pleasure sparked at her touch. He tried to grab her, but she moved quickly out of reach, as light-footed as a doe. She gave him a coy smile, then slid her arms out of her dress and let it flutter to the floor. It caressed her hips on the way down, and she gave a little shimmy that made his head spin.

His mind flashed back to the first time he'd seen her naked, when she was bathing at the inn after escaping from Glabrio. Her skin then had been bruised and scratched from their ordeal, but he'd still been dumbstruck by her beauty. Now, she was flawless, all blushing ivory skin and soft curves. He itched to fill his hands with her perfect tits, but he forced himself to hold back. She'd made it clear she wanted to set the pace tonight, and he was hers to command.

She ambled over to the bed, moving much more slowly than he thought necessary, and pulled back the blankets. She climbed into the center of the bed and lay down, then spent an interminable moment rearranging the pillows and adjusting the blankets. When her thighs parted, revealing the pink softness between them, Max could wait no longer. He crossed to the bed in several long, urgent strides, and a moment later covered her body with his own. Skin brushed against skin, and heady pleasure dizzied him.

"Max!" Volusia gasped, wriggling beneath him. "I did not say you could—"

He snared her wrists and pinned them next to her head. "I thought you knew I was never much good at following orders."

She gave a last hopeless little squirm, but only succeeded in wedging herself more securely beneath him. Triumphant, he lowered his head to claim her mouth. He released one of her wrists to better enjoy her, squeezing her plump breast. Her free hand twined in his hair, pressing him ever closer.

Her thighs widened, sliding open to make room for him between them. His cock nudged against her core. Her warmth beckoned, but he stilled himself. His hand traveled down to brush her folds. Fuck, she was soaked for him.

Even so, he paused. "Awaiting orders."

"Take me, Max." The words came without hesitation, her voice high and breathy.

He grabbed her thigh and angled it back, opening her even more to him. One last question stilled him, possibly the only thing important enough to steal his focus at this moment. "Children," he said. "Do you want me to, uh…like before?"

She met his gaze for a long moment. "If the gods choose to bless us with a child, I'll be very happy. But what about you? Are you ready to be a father as well as a stepfather?"

He blinked stupidly. He had always assumed she would dictate if or when they had a child, especially since she had a son already, and had never expected to be asked for his opinion. The idea of fatherhood terrified him, but he had already agreed to take on the role for Lucius. And with Volusia as his wife, he could do anything. He nodded. "Yes. I would like that."

She wrapped her legs around him. "Then take me, and stop talking."

Slowly, he eased himself into her warmth. She let out a little moan, and her eyes fluttered closed. Multiple words of profanity rose to his tongue as her slick warmth sheathed him, but he wasn't capable of speaking.

His body urged him to move, to thrust, to chase the pleasure that awaited them both, but he took a deep breath and forced himself to be still for just one moment more. He gazed down at her, her eyes closed, cheeks flushed, her lips slightly parted. He wanted to remember this moment. Volusia was his future, his forever, his everything. He didn't know what adventures the years ahead of them had in store, but with her by his side, he couldn't wait to find out.

Thank you for reading! If you enjoyed Max and Volusia's story, please consider leaving a review wherever you found this book.

Want more of the Roman Heirs universe? Scan below or head to jennabigelow.com/legionary for a free prequel novella, *The Merchant Match.*

Turn the page for a sneak peek of Book 3, *The Fortune Flirtation,* which picks up twenty years later and follows Volusia's son as he finds an unlikely love with his business rival Lucretia.

Sneak Peek: The Fortune Flirtation

He trades in foreign goods, not love—but when his greatest rival offers an erotic education in exchange for a truce, both their hearts may be captured in the bargain.

In the Roman port city of Ostia, a fierce rivalry wages in the world of trade. After losing her husband to a shipwreck, Lucretia has devoted herself to keeping his shipping business afloat, clinging to the independence it offers her. Felix, her scheming rival, strives for total control over commerce in Ostia, which requires toppling Lucretia's enterprise and seizing her ships for himself.

Unfortunately for Felix, it's not just Lucretia's ships he desires. Her cool smile and calm competence shred his focus and scramble his thoughts, even as he plots sabotage. Even worse, he's been too busy building his business empire to dally with women…ever.

When Lucretia discovers both how much he wants her and that he's as inexperienced as a Vestal Virgin, she decides to use this to her advantage—proposing a truce in exchange for initiating Felix into the ways of the flesh. Their heated encounters blur the line between business and pleasure, and soon pleasure turns to something deeper. Despite never wanting to remarry, Lucretia finds herself contemplating a partnership with Felix, in business as well as life.

But when Felix uncovers a secret that could vanquish Lucretia once and for all, he realizes the unthinkable has happened: he's falling for the woman he should want to destroy. His dream of ruling trade in Ostia is finally at his fingertips, but he must decide what he wants more: Lucretia's ships, or her heart.

Chapter 1

Lucretia frowned at the results on the abacus before her. Calculations worked themselves out in her brain. A small sum of money—about twenty sestertii—was missing from her accounts. She hoped she'd just made a mistake with her accounting, but such a calculation error was unlike her. As the second most powerful merchant in Ostia, she couldn't afford mistakes, even over a few sestertii.

She had a sneaking suspicion as to where the money went, but she was loath to admit it to herself. Surely Marcus, her fourteen-year-old son, knew better than to pilfer from her accounts.

But it was the sort of thing a rebellious adolescent might do, and ever since his father's death last year, Marcus had been even more prone to such unruly habits. His great passion these days was chariot racing, and he was constantly betting on the latest races. To be fair, he did win more than he lost.

With a sigh, she pushed the wax tablet away and pressed the heels of her hands against her eyes to soothe the persistent throbbing in her skull. A thieving son was the last thing she needed.

A tap came at the door, and Lucretia lifted her gaze to see Dihya, her friend and colleague, poking her head into the back room of their two-room office. "Lucius Avitus Felix is here.

Again." Dihya's expressive mouth twisted in distaste. "Shall I tell him you're busy?"

Lucretia groaned. Lucius Avitus Felix was one of the richest men in Ostia and the proprietor of the city's largest shipping venture. He had been her late husband's perpetual rival, locked in a never-ending competition for who had the most ships, the best profit margins, the fastest shipments, the most sought-after products. Felix, somehow, had always managed to maintain a slight edge over Cornelius.

Now that his rival was dead, Felix had turned his attention to Lucretia. But he wasn't just trying to beat her. He was trying to remove her from the game entirely.

"I'll see him," she muttered. If he wanted to speak to her, he wouldn't leave until he did, so better to get this over with.

Dihya nodded and withdrew. Lucretia busied herself tidying her desk, pushing aside the abacus and neatening her stacks of paper. Her office was small, little more than a cell, with most of its space taken up by crates and boxes full of records going back decades, to the very start of Cornelius's business. A few chests contained money for everyday expenses, though the bulk of her capital was stored at the temple bank, safeguarded by priests and the gods. On the corner of her desk, a lamp burned lavender scented oil, diffusing a pleasant smell into the air and providing some extra light in addition to the single window cut high into the wall.

Lucius Avitus Felix entered her office. Tall and lean, he wore an ankle-length tunic of dark blue, which complemented his fair complexion and dark hair.

She chided herself for noticing such things. "Felix," she greeted him, gesturing to the chair opposite her desk.

He nodded to her and sat. "Lucretia." His eyes, the gray of a bleak winter morning, moved over her and their surroundings with dispassionate efficiency, as if cataloguing every detail to file away in his head for some future purpose. She hadn't given him much to notice—or so she thought.

His eyes fixed on her face. "You look tired."

Her eyebrows shot up, but she forced herself to moderate her expression. He wasn't usually outright rude, but everything Felix said and did was calculated several times over. So if he was being rude, it was likely to get a reaction from her.

She levelled her chin at him. "If there's something you wished to discuss other than my appearance, please get to the point. I'm busy."

He surveyed her for another moment, eyes flicking from her face to her left hand, where she used to wear Cornelius's ring. She resisted the urge to slide her hand beneath the nearest piece of papyrus.

"I've come with a proposition for you," he finally said. His voice warmed, losing its cool, clipped quality. "I would like to offer you something of great value." He even smiled at her, a charming mask settling over his face as if they were making conversation at a dinner party.

Lucretia tried to ignore the flip her stomach gave at his smile. She had always—guiltily—found Felix handsome, even when she'd been happily married to Cornelius. Felix's cold, scheming personality irked her, but she couldn't deny that his face didn't generate quite the same reaction. "And what is that?"

He leaned forward, bracing his forearms on the edge of her desk. "My hand in marriage."

She choked on a laugh, which made her cough. When she recovered her breath, she grinned at him. Triumph rose in her chest. "You are really so threatened by my business that you would tie yourself to me in marriage just so you can control my ships?"

She knew better than to think there was any romantic feeling underlying this ridiculous proposal. Once, several years ago, he had attempted a flirtation, but her quick rejection had ended any further overtures of that sort.

No, this proposal had a different motivation. In the year since Cornelius died, Felix had been steadily trying several different angles to induce her to sell her ships to him. First, a generous cash offer. Then an even more generous one.

When simple money didn't work, he became more persuasive, trying to remind her how difficult and time-consuming it was to manage a business operation like this. Surely she would prefer to devote her time and energy to raising her son or securing a new husband. Surely she didn't want the hassle and stress of managing a business.

While it could be stressful at times, this business was Lucretia's greatest chance at independence, at carving out a life for herself and Marcus where they were beholden to no one. Cornelius had given her a great gift in leaving the business to her, and she wasn't about to squander it. One day, her ships would be her son's legacy, and she was determined to make them as successful as possible.

Felix, composed as always, showed no discomfiture at her reaction. "I can give you security. A comfortable life. My house is twice the size of yours, if I'm not mistaken. Additionally, I have a summer residence at Baiae with sweeping water views. You and Marcus could spend as much time there as you wish. Speaking of Marcus, it could benefit the boy to have a stepfather to smooth his path as he comes of age. And you must be lonely without Cornelius. I could offer you companionship, should you wish it."

A blush stole across her cheeks at his last words. Did he mean social companionship, or was he suggesting companionship of a more...*marital* sort?

Either way, it was impossible.

"Of course, your shipping enterprise would serve as dowry, as your father is no longer living and cannot provide you with one," he continued.

She raised an eyebrow. "If I were to divorce you, I would take everything back." And while she might legally retain control of her own property in marriage, her husband would become her legal guardian and would have to consent to any decisions she made. That would effectively give Felix total control over her holdings.

He nodded. "A risk I am willing to take—that I will give you no reason to dissolve our marriage. You would have complete freedom. You would not have to spend your days poring over account books or negotiating with suppliers. You could do exactly as you please."

"I am doing exactly as I please," she replied. "If you really think I would give up everything I've built just for the promise of a bigger house and some vacations to Baiae…" She shook her head. "I refuse your proposal."

His eyes narrowed, the charming mask slipping. "I have made you several generous offers, Lucretia, this last one being the most generous of all. I have treated you like a respected associate. But allow me to advise you that this will be my last offer. If you maintain your refusal, you will no longer be my colleague, but my adversary. And my adversaries do not last long."

That was true enough; for the last several years, Felix had dedicated himself to picking off competing shipping enterprises one by one, whether through undercutting their prices, overtaking their supplier relationships, poaching their investors, or simply convincing them to sell their ships. Lucretia was now the last major competitor in Ostia. If she folded, Felix would control the entire flow of goods into and out of the port city, which could have disastrous consequences if his greed took over.

So she would stand against him, if it came to it. She would risk whatever it took to maintain her independence, and she certainly wouldn't accept his offer of marriage.

"My refusal stands."

"Perhaps you wish to think about it."

She rose to her feet, a gesture of dismissal. "I trust you'll have no further reason to speak to me again."

A muscle pulsed in his jaw. He stood in a quick, spare movement, and cast her one long, dark glance before he turned for the door.

Lucretia waited until she heard the outer door to their office open and close before sinking back into her chair. She let out a long breath. She wasn't thrilled at the idea of having Felix for an enemy, but she owed it to Ostia—and possibly the entire Roman economy—to stand against him.

Felix walked away from Lucretia's office, passing through the Square of the Guilds where all of Ostia's commerce centered. He tried and failed to unclench his jaw. He had planned to return to his own office, on the opposite side of the square from Lucretia's, but now he was too irritated to get any work done. Better to take a brisk walk to work off his frustration.

Lucretia's calm refusal of his best offer rankled him. Who did she think she was playing with? She had to be the only woman in Ostia who would refuse a marriage proposal from him.

Unluckily for him, Lucretia was the only one he had any interest in marrying.

Purely for business reasons, of course. If he couldn't convince Lucretia to sell her ships to him outright, then he'd thought offering a lifetime of security and a respected stepfather for her son would sway her.

His proposal had certainly had *nothing* to do with the fact that thoughts of her had filled his mind ever since they first met years ago, when she was still married to Cornelius. Her shining auburn hair, her quick wit and delicate laugh. Her tempting figure, always hidden beneath a loose dress.

Five years ago, she had also refused him—though that proposal had been of a more prurient nature than the one he'd made today. His inelegant, fumbling advance had left him deeply embarrassed, and he had never approached her again in such a manner.

It had been a simple thing to quietly lust after her when she was nothing more than his rival's wife. But now, a year after Cornelius's death, Lucretia herself had become his greatest rival. A layer of regard had built—unwillingly—alongside his attraction to her. She had managed to maintain and even grow her husband's business. Somehow, she had convinced the captains of her ships to stay with her and had preserved Cornelius's relationships with merchants and suppliers from Massilia to New Carthage. It made him wonder if perhaps she had been more involved with the business during Cornelius's lifetime than Felix had realized, if her husband's key contacts were willing to trust her without batting an eye.

He hated the way he felt around her. Though he strove to avoid her, Ostia's small social circle threw them together more often than not. Whenever they were in the same room, his attention was drawn to her like a hapless moth to a flame. She scrambled his focus, rendering his other conversations a blur of half-understood words.

On a few occasions, in a particularly crowded room, they'd touched, and each brief moment of contact was branded onto his mind. There was the time her shoulder had brushed his arm when she'd stepped aside to make room for someone to pass. Then the time when her knee had bumped him as she'd risen from the dining couch. Most memorably, she'd once stumbled into him, jostled by someone behind her, and her entire body had pressed against his for one breathless, heated moment. Much as he resented his reaction to her, he hoarded those little moments like Croesus hoarded gold.

But Felix would not let Lucretia's allure blind him. She was standing in the way of his goal to monopolize shipping to and from Ostia, and he would find a way to remove her from his path.

As he made his way through the streets, leaving the colonnaded central square behind, a commotion down a side street caught his attention. He paused, glancing into the shadowy alley. It was just a group of adolescent boys, embroiled in a scuffle.

He made to keep walking, but the nature of the scuffle kept his focus. It didn't seem to be an ordinary, evenly matched brawl, but a three-on-one beating. The boy at the middle of it all was curled into a ball, trying to protect his face from the kicks and punches of the others.

Distaste curled in his stomach. Felix had occasionally been the victim of such torment as a child. If there was one thing he couldn't abide, it was an unfair fight. Nowadays, he visited the gymnasium twice a week to spar with his fists and had developed into a highly capable boxer, but as a boy, he'd been too often targeted for beatings, until his mother, Volusia, had removed him from school and secured private tutors.

Well, he was overdue for a training session, so dispatching these bullies would serve two purposes.

Felix strode into the alley and grabbed the closest boy by the neck of his tunic. He hauled him off the victim and shoved him toward the wall of the alley. The second boy turned to Felix with a snarl and aimed a punch, but Felix deflected the blow easily and rewarded the boy with a cuff to the side of his head that sent the boy reeling to the dirt.

The third boy took a step back, his gaze flicking between Felix and his two comrades, both attempting to drag themselves to their feet.

Felix narrowed his eyes. "Go."

The boy turned and ran. The other two stumbled after him, leaving Felix alone in the alley with their erstwhile victim.

The adolescent hauled himself to his feet, brushing dirt off his knee-length tunic. A few scrapes and bruises marred his arms and legs, but he didn't seem to be seriously injured. "Thank you," he muttered.

Based on the tenor of his voice, Felix put the boy's age at fourteen or fifteen. He was scrawny for his age, though, which was likely at least part of the reason he'd been targeted. Boys like his attackers loved an easy victim.

"I've been in your position more than I'd like to admit," Felix replied. "Not particularly enjoyable, is it?"

The boy shook his head, inspecting a scrape on his elbow with a frown. There was something about him that seemed familiar. Something about the coppery sheen of his hair tugged at a thread of recognition, but Felix couldn't place it.

"Do I know you?" Felix asked. "What's your name?"

The boy glanced up, meeting his gaze with hazel eyes that sent another pang of familiarity through Felix. "Marcus Cornelius."

Cornelius. "Lucretia's son," he realized out loud with a jolt. He had never actually met Lucretia's fourteen-year-old son, but now he clearly saw the resemblance. Marcus's hair was a few shades browner than Lucretia's rich auburn, but they had the same eyes and even the same pointed shape to their chins.

Marcus narrowed his eyes. "You know my mother?"

"Yes." *And I'm trying very hard to ruin her.* "My name is Lucius Avitus Felix."

Recognition dawned on Marcus's face. "I know you. Mother says you—" He bit back the words, flushing. "Never mind."

Felix could imagine the sort of things Lucretia would say about him. *Grasping. Greedy. Money-grubbing. Ruthless.* "You should get home," he said. "Before she starts to worry." He nodded to the boy, then turned and left the alley.

To keep reading, head to jennabigelow.com/legionary for purchasing information!

ALSO BY JENNA BIGELOW

THE IMPERIAL GAMES SERIES

Set in the early days of Caligula's reign, the Imperial Games series follows three gladiators during a stretch of games held to celebrate the new emperor's accession. Win or lose, one thing is sure: love will be found where they least expect it.

Gladiator's Embrace (Book 1)

A retired gladiator reluctantly returns to the arena for one last series of fights, only to fall for his manager's ambitious niece when she hires him to train the up-and-coming gladiator she's taken on.

Gladiator's Beloved (Book 2)

She's Rome's most feared female gladiator. He's the emperor's personal physician, commanded to heal her latest injury. Sparks fly when they're together, until the machinations of the imperial court threaten to tear them apart.

Gladiator's Touch (Book 3)

A former Vestal Virgin seeks out the gladiator-turned-sculptor whose life she spared. He wants nothing to do with her after she ended his fighting career, but the heat that blossoms between them is impossible to escape.

THE ROMAN HEIRS SERIES

The Roman Heirs series follows the love stories of three generations of an unconventional family in the last decades of the Roman Republic. There's a politically motivated marriage of convenience, forbidden pining between a soldier and a governor's wife, and a pair of business rivals who somehow find themselves trading sex lessons for a truce.

The Merchant Match (free prequel novella)

After gaining her freedom from slavery, Gaia will do whatever it takes to build a new future for herself and her son—even infiltrate a dinner party under an assumed identity to extort money from her former mistress. There, she meets Herminius, a wealthy merchant in search of a respectable bride. Despite her subterfuge, Gaia can't ignore the heat that sparks between them. She knows she should keep her distance, but what's the point of freedom if she can't enjoy the pleasurable attentions of a man who makes her heart flutter every time they touch?

The Tribune Temptation (**Book 1**)

In the cutthroat world of Roman politics, family is everything. Aelius, a freed slave turned ambitious politician, enters into a marriage of convenience with a disgraced patrician divorcee, hoping her powerful family name will bolster his chances in his next election. Prickly one moment and icy the next, Crispina is determined to keep her charming husband at a distance. That is, until Aelius undertakes a campaign to win not just the city's vote, but his wife's heart.

The Legionary Seduction (**Book 2**)

Max joined the Roman army in search of glory and adventure, but soon finds himself stuck in the provinces, unable to land even one promotion. During a stint on guard duty at the new governor's residence, he comes face-to-face with Volusia, the girl he loved ten years ago. Only now, she's married to the governor. But when her husband mysteriously dies and she suspects foul play, the only person Volusia dares trust is Max, and she begs him to help investigate. Their love is strong, but can it withstand a killer's blade?

The Fortune Flirtation (**Book 3**)

After losing her husband to a shipwreck, Lucretia has devoted herself to keeping his shipping business afloat. Felix, her scheming rival, strives for a monopoly on trade, which requires seizing Lucretia's ships for himself. Unfortunately for Felix, it's not just her ships he desires. Even worse, he's been too busy building his business empire to dally with women...*ever*. When Lucretia discovers both how much he wants her *and* that he's as inexperienced as a Vestal Virgin, she decides to use this to her advantage—proposing a truce in exchange for initiating Felix into the ways of the flesh.

OTHER WORKS

A Princess's Ransom (Tales of Timeless Romance anthology)

After the sack of Rome, Galla Placidia, the emperor's sister, becomes the Goths' most valuable hostage. While awaiting ransom, the ambitious princess, tired of living in her brother's shadow, realizes the Goths could be the key to the power she craves. Allying with the Goths could also allow her to indulge her forbidden attraction to her captor—the stoic, noble, and irritatingly handsome Athaulf. Placidia must decide how far she'll go to secure both the man and the future she desires, and if she's willing to turn her back on Rome forever.

Acknowledgements

Firstly, thank you to Stanford University for creating ORBIS, the Stanford Geospatial Network Model of the Roman World. It was an invaluable resource for planning travel times and routes for all of the various journeys that take place in this book. It's also just a lot of fun to play with.

Thank you to my author colleagues who provided feedback and encouragement on various drafts of this story from its inception in 2022 to the present, including Maggie Sims, Anne Knight, Katy Jakes, and Faye Delacour. Thank you also to editor Emily Keyes for helping to bring this manuscript to its finished state (and for calling Max a "total simp king").

Finally, thank you to Frankie, my proofreader and husband, who caught a typo in the very first sentence, among other things. What would I do without him?

ABOUT THE AUTHOR

Jenna Bigelow is a historical romance author based in Wilmington, DE. She has eleven years of Latin classes under her belt, as well as a minor in Classical Culture and Society. When not writing, she enjoys sewing, especially recreating historical fashions of the 18th and 19th centuries. She thinks about the Roman Empire every day.

Connect with Jenna at her website, jennabigelow.com, or on Instagram/Threads at @jennabigelowwrites.